I0659284

Kolu & Sayzay

An Enduring Love Story

Sakui W. G. Malakpa

Forte Publishing

First Published in 2018 Published by:

FORTE Publications
#12 Ashmun Street
Snapper Hill
Monrovia, Liberia
[+231] 777155-923
[+231] 881-106-177

FORTE Publishing
7202 Tavenner Lane
208 Alexandria
VA, 22306

FORTE Press
76 Sarasit Road
Ban Pong, 70110
Ratchaburi, Thailand **[+66] 85-824-4382**

http://fortepublishing.wix.com/fppp

fortepublishing@gmaill.com

ISBN-13: 978-0-9945347-8-1

Kolu and Sayzay

Dedication

To my lovely children.

Contents

PROLOGUE

Mr Fahpeh was prepared to commit murder to protect his daughter from a peasant kid whom he called a dog. This was no empty threat. He not only vowed to his wife that he would carry out the act but he alsoloaded his three guns and set aside a considerable supply of ammunition. He only needed to know when and where he would spot "the dog" with his daughter. He was likely to succeed because fact that murder was a serious crime did not matter to him. His enormous wealth and stupendous social status in a rural region made him an outlaw who committed many heinous crimes with impunity. Determined to show that this would be no exception, he did not hesitate to pull the trigger.

CHAPTER ONE

Growing up" and "maturation" often are used interchangeably but, more than increases in stature, maturation is the process of gaining maturity. Among other things, this status requires one to deal logically and aptly with external forces--interpersonal relations and other challenges of the world--as well as internal realities--personal preferences, feelings, ambitions, pains, and needs, including the need to belong, love and beloved. Stated differently, increasing in stature is not synonymous to becoming mature. Maturity implies ability to deal aptly on one hand, with oneself while on the other, building and maintaining interpersonal relationships irrespective of human differences, abiding by laws and regulations, dealing carefully and judiciously with nature, and, depending on belief, being mindful of a Supreme Being Who knows the strengths and limitations of mere mortals.

At sixteen and five feet six inches tall, there was no doubt in the fact that Kolu was not only growing up but that she was an extremely beautiful young lady who was striving toward maturity. She was the uncontested beauty queen of her school, the apple of her father's eye, and the darling of her mother's.

Kolu also was maturing logically and physically. As she experienced increased gonadal activities, she was beginning to think about boys but she was not sure. In actuality, her social status or, more correctly, her parents did not give her much opportunity, if any, to interact with other teenagers, boys or girls.

On the morning of the first day of school after a long summer vacation, Kolu once more showered in the big bathroom of the Fahpeh residence. It was a huge bathroom with an incredibly large shower room, a separate big bathtub both with exquisite display of bath soaps, body lotions, and various items for bathing. There was a separate room for towers, bathrobes, and more. Between the shower room and the bathtub was a humongous mirror. A similar mirror was place in the opposite direction so one could see oneself in both the front and back. The floor was made of a special marble laced with rare stones. The commode was different. The seat was always down but if a gentleman wanted to take a leak, he only had to step on a special spot on either the right or left of the commode and the seat would lift up. After peeing, or going number two, the commode not only flushed automatically but it also sprayed a wonderful fragrance of air freshener.

In that big bathroom, Kolu got out of the shower and stood in front of the huge mirror to examine her beautiful body. To her, it looked just right although she had to work hard to maintain this gorgeous magazine figure. "Hmmm," she whispered softly. "Five feet six inches and a hundred and fifteen pounds is not bad although could be better. I'm working on it." This emphasis on body weight and mass was baffling in that, for people of her age, being thin and slim was a sign of beauty. Conversely, to older generations, a full body was a sign of beauty and satisfaction but such was the essence of the generational gap.

As Kolu looked at herself in the mirror, she thought about dating guys. It is difficult to overemphasize the fact that she was a stunning beauty. As she visually surveyed her gorgeous body, she examined herself carefully and unapologetically admired her own beauty although not in a narcissistic manner. "Someday," she whispered, "I will be giving this body to a well-deserved man. Of course, he must be the right man, the right man who will be mine and I, his forever. I will do anything to get such a man regardless of threats, intimidations, oppositions, obstacles, or any other hazards."

"How long will you be in that bathroom?" shouted Mrs. Kebbeh Fahpeh, Kolu's mother who was dressed in a very nice gray and white dress although she had no plans for leaving the house. "Are you trying to be late on the first day of school?" Mrs. Fahpeh pushed her daughter.

"Coming Ma," Kolu shouted back. She put on her make-ups, did her hair, and took another look at her body before putting on her bath robe.

She went to her room, dressed elegantly, and headed to the family dining room, which exuded an aroma of delicious breakfast food. Her parents and brother Akoei (17) were already at the breakfast table each dressed elegantly as well. "Good morning Mom and Dad, good morning Akoei," she greeted. The family returned the greeting as Kolu took her usual seat at the breakfast table. A maid came over to serve her.

Mr. Kolubah Fahpeh, usually in a business suit, wanted to know what was up for the young ones on the first day of school. "So what's the schedule for today?" he asked.

"The usual opening day routine," Kolu answered just before she took her first bite of scrambled eggs placed carefully near a serving   of cassava and fish gravy. She had a separate bowl of fruits next to a glass of freshly squeezed juice. Unlike her parents, she never cared for coffee or tea, except ice   tea.

"And what is that?" Mr. Fahpeh pressed on.

As Kolu chewed, her brother went to her rescue. "Well Dad, first, it will be great to see old friends. Then, the principal will tell us what to do before we go to our classes for books, assignments, and so on; but on the first day, we do not expect to do much."

The room was quiet for a moment before Kolu concurred adding,   "I can't wait to see my friends from the ninth grade. I'm sure we will have fun together this year again. Now, it's tenth grade you all!" she emphasized excitedly as if her parents already did not know.

"That's right," Akoei also concurred. "It's eleventh grade for me! I too can't wait."

"I hope both of you are considering college. Now-a-days, it's difficult to make it without a college degree although I think most of those so-called college graduates are educated fools," Mr. Fahpeh opined. Then he added, "After all their degrees, those educated fools will be working for me. That's when they will learn that they do not know a thing and that my bank book is mightier than their stupid degrees."

"Stupid degrees Dad?" Kolu seemed flabbergasted. "If degrees are stupid, then why are we going to school? Why do you and Mom pay so much money for someone to tutor us regularly?"

"To get stupid degrees so you may work for people like me who do not have stupid degrees," Mr. Fahpeh would not light up. "You see Dear, it just goes to show that all that talk about education is pure nonsense. This is why I have never supported the rigorous tutoring of you kids; that's your mom's idea but I'm glad to pay for it. After all, I can afford it and much more; so it is nothing to me financially."

Kolu could not believe her ears. "Thank you Mom because the tutoring has helped us tremendously," she said although in actuality, the use of four private tutors emphasizing different subject areas benefited her far more than Akoei who often skipped sessions. Turning to her father, she asked, "Nonsense Dad? If you had not gone to school, how would you run your business?"

Mr. Fahpeh sipped on his coffee and looked around the table. He smiled lightly before stressing that Kolu and her brother would never understand his view because they had been brainwashed into believing that education was everything. He pontificated that, far from it, education was not everything. "In fact, in some instances, no, more correctly, in many instances, education is purely nonsensical. Take for example, a biologist studying the mating life of flies or the reproduction of worms. What do you get out of that? Likewise, what do you get out of the history of a thousand years ago?" Without waiting for answers, Mr. Fahpeh laughed mockingly. "Pure nonsense!" he mocked further.

Taking on a serious face, Mr. Fahpeh informed his children as well as his wife who was listening intently that with or without even minimal schooling, he would have run his business with common sense. "You see," he continued with a serious face, "it does not take formal education to get a genius like your dad, and that's the truth. Informal, I mean street-smart education, is the way to go if you really want to make for a rich and successful life, not merely exist for the sake of existing."

"Really Dad?" Kolu asked. "I'm sure you are kidding; you could not possibly be serious."

"Of course I am dead serious," Mr. Fahpeh, answered. He said this was why those empty-headed and broke professors out there who preached education and all that nonsense should have been taking lessons from a genius like him. Challenging his kids, he said, "If you doubt me, count the number of college graduates who work for me although I never went to college and never wanted to. In fact," he stated as a matter of truth, "I did not graduate from high school but look at me and look at those educated fools. Some have bachelor's degrees, others, master's degrees and still others, PhDs. But what do they have? Nothing," he answered his own question. He said such so-called educated people were frequently at his door to borrow one amount or another. "I mean, he mocked, "the fools have nothing but their stupid degrees. They ought to be ashamed for wasting such valuable time on so-called education, an end-product that gets them nowhere." He said he was truly embarrassed by the stupidity of people who ought to know better. "Worse," he continued, "society listens to them as if they are geniuses; nonsense! Absolute nonsense," he vented out his anger.

Kolu and her brother looked at their father in total amazement but Mr. Fahpeh was not finished. As if what he had said did not sink in, he once more said all so-called educated people were blockheads who only had pieces of paper they called degrees, degrees that did not mean a thing to the bank. As a result, he could hire them if he wished and fired them at will. He could push them around by their noses anytime and anyhow he wanted. He could even kick them in the rear and get away with it in court where he could simply bribe lawyers and judges who were broke as well. "They will never touch me in life, no, not those fools," he concluded his vexatious remarks.

As Mr. Fahpeh bragged, his wife nodded admiringly. Caught up in himself, he smiled immodestly as if patting himself on the back for a marvelous achievement especially when he reached such a milestone without graduating from high school, not to mention a degree.

Akoei did not know how to respond forcefully to his father's braggadocio. Nevertheless, he spoke briefly for himself and his sibling. "Dad, we find it baffling that you think education is a waste of time and yet you want us to go to college. For now, we are just thinking about graduating from high school. After that, who knows?"

"That's right!" Kolu supported. "I am looking forward to going back to school and meeting my old friends." Apparently trying to change the subject, she added, "Also, I'm glad that, in tenth grade, I do not have to deal with Mr. Zoevor, that horrible ninth grade math teacher." She smiled triumphantly as if she had conquered the world by completing ninth grade and leaving Mr. Zoevor behind.

Akoei laughed. "I had to deal with him for two years."

The teenagers' father warned that as they got rid of one tough teacher, they would contend with another; that's just how life went. He still thought that teachers and college graduates were educated fools but on second thought, he modified his position lightly, stating, "Maybe not all of them. I guess there are a few good teachers out there. In fact, I remember one or two from my high school days." He looked at his wife who smiled lightly as if she knew what he was talking about. He then fed himself with a mouthful of cassava gravy. "That's the reminder we need," Kolu, cheered up. "As I said, for now, we are just excited about returning to school and meeting old friends." Looking directly at her father as if delivering a major lecture, she stressed that meeting new challenges in life was natural especially since such challenges were expected at different times, in different ways, and in different clothes.

Kolu's dad directly addressed her point. He averred that whenever and wherever he was confronted with life's challenges, he would be ready for them without a degree, not even a high school diploma. He asserted confidently that he would conquer every life challenge, regardless of its type, strength, magnitude, or anything else. "That's what common sense does," he emphasized. "I have the money and other means to combat any challenge in life. On the other hand," he continued, "when life's challenges come to those educated fools, their degrees, unlike my bank book, will be totally meaningless. That's why I say they are fools. Maybe they are not all bad people; they are just fools who do not know how to make a living for themselves. I honestly think they ought to take lessons from people like me; people who deal with everyday crises, people who know how to get around earning a living, and peopling who know how to work our way smartly around the system."

As Mr. Fahpeh condemned education while Kolu and her brother expressed excitement about returning to school, Mrs. Fahpeh constantly looked at her daughter. "You look gorgeous my dear," complimented Mrs. Fahpeh. "After Kolu thanked her mother, Mrs. Fahpeh added, "My goodness, my little one is maturing right under my nose; I can't believe it. Soon, I hope, she will be married to a handsome and wonderful young man." She laughed. "I can't wait to hold their baby in my arms."

"Oh Ma," Kolu protested mildly. "We are talking about school. Please let's keep the conversation at that and that alone, at least for now."

"You will be very lucky if he's even a slight image of your Pa," Kolu's father said in a serious tune. He said most boys out there were good-for-nothing vagabonds. He threatened to cut off the tail of any good-for-nothing vagabond rascal he caught at his door. "They are all useless, I mean totally useless fools," he murmured as he managed to control a mixture of anger and disgust.

Kolu was getting irritated and her brother was not only unresponsive but absolutely disinterested in the topic. Their mother did not comment on her husband's statement either.

Kolu and Akoei quickly finished breakfast. They did not eat half of the food on their plates. Without returning to their rooms, they jumped in a luxurious car to be driven to school.

The school ground was as familiar as they had left it at the end of the previous school year. The two-floor brick school building was the same. It had a small library and an auditorium on the first floor. The school also had two small labs, a faculty lounge, a student store, a small cafeteria, a place for students to congregate if necessary, and the principal's office. There were several bathrooms—bathrooms for guys, girls, teachers, and the principal. There were classrooms for grades one through twelve. There also were decorations and pictures along the walls, some encased in glass holdings.

The green field around the school was particularly welcoming. The few trees around the school building added to the beauty of the school grounds. In those trees, birds flew back and forth as if they had businesses of their own and maybe they did. Whatever the case, the truth was, no doubt, everything was ripe for a new school year.

For Kolu and other returning students, it was wonderful to see old friends. Each time old friends showed up, they embraced and laughed interminably. As quickly as they could, they tried to catch up on the activities of the long vacation. The stories, however, seemed similar as very few traveled away from Fasawoba. On the other hand, Kolu and a few students from well-off homes did travel to Coastal City, the nation's capital and other big cities to visit, shop, or simply be there as their parents transacted one business or another.

As returning students caught up with old friends, new students just stood around, some looking very strange, perhaps uncertain as to whether they truly belonged here. Some talked with family or friends they knew from elsewhere.

When a new student, Sayzay Yakpazuo Kargbo, 17, spotted Kolu, he was mesmerized. "Who is that beautiful girl?" Sayzay asked his friend.

"That's the school queen," Golo replied. "As you can see, apart from her high social status, she truly deserves that title. I mean, the lady is gorgeous; I do not need to convince you or anyone on that count."

"I absolutely agree," Sayzay said. "I like that girl. No, that's false; I love her and love her deeply. No doubt, that's Zeemai. I do not know when and where but I am very sure that's the girl I will marry," he emphasized without hesitation. "Yes, yes, I will marry that girl, no matter what," he further stressed with unadulterated certainty and unapologetic excitement.

"There's a difference between saying 'that's the girl I would like to marry', and 'that's the girl I will marry'," Golo reminded his buddy. "You are correct," Mr. English Major," Sayzay teased lightly. "That is the girl I will definitely marry," he emphasized once more with unbending and spotless certitude.

"You are crazy, absolutely crazy," Golo mildly reprimanded. "You do not even know the girl." Without waiting for any response from Sayzay, he questioned him in frustration. "Do you know the girl you are talking about? Do you know the family she's from?"

"I hope she is from a good family because she will be my wife," Sayzay declared with an emphasis on 'will'. He said her family background aside, all he knew was that he loved the young lady deeply. "What is her name?"

Golo said the girl's name was Kolu Fahpeh. He then disclosed that Kolu's dad, Mr. Kolubah Fahpeh, was one of the richest people in the region. Because of that and Kolu's stunning beauty, every young man with half a brain in the region wanted her but to the best of his knowledge, Kolu was not interested in any. "Who are you in the world to think you will beat all the other boys and marry her?" Golo asked indignantly. Again, without waiting for a response from Sayzay, he added, "You and that young lady are not close in social status; there is no way you will be able to date her, let alone marry her." Laughing lightly, he advised Sayzay to look elsewhere instead of hitting his head against the wall. "My friend," he said, "I am sure you do not want to be like a fool fishing on dry ground instead of fishing in a deep river. If you truly want to catch fish, you better fish in the right places."

Sayzay shook his head in disagreement. "I'm telling you, I will marry that girl. Yes, that's my wife. There's something about her that strikes me strongly, deeply, and deliciously. I am hooked on her for life; therefore, except God, nothing and no one can keep me from marrying My Heart's Desire."

"I do not think you are listening Sayzay," Golo scolded mildly. "You and the lady are not close in social status. I know her family and based on what I know, you will not be able to get close to her. They do not even allow us in their house. Do you know that?"

Golo was right; Sayzay was not listening. His friend's doubts and opposition went in one ear and out the other. He maintained that when genuine love appeared, social status and any other difference had to give way. "I tell you Golo, I love her and that counts beyond anything else. Whether you understand it now or later, that's the truth and nothing else," he once more stressed with certainty.

"I hear what you say Sayzay but it will take nothing less than a miracle for you to even date that girl, not to mention marrying her. Look Sayzay," Golo stated as if he had just thought of something, "You do not even know what love and marriage are. What makes you think you love her and will marry her?"

"I'm not sure if there are specific definitions of those words but I can tell you for sure that deep down in my heart, I love that young lady and would like to spend the rest of my life with her. To me, that's love and marriage."

Golo was undoubtedly frustrated, even angry with Sayzay for allegedly being such a blockhead. He nonetheless wished his buddy good luck although he said he just did not see any possibility of Sayzay dating Kolu. On the other hand, he underscored his admiration for Kolu. He explained that unlike some ladies in Kolu's position, Kolu was different. She volunteered with little children and loved to bring gifts to elderly people in town, especially those who live alone. "She is not just pretty but very kind too."

"That is music to my ear," Sayzay smiled. "I want my wife to be kind, generous, hard-working, respectful to others, and God- fearing. Of course, I pray to God to bless us with a child or two."

"I say, you are definitely crazy, absolutely insane," Golo laughed. "You have not even said a word to the young lady and now you are telling me what you want her as your wife to be and even talking about children? That's nothing less than insanity. Get back to reality my dear friend; otherwise, we will soon be taking you for a mental health check-up. I mean that for no sane person sees a young lady for the first time and says he will marry her; that's total nonsense." Sayzay was not perturbed. "Say what you may but I mean what I say; that beautiful queen will be my bride and lifetime partner. By the way, you are invited to the wedding." Still in disbelief, Golo laughed again and the two entered the school building.

In comparison to the size of the building, the auditorium was huge. It had flap back seats on both sides of the isle, the types of seats that snap back up when one stands up. The front of the auditorium had a podium on an elevated stage. At the back were comfortable rows of seats where teachers and visitors sat. The auditorium was decorated beautifully mainly with the school's colors, green, white and gold. When students and teachers gathered in the auditorium on the first day, the principal welcomed everyone back and introduced new teachers. He outlined the usual school rules and regulations before sending students and class sponsors to their respective classes.

CHAPTER TWO

The first day of school flew by quickly especially for Sayzay. At home, he sat still as he thought over events of the last two months and few weeks. At the end of his school year in Kizehbu, a town much bigger than Fasawoba where he lived with his uncle, Mr. Kawvah and attended school, his father, Mr. Siefa Kargbo, showed up. He thought this was strange for normally, parents and family show up for graduation or important ceremonies but going from tenth to eleventh grade was not out of the ordinary. He therefore was suspicious, even apprehensive.

When Sayzay, his dad and uncle returned to his uncle's house from the school-closing program, his uncle called him for what he called "a small talk." Sayzay knew then that his father's presence must have had another purpose.

"As you know Sayzay," Mr. Kawvah started. He cleared his throat and waited a few minutes before continuing. "As I was saying, you know that my sister, your mother has not been well."

Sayzay sat up straight. Did something happen to his mother? "Is she alright? Is she?" he asked as his heart beat faster and faster.

His uncle sought to reassure him. "She's alright, considering …"

"Considering what?" Sayzay uncharacteristically cut off his uncle as his father sat without saying a word.

"I do not want to imply anything bad," Uncle Kawvah assured his nephew. "Your mother is alright. It's just that …"

"What! It's just what?" Sayzay cut uncle off again this time standing up. "Please tell me. Is my mother alright?"

"I assure you Sayzay, your mother is alright. Your father says however that her condition is beginning to worsen and doing farm work and taking care of her has become much too difficult for him alone."

Finally, Sayzay's father spoke. "That's true my little one. It has become difficult to farm and take care of your mother alone. Do not forget; her mother and brother are also up there in age and I have to care for them also although they do not live under my roof."

Sayzay relaxed, as he knew exactly what was coming. "So you want me to come with you to help with the farm and take care of Mom?"

"Yes," his uncle and father said at once.

Sayzay stood silent for a while and the silence was frightening for his uncle and father. "Did you hear us Sayzay?" his uncle asked.

"Yes Uncle, I did." The silence was once more frightening. If the teenager refused to go back home, his uncle and father could do very little about it. There wasn't the faintest likelihood that, because of such refusal, his uncle would put him out. On the other hand, this would be disastrous for his father who was under tremendous stress not only because his wife's situation was worsening but also because of all he had to do.

"O.K.," Sayzay broke the silence. He dragged his words in what was clearly a reluctant acquiescence. "I will go to take care of Mom." He went silent for a few minutes while his uncle and father looked at him wondering what was coming next. "But I will miss my friends here dearly. I will miss Uncle and Auntie too."

"We know," his uncle assured him. "Doubt it not, Auntie and I will miss you too Sayzay." He complimented Sayzay by stating that Sayzay was a wonderful young man and a big help at home. Unlike many people of Sayzay's age group, the young man did not drink, smoke or anything like that. He never left home to wander aimlessly. Instead, from school, he was back home, doing his schoolwork and helping around the house. "Believe me," Uncle asserted, "we will miss you dearly but it's important you return home and help take care of my sister. As your father has explained, my mother and older brother need help too." Uncle thanked God there was a good school in Fasawoba. "I hear students in the high school there speak like college students; like the high school here in Kizehbu, it is indeed a very good school." Uncle Kawvah said Sayzay could attend that school until he graduated from high school. "When you graduate, although we are limited to meagre resources, we will figure out what to do next if you want to go beyond high school."

"I do not want you to miss your uncle and friends either," Mr. Kargbo said. "However, I truly need help." Sayzay nodded in agreement.

After his father returned to Fasawoba, Sayzay waited another month or so before returning home. It actually no longer seemed like home but he could not deny the fact that this was his birthplace.

For the rest of the summer vacation, Sayzay helped his father on the farm and also helped take care of his mother. He regularly visited his grandmother and uncle to assist them in any ways they needed.

When school reopened in Fasawoba and Sayzay saw Kolu on the first day, he was glad after all that his father asked him to return home to continue schooling and help take care of his ailing mother. In fact, he praised God for the move. "I now believe what they say; 'God moves in mysterious ways'," he said. "I have no doubt God led me to come home to meet my future bride, my true Zeemai. I can't thank Him enough."

The first week of school was hectic. Like other students, Sayzay picked up assignments here and there, but his mind was fixed firmly on Kolu, the love of his life, the lady of both his dream and waking hours. He dearly wanted to talk with her, even if that meant just saying, "Hello!" but he could not even do that. While he walked to school, their father's driver dropped off her and her brother. She was in tenth grade and he, eleventh grade but their classes were not close. The tenth grade class was at one end of the floor while the eleventh and twelfth grades were at another end.

During recess breaks, she always hung around other rich students; he just could not come close to her. Although this was frustrating, he was willing to bear any pains, go to any lengths except the commission of crimes, sacrifice anything except character and integrity, and wait as long as it took to get Kolu as his sweetheart, bride and lifetime partner.

At the end of the first week of school, Golo asked Sayzay if he had succeeded in talking with Kolu. "Not yet," Sayzay replied. "I just cannot get close to her. It's truly frustrating but this is temporary. I mean, it's a matter of time. I will have that lady as my bride, no doubt. You know what they say; 'a patient dog eats a fat bone'."

"True," Golo concurred "but you also ought to remember that by waiting patiently over time, the patient dog most likely ends up with a rotten bone." Sayzay shook his head in disagreement. He was baffled by Golo's failure to see possibility and the reality of him marrying Kolu.

Golo too was amazed by the certainty in Sayzay's voice and demeanor. Sayzay seemed sure, undoubtedly sure. Yet, Golo felt forced to redirect Sayzay to reality. "I told you Buddy," Golo reminded. "That girl is in a different class and there's no way you and she will ever mingle together, let alone date."

"I know she is in tenth grade while you and I are in eleventh grade."

"Don't be silly," Golo scolded. "I mean social class and that's why she only hangs around students from a similar social status as hers; as you know, that does not include you and me. That's the reality Buddy; accept it now or later."

"Never!" protested Sayzay. "I will not stop wooing that beautiful angel on account of differences in social status or on account of anything or anyone else. What? Is she not another human being? Nothing will stop me and no one will intimidate me," Sayzay emphasized. Without saying a word, Golo once more shrugged in amazement.

Seeing that he could not come close to the love of his life, Sayzay wondered what he could do to get Kolu's attention and admiration. In that regard, academic performance was not an option. While Kolu was an A student, he was a C student with occasional B's. Consequently, he had to look elsewhere. He therefore inquired and found out that Kolu loved music and sports. That settles it, he thought to himself. "I will be a musician, and a very good one; no, an excellent one."

Often, wise elders advise youngsters not only to be ambitious in life but to reach for the sky and dream big. Grandiose dreams, however, must be backed by abilities, opportunities, and sometimes luck to embrace reality. In Sayzay's case, he had no musical talents and no opportunity or luck for developing any, if he could. His dream of becoming a musician therefore ended in a dismal failure. He was nonetheless thankful to God Kolu was not present for his debut appearance as a musician because, although he worked very hard on becoming a musician, he made a total fool of himself. Evidently, he was not a musician and had not the slimmest chance of becoming one. Nope, he was not for music nor was music for him.

After failing miserably with music, Sayzay had only one means of attracting Kolu's attention and impressing her; he had to excel in sports. He therefore started practicing football (some call soccer) with the boys, including Akoei. Again, he was bad, really awful on the field but he did not give up. He worked daily to improve his football talent. Often, he was not only teased but insulted and humiliated for bad plays; it seemed he just could not do anything right on the football pitch. In spite of it all, he refused to quit. Anything for Kolu was worth pursuing. Likewise, for Kolu, he could withstand any insults.

As Sayzay continued to perform dismally in football, it became increasingly difficult for others to choose him on their practicing teams. One day, when all the players were selected for another practice session, the only position left unoccupied was the goal. As no one wanted that position, the coach took a chance on Sayzay. Amazingly, Sayzay did well, surprising everyone including himself. The coach therefore spent extra hours coaching Sayzay regarding the dos and don'ts of goalkeeping. The new goalie learned quickly and it showed in his performance. He was outstanding between the poles.

Sayzay's newfound talent gave him renewed hope. Many students were delighted that the school finally found a talented goalkeeper. It was the talk around the school and at home. For example, Akoei talked about him ad nauseam at home so much so that Kolu wanted to see Sayzay play. Therefore, one day she went to him. "Are you Sayzay?" she asked.

When Sayzay's true love addressed him directly, his heart started beating rapidly, his blood pumping as fast as it could. For a moment, he was speechless. He could not believe he actually was talking with not only Kolu but also the angel of his life. To sweeten the pie further, she started the conversation. He could not be happier. He was sure this was the break he needed to start a strong and durable relationship with Kolu, his True Heart String.

"Yes I am Sayzay and I am pleased to talk with you finally," the young man spoke in the smoothest voice he could muster. Without Kolu having the faintest idea as to what he meant, she asked when the next big game was. "In two weeks, we are facing one of our arch rivals. Are you coming? I really want you to come and be my special guest."

"I will not miss that game," Kolu promised. "My brother and I will be there; I can't wait. Also, I will convince my parents to come; they too love football."

Talking with Kolu made Sayzay's day, week, and month; he could not be happier. She was to be his special guest; incredible, fantastic. He then stopped himself in his tracks. This meant he had to perform superbly as he could not afford to disappoint his special guest. The thought put a heavy burden on him but for Kolu, he was armed and ready to take on any task and win. "I will practice over and over to make sure we win," he voiced his determination.

Indeed, the Fasawoba team practiced vigorously for the big game. Sayzay was impressive during practice and therefore a huge hope for the team. The day finally came. The host team appeared in elegant jerseys to the applause of Fasawoba students, teachers, parents, and well-wishers. To Sayzay's utmost delight, Kolu and her parents were in the stand. This meant he could do nothing but his very best. He was determined to do just that.

The visiting team, also elegantly dressed, was aggressive from the first whistle. Within the first thirty minutes of the game, Sayzay had narrowly saved the team a goal at least ten times. Unfortunately, this stance did not last forever. Five minutes to the end of the first half, the visiting team scored. Sayzay was crushed but not panic; he had to ensure victory for Kolu.

The second half was equally tough, if not more so. The visiting team continued its aggressive attacks but thanks to Sayzay, it did not score. Instead, Fasawoba equalized to a thunderous applause of students, teachers and parents. Less than ten minutes after the equalizer, Golo, an incredible ball handler, displayed his magic. He skillfully dribbled past four players and landed the ball at the back of the net. The stadium went wild. Doubtless, it was a beautiful display to see.

Naturally, being down a goal angered the visiting squad, which became more aggressive than ever. Fortunately, Sayzay was up to the task, saving every ball sent his direction. Yes, Fasawoba had to win but more importantly, at least to Sayzay, he had to win for Kolu.

Sayzay's hopes of winning appeared unlikely when, less than a minute to the end of the game, a penalty was called against Fasawoba. Initially, the Fasawoba coach and teachers rejected the call but the referee did not relent; he kept blowing his whistle continuously and waving people off the field. Eventually, the Fasawoba coach, teachers, and supporters capitulated and the stadium became as quiet as a graveyard. The ball was placed on the penalty spot and all hopes rested on Sayzay.

Interestingly, he welcomed this opportunity as his last chance for winning Kolu over. He therefore stood calmly between the poles eyeing the football and the opposing player who was to kick the penalty. On the other hand, for Fasawoba fans, stress was not the word. Some were actually trembling while others were in tears.

As anticipation mounted, fans shouted words of encouragement to Sayzay but the goalkeepers resolve was rekindled doubly when he heard Kolu shouting from the stadium, "Go Sayzay! Go!" That did it. He had to do his best or die and he was not about to die and leave Kolu. So he was prepared.

The coach of the visiting team called his captain for a brief conference. The crowd waited anxiously but the referee did not have to wait for the visiting coach. The referee kept looking at his stopwatch.

At a certain time and apparently only the referee knew when, he signaled for the kicker to move toward the ball and the captain of the visiting team did. Since the captain knew that generally, goalkeepers study the eyes of kickers to figure out the possible direction of the ball, he turned his back to Sayzay and the ball. At the sound of the referee's whistle, the captain of the visiting team, an extremely talented player, quickly turned around, ran toward the ball, and put his left foot into it. "Saved!" the crowd shouted and spectators thronged the field. Sayzay remained calmed as if to say, "I knew I could do it for Kolu."

It took a while for the referee and linesmen to get the crowd off the field. About thirty seconds after the gamed resumed, the referee blew his whistle to end the game. Once more, the crowd took to the field. People lifted Sayzay up high but nothing meant more to him than when Kolu hugged him jubilantly.

"That was awesome Sayzay," she said excitedly. "Thank you, thank you Sayzay; you saved the day."

Sayzay was all smiles and the smiles turned to laughter. To him, she was his special guest and wanted to express her appreciation for the invitation. More importantly, without a doubt, he was sure she wanted to register her admiration and affection for him. He could not be more pleased. He therefore looked forward to a close and open relationship.

As Sayzay anticipated a better relationship with Kolu, his outstanding goalie performance catapulted him to stardom. Increasingly, he became a Fasawoba celebrity as his team inched closer and closer to the regional championship. However, Sayzay never accepted lone credit; he always said it was a team effort and indeed, it was.

The team effort led Fasawoba to the regional championship. To say it was a milestone for Fasawoba would be a gross understatement; the school had never won more than four games in a season. Now, they had won nineteen games and drawn three. They were scheduled to face the talented boys of Suo-mee-lazu who, in nine years, won the regional championship seven times although they had never made it past the first round of national championship games.

Announcements about the Fasawoba-Suo-mee-lazu regional championship game were broadcast on regional and national radio stations and covered in various daily newspapers around the country. Each time, Sayzay was cited as a rising football star who had led his team to an unprecedented northern regional championship. "Sayzay Y. Kargbo," one newspaper editorialized, "is the big D in Fasawoba's defense." Other newspapers and radio stations sent journalists to Fasawoba to interview Sayzay Yakpazuo Kargbo. In each interview, he was modest and sportsman like, not only praising God and giving credits to his teammates and coaches, but also showing respect and admiration for opposing teams.

As Sayzay's celebrity status swelled, beautiful girls in Fasawoba, the region and around the country sought his attention. He received a series of letters and sometimes pictures from extremely attractive young ladies. This was much to his parents' delight. They really wanted a prospective daughter-in-law for their only child.

It goes without saying that, all things being equal, every young person deserves a lifetime partner and Sayzay was no exception. Beyond his goalie celebrity status, he held his grounds in looks and appearance although not Mr. Universe. Besides, he was well mannered as he was raised well.

As beautiful girls sought Sayzay's attention, he was only interested in Kolu, the love of his life. During one football practice, he asked Akoei, Kolu's brother if the Fahpeh family was going to the regional championship game. "Of course," Akoei assured. "My sisters, parents and I love football a lot. With the exception of one sister, we will not miss the game for anything."

Sayzay was delighted to know his true love would be at the game but was surprised to know she had a sister. "Your sisters?" he asked Akoei.

"Oh yea," Akoei replied. Fahzie Lawuo Fawkpa is the daughter of my father's late brother, Fawkpa." Sayzay nodded, as he instantly understood. He knew that in this culture, one's father's brother was not uncle but father; therefore, children of two or more brothers were true siblings. Likewise, one's mother's sister was not aunt but mother.

Therefore, children of two or more sisters were true siblings. As he marveled at the family relationship in his culture and wondered how other cultures categorized family members, he could not take his mind off Kolu's family. "Where is Fahzie?" he asked. "She lives here in Fasawoba but, although my father raised her as a true daughter, she no longer lives in our house. She owns a house and a little store at the edge of the town."

Sayzay nodded again. He knew the location of the store but hitherto, did not know the owner. "I wonder, just wonder if through Fahzie I might be able to connect with Kolu," he whispered. "It's worth giving it a try. After all, they say he who ventures not gains naught and God knows in this case, I will not go empty-handed."

Sayzay and the Fasawoba boys practiced very hard for the regional championship game. They knew all eyes were focused on them especially since they were rated as the Cinderella team that was likely to capture a regional championship. Youngsters in Fasawoba therefore wished them the best while elders prayed fervently for their success.

CHAPTER THREE

Sayzay and his teammates practiced hard and long for the regional championship match, the day of the big game came. Spectators from parts of the region gathered in Biahlaw, the regional capital for the match. Coaches, players, and spectators could not be more anxious. While some players were nervous, others were relaxed and confident but none more than Sayzay. His confidence was not derivative of arrogance but determination to win another one for Kolu. "If only we could win a regional championship," he thought, "who knows; maybe Zeemai will finally come around. So help me God," he prayed.

The game started with a bang. The Suo-mee-lazu boys showed their superiority by taking an aim at Sayzay seconds after the whistle blew to start the game. Sayzay was prepared; incredibly, he saved the goal to the jubilation of Fasawoba spectators. However, this was certainly not the last shot toward Sayzay. In fact, it seemed the Suo- mee-lazu boys were playing half field with Fasawoba. Again, and again, Sayzay saved the day with his acrobatic performance between the poles. Each time he glanced at Kolu, her family, his energy was renewed, and his resolve invigorated.

The second half was no less hectic for Fasawoba. Suo-mee-lazu took them to task repeatedly. But for Sayzay, the game would have been a disaster. Finally, the whistle blew to end the game; it was a nil-nil draw and spectators from both sides flooded the pitch. Once more, Sayzay was lifted high in the sky but he dearly waited for a hug from Kolu. Unfortunately, that was not to be. The crowd was too big for her to reach him. It was also unfortunate that Suo-mee-lazu won the regional championship on points. This did not dampen the jubilation of the

Fasawoba crowd for never in the school's history had it come this far; receiving a second place trophy was a huge victory indeed.

When the field cleared a little, Mr. Fahpeh and his family walked toward Sayzay; everyone gave way. When they reached him, Mr. Fahpeh addressed him directly. "Sayzay my son," he said, "you are an outstanding young man; we are very proud of you. My family and I brought you a small gift to congratulate you for your amazing athleticism. I have no doubt you will be a great athlete and a wonderful man. Congratulations!" Kolu, her mother, and brother also congratulated Sayzay. Akoei joyously patted him on the back while Kolu and her mother embraced him warmly.

Sayzay once more thought he was dreaming. He dearly wanted to meet Fahzie but although she did not make it to the game, he was particularly delighted to know that his soon-to-be father-in-law thought he was bound to be a wonderful man. He could not be more pleased. He thanked the Fahpeh family as he enjoyed his moment on cloud ninety-nine.

The Fahpehs talked positively about Sayzay in their commodious car as they rode back home. "That young man is bound to go somewhere," Mr. Fahpeh predicted. "He is just an awesome player; I mean the kid is good." Kolu and her mother agreed for they both admired Sayzay's athletic performance.

Akoei also agreed with his father but when farther. He said he had never seen a goalie like Sayzay and he doubted whether, in his lifetime, he would find one with such limited experience but unmatchable skill. He emphasized this point and provided as evidence, the fact that he had watched many national and international matches but had never seen anyone like Sayzay; no one was close. "The gentleman is just great," Akoei declared once more with emphasis. "That's why I am proud to be his buddy. Yes, it is a true honor to practice on the same field with him. One day, when he becomes famous, I will show people pictures of me practicing football with him. Without such pictures, no one will believe me." Laughing, Akoei's family agreed.

The regional championship game brought the school year to an end. This meant Sayzay had no opportunity of seeing Kolu daily. Of course, this bothered him. He handled this bother by being busy. He took care of his mother and regularly worked on his father's farm. As he never took his goalkeeping talent for granted, and since excelling in sports was his only means of winning Kolu over, he practiced football regularly and vigorously with the boys. When everyone left the field, he spent considerable time practicing by himself. He did so by jumping from one end of the goal to another as he imagined balls coming his way from various directions. He would do this for another hour or two always with his mind fixed on Kolu.

During one afternoon practice session, Akoei showed up. As usual, he seemed to be in a new outfit with a new pair of expensive soccer boots. "My goodness, I have not seen you since the regional championship game," Sayzay said excitedly. "How are you and how is your family?"

"Just fine, thank you," Akoei replied politely. "We all enjoyed the championship game and still talk about it. We truly admired your superb performance."

"Thanks," Sayzay returned the courtesy. "But how is your sister Kolu? Is she alright?"

"She is fine," Akoei said. He relayed that in his entire family of four, Kolu talked about the game the most. She appeared to relive the game repeatedly, enjoying every minute especially those moments Sayzay saved one goal after another. "I mean, she just cannot get enough," Akoei laughed.

"I'm glad to hear that," Sayzay averred. "I think of her every waking moment of my life and probably when I'm asleep as well."

"You do?" Akoei asked surprisingly. "And why is that?"

Sayzay grinned sheepishly before coming back boldly. "I love Kolu, Akoei and I'm sure I will marry her. Yep, it's Kolu or no one else. I feel the love for her deep in my heart and soul; she is a truly God- sent to me and I thank God for her every day!"

Akoei was speechless, utterly shocked. Then, he burst out in an interminable laughter. He tried to stop but could not control himself; he just could not bring himself to stop laughing. "What!" he said. "You marry my sister?"

"Yes, me!" Sayzay answered with confidence, pointing to himself. "I will marry your sister or no one else, and I mean that."

Akoei finally stopped laughing and took on a serious face. "Look Sayzay, my family and I admire you for your wonderful athletic performance but do not mistake that for anything else. You and my sister are so far apart that your illusion of marrying her could not be more hilarious." Akoei further lectured Sayzay about his sister's stunning beauty worthy of a prince, his family's socio-economic status that would not allow his sister to stoop to a lowly one like Sayzay, etc... "Let's face it Sayzay," Akoei continued, "off the football field, you have nothing to offer anyone. If you do not play professional football, you have no future other than taking care of your father's farm. If you play professional football, and that's unlikely despite your talents, you still will make peanuts compared to what Kolu and I will inherit from our father. So, frankly speaking, why should my sister stoop down to someone like you? To get what? Quite frankly, the thought is nauseating."

Akoei stopped and looked at Sayzay to see if there was a change in his demeanor. Seeing none, he continued. "I assure you Sayzay, until you and I die, we will never come close in social status. So, just get it out of your mind. It is a stupid dream that you will ever come close to marrying my sister. No, never; not one like you."

Sayzay surprised Akoei by nodding his head as if he agreed with him. He said for Kolu's sake, he was willing to endure any pains, including Akoei's insults. He said

Akoei was right in that he, Sayzay, had nothing, and could do nothing. It was possible he did not have a great future but only God knew that. However, he assured Akoei beyond doubt that he had something to offer his sister, something he was sure, very sure, no other man could match, not even come close. "I have a deep, untainted, unadulterated love for her. No one else can offer her that kind of love, not the way I do—no, nothing or no one comes close."

"You are absolutely crazy," Akoei chastised with emphasis on 'absolutely'. He was sure that, in light of his sister's stunning beauty and with his family's wealth, there was not a single prince in his right mind who would not want to fall in love with his sister. Laughing lightly, he said for the same reasons, there was no princess in her right mind who would not want to marry him. "It is amazing that you do not understand these glaring facts but rather continue to dream. Yes, no doubt, you are not only a dreamer but a dumb one. You must be dumb to think someone of your stature can even come close to my sister. You are even lucky to be talking with me. As lowly as you are, I ought not talk with you but I do so for the sake of sports and nothing else. Haven't you heard that birds of the same feather flock together?"

"I definitely have," Sayzay said with a smile. "The fact that they have the same feather is only a minute part of the reason why they flock together."

"What do you mean?" Akoei shrugged his shoulders. He smiled at Sayzay's inability to understand such a simple statement.

Sayzay looked away as if trying to find the answer to the question elsewhere. He smiled again. Looking back at Akoei, he spoke as clearly as he could. "The real reason why they flock together centers on insecurity, fear, and outright laziness."

"You are crazy," Akoei said with a mocking giggle. "It's unbelievable that you cannot understand such a familiar saying."

"You don't understand," Sayzay retorted with an emphasis on 'you'. He elaborated that birds of the same feather flocked together because individually, they were incapable of protecting themselves. They flocked together because they lack self-confidence and ability to fend for food and other needs. He stressed that singly, none of them was capable of overcoming hurdles and accomplishing goals. "In other words," Sayzay clarified, "insecurity, lack of confidence, laziness, and dependence force them to flock together."

"I say, you are absolutely crazy. What's difficult to understand that 'Birds of the same feather flock together'?"

"It's not difficult Akoei. When was the last time you saw a flock of eagles?"

"What does that have to do with it?"

"Just answer me," insisted Sayzay. "When?"

"Well, I haven't. Have you?"

"Actually, a group of eagles is referred to as a convocation but in general, eagles, especially bald eagles do not flock together." He explained. "While eagles sometimes gathered to mate, they seldom flocked together; rather, they competed with one another." He said this was because a kingly bird like an eagle did not need a flock. "It is confident, strong, adventurous, smart, and knows what it wants and needs. With its sharp vision, mighty wings, and strong body, it does not allow anything to deter him; so are some people."

Akoei was very puzzled. Sayzay explained that because of the self-confidence of determined people, they allow nothing to deter them. Rather, they persist in spite of obstacles and seeming impossibilities. They venture when others don't and setbacks only solidify their resolve. "When you find such a determined spirit, you have found success."

Akoei stood in total numbness. He wondered what it took to get a simple statement into the skull of this peasant young man. If he could not, he could at least direct the conversation to the issue at hand. "But what does that have to do with my sister? What does that have to do with a lowly peasant son dreaming stupidly about marrying my sister? It is precisely because of such stupidity that we oppose lowly peasants like you and ensure that you do not associate with us much, so some of that stupidity does not rub off on us."

Akoei looked directly at Sayzay expecting a change of facial features or even an outburst of anger; there was none so he went on. "There can be no love where you are socially far apart. To make things worse, you do not have the looks for a queen half as beautiful as my sister."

Sayzay's smile turned into a giggle. "I say … God help us all."

Though he suspected why Sayzay laughed, Akoei asked nonetheless. "What are you laughing about?"

Sayzay continued laughing softly. He gave no reason for his laughter but rather said, "That's the thing you do not understand Akoei. It is not love when one loves because of beauty, wealth or any other factor. Love is only love when you love because of love." He caught Akoei grinning mockingly but paid no heed. He explained that love at that level ignored everything else and took hold permanently and deeply. Without such love, there might be infatuation or a relationship of dependence, convenience, self-promotion, sexual satisfaction, or even exploitation, but nothing in pure love. "This is why, in one way or another, pure love always conquers," Sayzay ended his brief lecture.

"How would you know pure love when you still are a virgin, let alone experience marriage and all its headaches and sweet juices?"

Sayzay was tempted to ask Akoei how he knew about the headaches and sweet juices of marriage when he too had never been married but he refrained from doing so. Rather, he confirmed that although he did not know how Akoei knew, he, Sayzay, had known no woman and, after seeing Kolu, thanked God for that. He said Kolu would be the first and only lady he would ever know. If he did not know her, on his honors, he would know no other woman. "I also cannot say how I know I will marry this angel but I can only say, I sincerely know."

Akoei had had it. "There you go again with your silly dreams." He said he had to go but before going, he once more wanted to make it clear that Sayzay and his sister were miles apart in terms of social status. For that reason, she deserved a man far better than Sayzay. It was therefore advisable, in fact compelling, Sayzay looked elsewhere. "I assure you without a doubt," Akoei bellowed, "regardless of who or what you ever become, and I am sure that will be next to nothing, you will never come close to Kolu, let alone marry her. Now, get that into that skull of yours and, for once, make an intelligent decision that will benefit you. Although I do not blame you for your peasant life has left you perpetually dumb and you're clueless about simple things, I hope you do just that."

Sayzay simply nodded and watched Akoei majestically walk away. If you do not know true love, you will never understand it, he thought to himself. In essence, he was alluding to the teachings of elders. Such wise elders teach that, "Love that is not based on love itself is by definition, fake, deceptive, and abhorrent."

CHAPTER FOUR

The brief encounter with Akoei did not discourage Sayzay; quite the contrary, it buttressed his resolve to marry Kolu. He only wished he could make Akoei and everyone else understand and even appreciate his dogged determination and his deep-seated love for Kolu. He no longer knew how to convince people, including his closest friends. Maybe I need not convince people, he thought to himself. Rather, I will let my actions speak for me.

On his part, Akoei was fuming with anger as he headed home. He did not understand why a lowly one like Sayzay could even dream of marrying his sister. "For sure, he is mad," Akoei concluded before walking into his home.

Kolu was on the phone when her brother entered. The living room was full of expensive furniture. There were pictures of the family in groups or singly. The recherché rug on the floor seemed like a huge mattress for someone's bed. The artwork in the living room alone must have cost tons, maybe tens of tons.

As soon as Akoei walked into the living room, Kolu hung up the phone. "Who was that? Your boyfriend?" Akoei asked laughing.

"What's that supposed to mean and why are you being nosy?"

"I just want to know if you were talking to your boyfriend."

"I do not have a boyfriend," Kolu snapped.

"Take it easy Little Sis," Akoei kept laughing softly. "I do not understand why someone as beautiful as you do not have a boyfriend. Evidently, being queen did not help."

Kolu, getting angry, emphasized that she did not have a boyfriend because she did not want to. Furthermore, she would have Akoei understand that she got letters and calls from guys all the time but was not interested in people Dad called 'vagabonds'.

"So there Mr. Nosy."

Akoei continued laughing softly. "Well, I'm asking because I found you a boyfriend, in fact, a husband."

"And who is that?" without waiting for an answer, Kolu questioned further. "Why should you be interested in finding me a boyfriend? I have not even met him and you think he will marry me? You must be crazy."

"You have met him and I am not the crazy one; he is."

"Who is this person?" Kolu's curiosity swelled. "Who is he?"

Akoei's soft laughter turned into a loud one and he could not stop laughing. When he did, he broke the news to Kolu. "Believe it or not, Sayzay says he is in love with you and will marry you and no one else."

Kolu sat up straight. "Wait, you're kidding right? You mean Sayzay the goalkeeper? That will be the last person I will consider dating even if he were the last man on earth. So, you must be kidding, right?"

"No, I'm not," Akoei, stated firmly. "I had a long discussion with him this afternoon and he is rigid in his decision; it seems nothing will deter him."

Kolu stood up. "What did you tell him? Please tell me. What did you tell him?"

Akoei started laughing softly again. "I told him he was crazy."

"Absolutely!" Kolu concurred. "I cannot believe my ears. Sayzay?" She too burst out in laughter and Akoei joined in the laughter. "He truly is crazy to think I can date him let alone marry him. That will never happen, even if I were to be on drugs or totally crazy and out of my mind."

As Kolu and her brother talked, their mother walked into the living room. "What are you two laughing about? Did someone win the lottery or a ticket around the world? It must be something like that."

"Ma, Kolu not only found a boyfriend but a husband, one I'm sure you will be very proud of, unless of course, you belong to the prestigious Fahpeh family," Akoei teased. "But whether you are a Fahpeh or not, this guy can't wait to marry your daughter."

"Wow! That's worth celebrating. Who is the lucky man?" asked Mrs. Fahpeh. "Have I met him?"

Akoei said, certainly his mother had met the suitor although she did not know him as such. "Believe it or not Ma, Sayzay the goalkeeper is sure he will marry Kolu or no one else."

Mrs. Fahpeh started laughing too. Suddenly, she caught herself and stopped laughing. She took on a serious face. "Come to think about it, this is no laughing matter. We have to set him straight; he is nowhere near the caliber of my daughter to even think he can date her. Who does he think he is? Has he forgotten where he was born and his lowly status? What! A peasant child to marry my daughter? Over my dead body."

"Calm down Ma," Kolu coaxed her mother. She said she was sure she could never come near Sayzay. In fact, no matter how well he played, from now on, she would avoid him. "I never ever want to give him the slightest impression that he can ever date me. No never!"

As the three talked, Mr. Fahpeh entered the house. When he heard the news, he too could not stop laughing. "What? A peasant child to marry my daughter? Where will he take her for their first date? Into the jungle or to his father's dirty farm? Unacceptable. The jungle fool must be out of his mind. If I ever catch him even staring at Kolu, I will cut off his ...," Everyone laughed again. It seemed the case was settled. The entire family was sure, absolutely sure, Sayzay would not date Kolu, not even come near her. Fahzie was the only person in the family who was not present to voice her opinion.

∞ ∞ ∞

As the summer vacation dragged on, Sayzay became increasingly uneasy about the fact that he could not see Kolu on a daily basis, even from a distance as he did when school was in session. "I would like not only to talk with her daily but touch her every minute; I'm willing to settle for seeing her at least once a day, even from a distance. For even then, I can feast in her beauty, be soothed by her presence, and be assured of a great future together. Yes, a future life together with Kolu cannot be anything less than great, I mean, absolutely awesome!" He rambled on and on as he walked sluggishly around his father's small house.

Sayzay regretted that he could not reach Kolu by phone. If my father had a phone, he thought, I would call Kolu every day to hear her angelic voice. Naturally, he had given no thought to whether Kolu would be willing to talk with him by phone.

Other than showing up at her house, and this was least likely, Sayzay's last choice for contacting Kolu was writing her a letter. This also seemed unlikely, as he knew no one who visited Mr. Fahpeh's home. This was because Mr. Fahpeh did not tolerate anyone from Fasawoba in his house although he and his wife were born in the town and grew up there. Similarly, they did not accept any mail from Fasawoba on grounds that people from the town only wrote to beg them for money and material things. "If we give once to those people," Mr. Fahpeh warned, "there will be no end. Like ants on a trail, they will come repeatedly, and worse, at odd hours. We should never give into their greed or feed their laziness. After all, we cannot change their status as they are bound to wallow in poverty till death."

In his harangue, Mr. Fahpeh never considered the fact that, in his many dubious business dealings, he added to, and actually deepened, the poverty of the people in Fasawoba. Of course, this did not matter because, as he saw it, it was all right to cheat, rob, and lie on business principles. As he often said, business was a matter of profit, profit at all cost—by hook or crook. He also said that business without profit was an exercise in futility, indeed a dumb exercise. To that, Kolu agreed that her father had a point although no one knew how he made his profits.

Sayzay could care less about Mr. Fahpeh's business dealings. To him, what mattered was seeing Kolu daily. Therefore, his inability to see or reach Kolu was frustrating. In that frustration, he vowed to himself. "When school starts, I will write Zeemai every day and hope one of her friends will take the note to her." In the meantime, as with any matter that regarded Kolu, he was not discouraged. He resorted to writing her anyway. Since no one could take the letter, after writing, he would put it in the small desk drawer in his room. He heard of a world leader who did a similar thing. When the leader was angry with someone-a journalist, who wrote horrible things about him, a fellow politician, etc.,- he would write the person a letter, getting everything off his chest about that person. After writing, he would not mail the letter but put it in his desk drawer. Sayzay found some solace in doing so himself.

Increasingly, Sayzay's boredom and frustration for not seeing Kolu intensified. He elected to visit Fahzie, Kolu's sister.

Sayzay seemed to be at Fahzie's store at the right time in that she was not busy. After a courteous greeting, he said, "Mam, I hope I am not bothering you but may I please talk with you a minute?"

Wearing a beautiful gray skirt with white tops and gorgeous chains, Fahzie replied, "Sure." She signaled the handsome young man at least ten years younger to follow her to the back of the store. "What's your name and what brings you to my store?"

Sayzay did not reply. Rather, he followed Fahzie to the backroom of the store. When they were seated, Fahzie repeated her questions. "What's your name and what brings you to my store?"

Now seated comfortably, Sayzay answered. "My name is Sayzay Kargbo."

"Are you Sayzay the goalie?" Sayzay nodded politely. "Wow! You are truly grown." Fahzie relayed that she knew the young man when he was very little but had not seen him for a long time. Since his return to Fasawoba, she had heard wonderful things about him but had never found time to see him play.

As Sayzay smiled at what he felt was great news from a future sister-in-law, Fahzie informed him further that her family talked admiringly about him and this was especially true of her little sister, Kolu. She further averred that once a week, Kolu visited the elderly and the poorest children in town. After the visitations, Kolu stopped by her store. When Kolu did, she could not stop talking about the regional championship game. Sometimes, she demonstrated how Sayzay caught one ball or another. Laughing, Fahzie wondered if her little sister talked about Sayzay in her sleep.

Sayzay's smile broadened. "I'm glad to hear that because I admire her greatly; in fact, I'm deeply in love with her."

"You?" Fahzie inquired surprisingly.

"Yes, me," Sayzay answered, pointing to himself. "Everyone seems surprised, even shocked when I say it but I will marry that girl or no one else. Yep, it's Kolu or no one else, I mean it."

Fahzie was even more surprised; in fact, she was speechless. "What do you think?" Sayzay pushed his luck.

Again, Fahzie was quiet for a while. Then, she spoke up softly. "I know for sure that love is a natural thing and when it's genuine, it knows no bounds, fears no foes, and is never, never intimidated by obstacles or opposition regardless of their source, size, strength, depth, or magnitude. I do not know you but you are not only a very good-looking young man but seem to have been raised very well. However, I'm curious. Have you talked with my sister or associated with her in any way?"

"No," Sayzay shook his head.

"Then how do you know you love her? What makes you think you will marry her?"

"I just know and knew from the minute I set eyes on her. She is beautiful."

Fahzie had never seen or heard anything like this. She was torn. On one hand, she thought this young man had to be completely out of his mind. On the other hand, she wanted to give him the benefit of her doubts and bewilderment. Before reaching any conclusions, she probed as much as she could. "I know my sister is beautiful but you have not answered my question directly. What makes you think you will marry her?"

Sayzay leaned back to relax. In simple but clear terms, he underscored that he had a strong inner feeling, a deep-seated love that did not lend itself to explanation, justification, or logical analysis. "I think that's a mark of sincere love. I do not know her and ..."

"Do you know anything about our family?" Fahzie interrupted.

"No," Sayzay once more shook his head. "I am learning a few things here and there but as of now, I do not know a whole lot. Give me time. No doubt, I will learn about Kolu and her family perhaps more than she would want me to."

Fahzie was lost again. She could not understand why a young man who had not spoken much with a young lady felt so strongly. Then she felt as if she had forgotten something. "Excuse me," she said, "may I get you something to drink?"

"I do not drink anything alcoholic; so water will be just fine, thank you," Sayzay replied politely.

"Actually, I do not keep anything alcoholic in my store," Fahzie informed. "But I do have juice and soft drinks. Wouldn't you like some of that?"

Sayzay still preferred water. Fahzie pulled a jog out of her refrigerator. Minutes later, she returned with a very cold cup of water. Sayzay had never drunk such cold water except from small streams deep in the forest where tree branches shade off the sun to render the water extremely cold. As he drank slowly, Fahzie took her usual seat and returned to the conversation. "Does my sister know you love her?"

Sayzay sipped on the cold cup of water again for he was unable to drink hastily. "I do not think so but I told Akoei, her brother."

"Ah, you can rest assured the entire family knows, that is, with the exception of yours truly." Fahzie sat thinking again. She wondered about her assertion of being a member of the family. In blood relations, she was but no longer lived in the Fahpeh home. To some extent, she therefore felt like, and certainly was treated as, an outsider.

Fahzie also thought of her own situation involving Seywala, the father of her children. He expressed his deep love for her but left her with two children to raise on her own. She did not want to generalize about all men for she knew there were good and bad men just as there were good and bad women.

"So what do you think?" Sayzay tried his luck once more.

Before Fahzie could answer, a customer appeared up front; she ran there. The middle-age gentleman inquired about prices, looked around and promised to come back. Before he left, he asked Fahzie if the gentleman in the back was her boyfriend. Fahzie could not believe the man's audacity. She fought hard to conceal her anger as she replied in the negative.

"Your husband?" the man pressed on.

"No, but why ask?" Fahzie continued to struggle with anger and appearing polite at the same time. After all, this was a customer, potentially a regular and long-term customer and the last thing she wanted was to scare such a customer away. On the other hand, long term customer or not, the man had guts to probe into her private life.

Paying no attention to Fahzie's ambivalent looks, the man smiled broadly. "I will come back. What's a good time?"

Fahzie still did not know what to make of this line of inquiry but, being in business, she had to be open-minded. "I open my store early in the morning and stay here till late but what is this about?"

The man smiled again before asking, "But what time of the day when business is slow and there are not many people around?"

Fahzie was beginning to lose it. "I'm busy all day so see you Sir," she tried to dismiss him. The customer was not deterred. He smiled once more and promised to come back. With that, the inquisitive gentleman left, and Fahzie returned to Sayzay with her mind firmly centered on the conversation with him.

"I asked what you thought," Sayzay pressed his luck once more.

It seemed Fahzie had had adequate time to think over the matter. "Frankly, I still do not understand why and how you fell in love without talking with the young lady about the matter. Forgive me but that does not make much sense to me. On the other hand, as I have said, love is a strange phenomenon. Whatever the case, I know my family well. I therefore advise you to be very careful, I mean very careful."

Sayzay thanked Fahzie and indicated that what she said was the most logical statement he had heard in years. However, although he thought her statement was logical, he sought clarification. "Forgive me but what do you mean? Please tell me earnestly and directly."

Fahzie was quiet again for a while as if searching for the right words to say. She cleared her throat and, as if giving herself time to think over the matter, she asked, "Do you want another cup of cold water?"

"No thank you," Sayzay answered. "The water was so cold that it took me a little while to finish it but it really quenched my thirst."

Fahzie sat quietly again before speaking. "What I'm trying to say is that I know my family; they will never accept you or, at best, let me say, it will be difficult for them to accept you." She said her father's opulence had transformed her little sister and brother as well as her parents into what they thought was a mini-god status. However, she was definitely sure Kolu was much less so. Conversely, to her little brother and parents, money was everything and the only thing second to that was socio- economic status, which was influenced by wealth and income. Naturally, she saw things differently and that was why she was glad her dad got her a little house and store where she and her two children could live in peace. It was Sayzay's turn to be speechless. "You mean you do not want to live in your father's rich house and enjoy all the things that come with opulence and high social status?"

"No," Fahzie surprised her guest. She explained that her biological father, Fawkpa, died mysteriously of a minor illness. His brother, Mr. Fahpeh did nothing to help him. She conjectured that out of guilt, Mr. Fahpeh took her into his home and raised her. Of course, she was thankful for that but knew from whence she came. Therefore, she was very happy in her little house and with the small store. With the store, she could earn a small income to raise her children and live in peace. She did not articulate the point that even if that was Mr. Fahpeh's way of getting her out of his house, she appreciated the gesture nonetheless.

"But this house is not very small," Sayzay stated as if trying to make a point.

"No it is not," Fahzie agreed. I have four bedrooms with two baths in the back, two living rooms, a conference room, a big kitchen, a good size dining room, and the store up front. My dad got it for me and he always likes to do things in a grandiose manner. Believe me, I am grateful for it but would have been happy with two rooms for my two boys and me."

Fahzie and Sayzay sat a while without saying a thing. Fahzie wondered if she had revealed too much to a complete stranger. Then she spoke up again. "Since you say you are deeply in love with my sister, I suggest you do not come to my house or store openly. Eventually, my parents will know your intentions toward my sister and believe me, will oppose you in the strongest way they can. In doing so, if they know you do come to my house or store, that will be the end of my business; so, please save me. If you must come here, please do so as discretely as you can; in fact, please avoid me as much as possible."

Sayzay nodded in bewilderment. As if she knew Sayzay's thought as to why she was discouraging him from visiting her, she explained quickly that she harbored no malice, animosity, or objection to Sayzay. "It's nothing personal but if my parents opposed your intentions toward my sister, and they definitely will, I too must go along or at least pretend to do so; otherwise, I will be out of their house and perhaps out of town." She said she could not afford either, as she was unable to raise her two children by herself without any source of income. Without specifics or examples, she stressed that she knew Mr. Fahpeh well and the extent to which he could go to accomplish anything he desired.

"I will do nothing to jeopardize your relationship with your parents but once more, please tell me earnestly; what do you think of my intentions toward your sister?"

Fahzie stared into Sayzay's face as if searching for the sincerity of his intent toward her sister. After a long pause, she took a deep breath and spoke softly, almost in a whisper. "As I have said true love knows no bounds and, in my humble view, should not be opposed, impeded, derailed, or affected negatively in any shape or manner because of external differences. True love is, or should be, internal and, by definition, genuine; anything less is hypocrisy." Fahzie therefore declared that if Sayzay's feelings toward Kolu were genuine, she would not advise him to give up wooing Kolu despite huge differences especially with regard to social status. She said she would be remiss to hide the fact that there would be opposition, insults, chastisements, threats, intimidations, and setbacks but if it was God's will for them to be married, nothing or no one could stop them. On the other hand, if Sayzay gave up quickly and easily, that would imply that his intentions were not deep and genuine in the first place.

Fahzie paused for a moment again before adding, "Remember Sayzay, nothing good and wonderful comes easily. Our people say it best: 'One whose property is beyond the river has wet bottom pants'." She therefore encouraged Sayzay to wet the seat of his pants if he truly wanted his prized possession, which was beyond the river, a river without a bridge. Breaking out into laughter, she added, "Sometimes you have to wet all your clothes to retrieve your property, unless that property is not worth the river-crossing trouble."

Sayzay stood up and shook Fahzie's hand. "Kolu is worth every trouble or inconvenience; she is Zeemai. Therefore, wetting the seat of my pants will not be a problem at all, not even wetting all my clothes in a bid to cross that river." He thanked Fahzie and assured her that she had said everything he wanted to hear and more. At the same time, he once more promised not to do anything to jeopardize her family relationship. He took one-step, stopped and looked at Fahzie. "Believe me, I will not come back here again or if I do, I will do so very discretely. Thank you again."

For days, Sayzay thought over his visit to Fahzie's store. He was sure, more than ever; Mr. Fahpeh and his family would oppose his suit toward Kolu but vowed never to give up wooing Kolu no matter the difficulty or possible consequences. He was convinced great achievements were monumental because they did not come easily. "Anyone as beautiful and worthy like Kolu, any love as deep as mine, is not only worth wetting pants for but even dying for and if I am to die for anyone, it will be for Kolu. If I am to die for anything, it will be for Kolu's love. I have no doubt that if I die for Kolu's love, I will die in peace," Sayzay underscored his unbending love and rigid determination.

The Bard wrote, "Love is blind and lovers cannot see the pretty follies that themselves commit."1 Whether Sayzay was committing a folly or not remained to be seen. For now, he knew he loved Kolu and no one else. He longed for the day school would reopen so he could see her daily. Even though the resumption of school was only weeks away, it seemed like centuries.

As Sayzay waited for the reopening of schools, he took care of his ailing mother and continued working on his father's farm. One day, his mother sent him to call her brother, Uncle Gayvlor.

Uncle Gayvlor was warming himself by a fireplace when Sayzay showed up at his house. It was a one-room house with a fireplace in the middle and three low wooden seats, each with three or four legs. It also had a bamboo bench and two mud beds on either side of the fireplace. There were two shelves and two small corners, toward both ends of the beds for storing personal properties. A large clay pot near the back door kept Uncle's drinking water cold no matter how hot the weather. Incidentally, the back door was seldom opened. Uncle, or a helper, kept the room very clean.

"Good day Uncle," Sayzay greeted as he entered.

"Nephew Sayzay," Uncle replied. "Did you bring firewood or palm wine for your uncle?" Sayzay laughed and said he did not bring either. He said, as he did not drink, he did not have a palm wine treequee but would bring firewood anytime Uncle desired. He then disclosed the purpose of his mission; his mother wanted to see her brother.

"I will be glad to see my sister," Uncle declared. He asked Sayzay to sit with him for a while. Then, Uncle struck a conversation. "You are a nice young growing boy Nephew Sayzay; do you have a girlfriend yet?" The older man laughed thinking about his own teenage years. Boy, boy, boy! Those were the days, he thought quietly.

Sayzay was taken aback. He wondered why his uncle wanted to know. Without hiding the truth, he told Uncle that the love of his life was Kolu. "Which Kolu?" Uncle asked.

---

1 William Shakespeare, the Merchant of Venice Act2, Scene 6.

"Mr. Kolubah Fahpeh's daughter," Sayzay said.

"Kpooo!" Uncle exclaimed. "You are up against a huge wall."

"What do you mean Uncle?"

"Well, I know Fahpeh well and believe me, he knows me too." Uncle Gayvlor smiled and reiterated his point, "He knows me in several capacities." Uncle further explained that though he and Fahpeh once were very close friends, they drifted apart because of Fahpeh's wealth and high social status. "He no longer talks to me but once more, I say, he knows me well. Although I'm older than him, we grew up together in this town. Need I say more?"

"I do not fully understand what you mean," Sayzay admitted, "but do you think I'm out of place to be in love with his daughter?

"Does Kolu know you are in love with her? Does her father know? How about the mother?" Uncle Gayvlor continuously asked without waiting for a response.

"I have not told Kolu how much I love her and believe me, when I find a chance, I will." Sayzay then disclosed that he had told Kolu's brother.

"Then she knows by now, I think," Uncle guessed.

"But you have not answered my question. Do you think I'm out of place to fall in love with Kolu? Is there any reason why I should not date and ultimately marry her when I am deeply in love with her?"

Uncle wanted to know in the first place if Sayzay knew what it meant to be in love. Sayzay said he was sure he knew. He therefore asked once more if there was anything wrong with being in love with Kolu. Uncle Gayvlor came back quickly. "No, no, no! True love is difficult to explain; in fact, when love is rationalized, it's based on something other than true love." The old man stopped and smiled as if once more recalling his younger days. "Ah yea, needless to say, I have been there, done that." He smiled again apparently rejuvenated by sweet memories. He explicated that people fell in love for various reasons--good looks, sexual appeal, social status, position or rank, real or potential financial holding, material possession, intellectual ability, and so on but true love was based on nothing but love. "Specifically," he clarified, "true love is within; external qualities are only fringe benefits. Of course, such benefits are appreciated highly."

"But Uncle, good looks and sexual appeals are important too."

"Yes Nephew; I agree. I just told you; they are appreciated but they come after true love, not before; they enrich true love, not cause it, or at least in my opinion, they ought not to be the sole basis of true love. True love is the love that blazes uncontrollably in the lover despite the looks, wealth or meagerness, popularity or unpopularity, strength or weakness, health or illness of the loved."

It was not clear if Uncle Gayvlor was aware of the difference between intuitive and sensual love but his distinctions were along those lines. It also was not clear if Sayzay fully understood the elder's drift.

Without considering, for a moment, if Sayzay understood him or not, Uncle sat a while thinking of his own experience with love. His eye turned teary when he thought of his late wife who passed away only two years ago. "You see Nephew," Uncle said, "I was deeply in love with your late aunt; so much so that when she passed away, I have not even thought of another woman and cannot fathom the thought of going out with anyone else, not in my old age." He went on and on as to the inner beauty of his late wife, Sawlaawu. "Sure she was beautiful. She turned heads when she passed but that external beauty was less than half of her real beauty. Her real beauty was within and believe me, I admired and appreciated that immensely," Uncle Gayvlor said in a low tune.

Sayzay knew Auntie Sawlaawu; and yes, she was an extremely beautiful and kind lady who loved Sayzay very much. As such, given Uncle's words that beauty did not, or ought not, trigger love, what, if anything was the hook that attracted one person to another? What was Uncle's definition of an inner love? Did he have inner love for Kolu? Sayzay's thoughts rolled on and on but he had no definitive answer. No, he did not understand it, not even in his own attraction to Kolu. Could it be that his inability to understand and/or explain his love for Kolu justified his love as true love? He did not know. Therefore, he was unwilling to dwell on that thought. Instead, he continued to seek his uncle's opinion and advice. "So, I am in my right mind to fall in love with Kolu. Is that right Uncle?"

Uncle Gayvlor smiled lightly. "No one can hold back true love Nephew; otherwise, it's not true love." Uncle nonetheless explained that Mr. Fahpeh's social status and wealth would be reasons for opposing any relationship between Sayzay and Kolu. "To him, you are nothing and therefore should not even look at his daughter, let alone dream of dating her; marriage is out of the question."

"Is that reason for me to give up Uncle? Is it?"

"No, no, no!" Uncle rejected again. "No matter what Fahpeh says or thinks, you ought to follow your true feelings. Only losers give up before they attempt; winners never give up."

I must be a winner, Sayzay thought to himself. However, as he dearly loved what Uncle was saying, he did not want to interrupt. Rather, he wanted to hear more. He moved his low seat closer to his uncle and nodded for Uncle to continue.

On his part, Uncle did not want to deceive his beloved nephew. He made it clear that, regardless of what he had said, it would be a tough battle because undoubtedly, Fahpeh would oppose Sayzay strongly. However, that was no reason for the young man to give up.

To complicate matters, Uncle said Sayzay's parents would likewise oppose the relationship not because they did not love him or because they hated Kolu. They would oppose the relationship because they did not think it would work out and therefore would not like to see Sayzay hurt. In addition, they would fear for their lives, knowing Fahpeh's status and clandestine activities in the community. "Believe me, your parents will not be out of their place to think so. I too know the man we are talking about."

"So, Uncle, regardless of what you know, you will not encourage me to give up, right?"

The older man once more thought of his teenage days and his young adulthood, especially about his beloved Sawlaawu, now regrettably deceased. He was mindful of the fact that times had changed and yet, he could not afford to discourage his nephew. He therefore directly replied Sayzay. "Never!" if that's your true love. In fact, I know that if your love is genuine, threats, intimidations, and seeming impossibilities will not deter you nor will my words, if I were opposed to the relationship. It's only true love that woos with irresistible force." He recalled that when he fell in love with the late Sawlaawu, nothing would deter him and, if necessary, he would have died in pursuing her. "That's true love my dear nephew and believe me, I had nothing less for your late auntie." With teary eyes, he narrated how much he missed his wife.

"You have no idea how much your words mean to me," Sayzay expressed appreciation. "Yes, Uncle, this means a lot to me for whether Kolu knows it or not, she means the world to me. It is my prayer that she will indeed be my wife, sweet wife and lifetime partner."

"If God wills it, nothing or no one can stop it," Uncle assured. Despite the assurance, Uncle warned Sayzay to be very careful with Fahpeh. He said he did not want to scare his nephew but knew for sure Fahpeh had grown callous, vindictive, and virulently vicious. "To put it bluntly, my dear nephew, the man is a cold killer."

"I'm sorry to hear that Uncle but that's no reason for me to stay away from Zeemai. Her father is, according to what you have said, 'the devil incarnate' but she is not. Quite the contrary, she is a saint, my love, and my lifetime partner. I can't wait to hold her in my arms."

"I say, this boy is in love. You already call her 'Zeemai'?" Uncle was amazed.

"Yes, I love her deeply and sincerely, and she's the only one I love."

Uncle Gayvlor did not understand how such a young man knew so much about love but he was convinced the young man was truly in love. He said a soft prayer for him, knowing Fahpeh. Next, he encouraged Sayzay to visit his grandmother and find out what she thought of her grandson's feelings toward Fahpeh's daughter, Kolu. "Your grandmother raised her three children very well and, even at a ripe old age, she still is sharp like a razor," Uncle said.

Sayzay thanked his uncle again. He and his uncle stood up at about the same time. Uncle put on his gown to answer to his sister's call and Sayzay headed toward his grandmother's.

"Maa, Yana?" or, "Grandma, are you there?" Sayzay greeted as he entered his grandmother's house. It was very much like his uncle's except that it had only one mud bed.

"Kpoo! Is that you Sayzay my little one? How are you and how is your mother?" Sayzay said he was well and his mother was trying, given her long-term illness. "I have not seen you for a while. Where have you been?" Grandma asked.

Sayzay said he was in town but, since school was not in session, he worked regularly on his father's farm. "So why haven't you brought me firewood lately?" Grandma questioned. Although Sayzay had brought firewood to his uncle and grandmother only three days ago, he apologized and promised to bring firewood the next day.

"But I came to ask you something Grandma." Without waiting for Grandma to ask about his mission, Sayzay spilled the beans. "Grandma, I'm in love with a girl and so wanted to know what you think."

Grandma fell over laughing. "You Sayzay? In love? I can't believe it."

"I just turned eighteen Grandma."

"That's another thing. Sayzay eighteen? It just seemed like yesterday when you were born into my arms and now you tell me you are eighteen? God be praised!"

Sayzay assured his grandmother that he was eighteen and in love. "Who is the lucky girl?"

"Kolu," Sayzay stated hastily. "Grandma, I truly love her and wonder what you think."

"Which Kolu?" Grandma was anxious to know.

"Mr. Kolubah Fahpeh's daughter," said Sayzay. "She's everything to me and I pray God permits me to marry her one day. I will need your blessings too Grandma."

"Kolubah Fahpeh, Kolubah Fahpeh" Grandma repeated to herself. She said she knew Fahpeh's grandparents. She and Fahpeh's mother were very good friends. "Now," Grandma continued in a disgusting voice, "everyone tells me that, because of his enormous wealth, he is firmly detached from the rest of society. He not only overlooks everyone but is staunchly against people with whom he grew, like your father and Uncle Gayvlor. Not only that but I hear he has become a real devil in the community. You say you are in love with his daughter?"

"Yes Grandma and what do you think?"Grandma repositioned herself in her chair as if preparing to deliver a major lecture. "Look my little one. Fahpeh is but a little child, regardless of his riches. Neither he nor anyone can stop true love. If you are truly in love, pray to God that the young lady eventually develops common sense and accepts you. I say 'eventually' because no doubt, initially she and her parents will oppose you. They will rather see feces than look at you."

Sayzay's faced dropped and Grandma digressed. "But to me, you are the best looking young man in the entire world; no one else comes close." She was sure any princess would be lucky, indeed blessed to have Sayzay for a husband. She said if, on the other hand, love propelled Sayzay to marry a peasant girl that would be no problem either but no doubt, that girl would be transformed instantly into a princess regardless of Sayzay's status. Laughing sarcastically, Grandma added, "That will be the day." She continued laughing as if to tease Sayzay. "Unbelievable," she said. "It is difficult to imagine little Sayzay with his own family; I mean, with wife and children? That's difficult to imagine but I certainly pray for it."

"Grandma, please tell me what you think of Kolu," Sayzay tried to redirect Grandma to the topic at hand knowing that without doing so, she would go on forever with something else.

"I was just saying, Fahpeh will oppose you in every way he can because he only prefers a young man from a family like his to marry his daughter." Grandma regretted that Fahpeh had forgotten where he was born and how he grew up. "I do not know what it takes to bring that boy back to reality," she bemoaned. In addition, she said Fahpeh had not been around long enough like her to know that genuine love required no prerequisites, qualifiers, or bases. It was what it was- true love and nothing else.

Grandma digressed again. "Ah yes, my little one, when I was young, lots of boys came knocking at my father's door. You should have seen them at the time." She said Sayzay's late grandfather was particularly headstrong about wooing her. Eventually, she married him and never regretted; he was a good and honorable man and hard working was not the word. "I mean, the man was a true workhorse who worked from dawn to dust." She laughed. "I could not get him to rest. He worked seven days a week. When I asked him ..."

Sayzay interrupted knowing that if he did not, Grandma would never continue the conversation. "Grandma please go on with what you were saying," he urged politely again.

"You see my little one; Fahpeh does not know what he is doing. I wish someone could knock some sense into his head to understand that money and material things are necessary for living but they are not the only things life's all about." Grandma further asserted that Kolu's mother was the same. She said she literally raised whom she called, "that little girl," and since Kolu's mother and her husband became wealthy, she had never footed Grandma's doorsteps.

Grandma made it clear that she did not need anything from Kolu's parents but only wished they remembered their roots, upbringing, and the precious principles their parents imbedded in them. "Again, my little one, I tell you the truth; I knew Fahpeh's grandparents and parents. They were virtuous people who adhered strictly to the norms, mores and invaluable values of our culture." Grandma prayed Sayzay would be the same.

Sayzay once more tried to direct the conversation to him and Kolu but it seemed Grandma would not be distracted. Referring to the Fahpehs, she stressed in a serious tune, "But they need to understand that gratitude is a peerless pearl. If we are not grateful to our fellow humans whom we see, how can we be grateful to God whom we do not see?" Grandma paused and looked at Sayzay, hoping the teenager understood her point clearly. Then she added, "They also need to learn the realities of life and living."

Still trying to direct the conversation to his one burning desire, Sayzay sought clarification, perhaps reassurance and encouragement. "So Grandma, you do not think it's wrong for me to woo Kolu? Do you Grandma?"

Grandma assured that it was not wrong for anyone to woo unless the purpose for wooing was deceptive and insincere. "When the fire of true love blazes in a young person like you, no force, intimidation, threat, opposition, mountain, valley, or river can squash it. Ah yes, I know."

Grandma laughed again. She added that, in the pursuit of a true love, a wooer was self-defeatist, insincere, and a coward if he or she gave up in the face of resistance from the wooed or opposition from others. She said the price a wooer paid for the gem he or she eventually got were the bumps and bruises, even wounds and broken bones as well as the derogations, humiliations, and inconveniences the wooer received and endured along the way. "In the end," Grandma stressed with conviction, "when you hold your precious gem in your arms, it will be worth the rejection, humiliation, and pain. Believe me," Grandma smiled broadly, "when you dive deeply into the pleasure of your true love, you will forget past obstacles nor will you think there are any problems on earth; that's what true love does."

Sayzay did not stop to think how Grandma, at her age and having lost her husband at least two decades ago remembered so much about love. Rather, he said jubilantly, "Well said, Grandma." He smiled broadly as if he had experienced the sweet juices of true love and was looking forward to a repeat of that experience. He also did not dare ask his grandmother what triggered her memory regarding love and romance. Rather, he looked at his her directly, addressing her as if making a vow. "I'm willing to bear any bumps, bruises, wounds and anything else to get Kolu; Grandma, she will be worth it all in the end."

Sayzay returned to his mother's house not only rejuvenated in his rigid determination to woo Kolu but also assured that, in his pursuit, the road ahead was bound to be rough, to put it mildly. Fortunately, his desire to see her daily would soon be realized, as school would reopen soon. Yes, once more, he would feast daily in her beauty, drown in her laughter—even if such laughter came from afar—and be rejuvenated by her sweet contagious smiles.

CHAPTER FIVE

The resumption of school made returning students happy, as they were eager to see friends they had not seen during the long summer break but no one was happier than Sayzay. He stood afar to await Kolu's arrival. Soon, her dad's car drove up. She and her brother got out. "Wow! She looked stunningly beautiful. What angel has god sent to earth? I'm very grateful to God for not keeping that gorgeous angel for Himself," Sayzay murmured in a blaspheming tune. He smiled broadly at Kolu and even waved but this was much to the disgust and resentment of Kolu. She hurriedly entered the building and went to her junior class where she joyously hugged old friends. They talked endlessly about the summer break but most people recalled the regional championship game. It still seemed fresh in people's minds but one girl noticed that uncharacteristically, Kolu showed no interest talking about sports. "Why do you keep changing the subject Kolu?" she asked. "I thought you were the biggest football fan."

"Nothing," Kolu came back softly. Her friend was not convinced but did not pursue the case further.

In the huge auditorium, the principal welcomed everyone back to school and laid out the usual guidelines. He introduced new teachers and plunged into a series of announcements. It seemed Sayzay was not hearing a thing. He was looking at Kolu as if feasting in her beauty. "That's Zeemai, the jewel of my life," he whispered. "Seeing her today means I will get a good night's sleep. Thank God she's here."

As Sayzay ruminated deeply, he did not hear the principal calling his name. When the principal called him the third and fourth times, someone standing next to him shoved him lightly. "The principal is calling you," the young man said. Sayzay trembled back to life as if awakened from a deep sleep and finally answered to the laughter of students and teachers. The principal congratulated Sayzay for an awesome performance during the regional championship game. "You led the team to new heights and put our school on a national map," the principal praised. On behalf of the Parent-Teacher Association, faculty, staff, and students, the principal presented a special award to Sayzay to the applause of students and teachers. Sayzay's teammates rushed forward and lifted him up once more to the applause of students and teachers. However, Kolu refused to look at Sayzay; she looked one way or another but not at him. Conversely,

Sayzay frequently glanced in her direction.

In brief remarks, Sayzay thanked the principal, teachers and fellow students as well as the Parent-Teacher Association. He also thanked the coach for his fatherly guidance. Above all, he thanked God and his teammates for an unselfish joint effort. "This award is for all of us for certainly, you made it possible so I thank you from the bottom of my heart," he concluded. Once more, he was lifted up high to thunderous applause.

During the first week of school, Sayzay arrived early every morning to wait for Kolu. When she got out of the car, he would smile at her but if she glimpsed at him, she would either frown, suck her teeth, or give him the finger before entering the building. On several occasions, she actually spat when he looked at her.

By the second week of the semester, Kolu's disdainful treatment of Sayzay notwithstanding, he wrote her a note expressing his love and asking to speak with her. "Kolu, I am sure you know by now that I love you deeply; I always will. I therefore will appreciate a minute, just one minute to talk with you Kolu; please grant me this humble request," he wrote.

To Sayzay's joy and amazement, Kolu replied his letter. "Dear Sayzay," she started and seeing those words made him stop reading and jump up and down with uncontrollable jubilation.

"She finally came around!" he shouted. "I knew it was just a matter of time."

He continued reading. "I have received your letter and perfectly understand ..."

Sayzay stopped reading again. He once more jumped up and down for joy. "She understands my feelings toward her. Yes, yes! Thank you God." He was breathing so hard that he had to sit down to catch himself from falling. "No doubt, there is a God and He answers prayers," he kept rejoicing.

He continued reading once more. "I perfectly understand your feelings toward me. However ..."

Sayzay started shaking. "However what?" He could not control himself. He picked up the note, which he had dropped on the bench on which he was sitting.

"However," Kolu continued, "at this time of my life, I am not interested in any relationships. Besides, you and I grew up so differently that I do not see how we could possibly have any reasonable relationship. I therefore thank you for your interest but respectfully beg to decline. Sincerely, Kolu."

"As our wise elders say, this follows the pattern--firm denial first and solid submission next," Sayzay whispered softly. He vowed to persist until he achieved firm and durable submission even if doing so imperiled his life. As he saw it, anything or anyone as precious as Kolu was worth dying for and anything worth dying for was worth pursuing tenaciously. He was determined to do just that. "I will do nothing less because Kolu is my Golden Fleece; any dragon between her and me will be defeated decisively. Yes, I will fight to get Kolu."

In spite of Kolu's clear rejection of Sayzay's advances, he wrote her a second, third, fourth and fifth letter but without response. He also did not stop arriving early to glimpse at her when she got off the car. Moreover, as the school's first game was scheduled, he was sure of another hug from her after the game. Unfortunately, Kolu did not show up for the game although Fasawoba won overwhelmingly—seven nil.

Once more, Sayzay performed superbly between the poles. Akoei relayed the news to Kolu who showed no interest.

After the game, Sayzay sent Kolu another letter stating how much he missed her at the game and how much he loved her. Kolu lost it. She sent Sayzay a response.

When Sayzay received another note from Kolu, he was all smiles but when he opened it, his jaws dropped. "Sayzay," she wrote, "this should be the last time you send me a letter. Never, never again! I do not ever ever want to hear from you. You must also desist from looking at me in the most disgusting way that you do. I tried to tell you in a friendly way that you and I have nothing in common for you to write me, talk to me, or even look at me. I hope you get this in your skull. I do not want you today, tomorrow, or ever; no never!"

Kolu's second letter did nothing to discourage Sayzay. He sent her one note after another. He got one more response. "Sayzay, I have warned you never to write me a note but your thick skull is obviously incapable of understanding. However, whether you understand or not, the next time you send me a stupid note, I will show it to my father. Then, you will know what it means to play with fire, and that's no empty threat."

"It's about time her father knew I am in love with her," Sayzay said. On that note, he sent her another letter expressing his genuine love for her. Kolu kept her word; she showed the letter to her parents. In tears, she explained how Sayzay had sent her many letters and that repeatedly, Sayzay harassed her at school with his stupid looks and smiles.

"Did you ever tell him not to write you?" Mrs. Kebbeh Fahpeh asked angrily.

Kolu said she did. "First, I sent him a friendly note declining his request for a relationship. After that, I sent him two nasty letters telling him never to write me or give me those stupid looks of his."

Wearing a brown suit, Mr. Fahpeh exclaimed, "It does not matter," as he arose quickly from his favorite chair in the house. "That stupid boy must stop and stop now; otherwise, he and his sickening peasant parents will learn a hard lesson." With that said, he took a swashbuckling dash toward the door.

On Mr. Fahpeh's shouting orders, his driver drove him to Sayzay's father's house. "Is Siefa Kargbo in that dirty house?" Mr. Fahpeh called from the car. Before anyone could answer, Mr. Kargbo emerged after hearing a car stop at his house.

"Kpoo my buddy Kolubah; this must be my lucky day. It's surely good to see you.

How are you Buddy and what brings you to my humble house?"

Mr. Fahpeh looked at Mr. Kargbo as if the latter were a piece of … For a while, Fahpeh did not even want to speak to Mr. Kargbo but he finally did. "Look here dirty dummy, don't you ever call me by my first name. You and I are nowhere close to be on a first name basis. When did you ever become my buddy? What's your status in society to be my buddy? You have nothing and worse, you will never get anything to be my friend. No, you will never reach my toe. You will remain the dirty dummy you are and nothing can change that. You are therefore lucky, indeed blessed that I am even speaking to you but I am here for a purpose."

Mr. Kargbo was flabbergasted. He could not believe his ears. "What? You Kolubah? Kolubah who and I did many things together when we were growing up? You Kolubah? You call me a dirty dummy? Ancestors please intercede for Heaven to save us. Kolubah, have you lost your mind or has an evil spirit possessed you?"

"Like I say, you must be a dummy. I just told you never to call me by my first name; can't you get that into your skull? I guess it's true what they say, 'idiocy is incurable' and yours is no exception. I cannot help you and doubt if even God can. No, I am sure you will remain in that miserable state till your dirty body departs this world."

As people gathered to witness the exchange, Mr. Siefa Kargbo laughed. "I can't believe my ears. Of all people, Kolubah Fahpeh? The Fahpeh I know? You talk about idiocy? You know Kolubah I have more than a few stories on you, your plenty money notwithstanding. No Kolubah, do not force me to wash your dirty laundry outdoors. For starters, do you remember how I saved your life in Gizisu? Have you forgotten what happened under the palm wine tree or in the … No Kolubah, please do not tempt me to talk."

Mr. Fahpeh looked at Mr. Kargbo without saying a word. The latter intimated that Fahpeh's deeds were not hidden. For example, it was an open secret as how Fahpeh's late brother, Yanquoi Fawkpa--who was progressive and would have far outshone Fahpeh--, met his demise with no account of his appreciable assets. Mr. Kargbo therefore warned Fahpeh not to throw stones if he dwelled in a glass house.

In addition, Mr. Kargbo regretted that Kolubah Fahpeh had forgotten everything, including the order of his name. Mr. Kargbo therefore lectured his hostile visitor. "Kolubah let me remind you that Kolubah is your second name. Your birth name is Fahpeh but, in a rather twisted fashion in line with your so-called quee[2] system, you took on your first name as your last name. That's how smart you are.[3] I know you Kolubah and regret that you have allowed your riches to inflict you with selective amnesia. Nor mind[44] yah but I rather live with rags in peace than with riches in perpetual torment."

Mr. Fahpeh was still fuming. "Look Siefa, I will not take any nonsense from you. If you go beyond limits, I will flog you with my bare hands."

"Kpoo Kolubah!" Mr. Kargbo screamed. "Clearly, you have forgotten many things but I refuse to believe you have forgotten the various times I whipped your rear end. If you have, I dare you make an attempt and I will punish you far more than our youthful days. Your money may have made you mad and forgetful but my bare hands will drive sense and memory into your skull. I dare you Kolubah; I dare you!"

"You are out of your mind dummy Kargbo."

"Whether I am or not, I dare you get out of that car; if I'm a man, you will know in an instant. What! You Kolubah dare challenge me? Come down if you are a man and I will refresh your memory as to what

---

[2]"Quee" refers to anything or anyone "modern," especially "Western."

[3] In this culture, when children are born, they receive one name; when they attend the poro society (for boys) or sande (for girls), they receive a second name. The second name is considered the adult name.

[4]"No mind" is a way of saying, "Sorry" or my regrets or sympathy."

happened during our youthful days; I can't wait." Mr. Kargbo moved closer to the car and dared Fahpeh on.

"Look dirt poor Kargbo," Mr. Fahpeh said, "I will not stoop to your low and miserable level but let me tell you the purpose of my trip to your dirty house. That dog of yours whom you call your son has been writing my daughter saying he loves her. The next time he even looks at my daughter, let alone write her, I will charge him with attempted battery and invasion of privacy, although I am sure you do not understand those legal terms." Without realizing the utter ridiculousness of his charges, Fahpeh further threatened that proving any of those charges, which was easy to do in court, would land Sayzay in jail for life. He repeated his warning. "Again, be forewarned. I do not want to see that dirty dog even looking at my daughter. Believe me, if he dares, you all will pay a heavy price. Get that into your idiotic skull. Your dirty dog and my daughter are not close in social status for him to speak to her; no, not such a lowly dirty dog. I know your skull is too thick to understand anything but, to save your life, you better understand this one; I mean it Dummy."

Before Mr. Kargbo could say another word, Mr. Fahpeh's driver took off. "My goodness, it's true what they say. 'Money can change people.' You mean Fahpeh? Fahpeh calls my son a dog and speaks to me as if I'm his slave? Good luck to him but he must also be thankful to God he did not carry through with his threat and attack me. He would not dare for he knows where and how we grew up." As he spoke, Mr. Kargbo shook his head back and forth in disbelief.

Long after Fahpeh was gone, Mr. Kargbo stood still thinking and wondering about the uncertainties and unpredictable twists and turns of life. Was he dreaming or was it true that Kolubah Fahpeh called him names, referred to his son as a dog, and even remotely entertained the thought of challenging him physically? "Life truly is an enigma," he murmured before going back indoors.

Mr. Kargbo's house had a big middle room with a fireplace and two wooden beds, which had locally made mattresses. The room had several shelves and three closets for storing personal properties. There were two smaller adjacent rooms, none of which had a fireplace. The smaller rooms also had wooden beds with storage closets. Sayzay slept in one room and the other was reserved for strangers.

Later in the evening, Mr. Kargbo called his son. "Sayzay," he said, "is it true that you are in love with Fahpeh's daughter? Is it?"

Sayzay did not know what to make of the question. He definitely would not lie about the situation but wondered why his father was asking. Without giving much thought to the reason or reasons behind the question, he answered directly. "Yes Papa, I'm in love with Kolu. As my Zeemai, she is the only person I love and will marry her or no one else."

"Her father came here today," Sayzay's father disclosed.

"He did?" Sayzay was surprised but remained calm. "What did he say?" Mr. Kargbo revealed that Mr. Fahpeh had called Sayzay a dog who was chasing Fahpeh's daughter. "He said if he catches you even staring at his daughter, he will charge you with some kind of battery and invasion of privacy. I do not know what those big law words mean but if you know what I know, you better be looking for another girl to date and eventually marry. After all, your mother and I never bore a dog; thanks to God, we have a handsome and well-behaved son of whom we are most proud." Mr. Kargbo revealed that Fahpeh threatened to confront him physically.

"The man is not a fool; he knows me from our young days. I'm sure he remembers the many times I whipped his rear end; therefore, he would not dare touch me," Mr. Kargbo stressed.

As Sayzay listened intently, his father insisted that no one, regardless of whom, was licensed to insult and humiliate him and his family irrespective of their social status. He underscored the point that no matter how poor they were, they had not lost, and would never lose, their dignity and self-respect. Continuing, he argued that no condition or station in society subjected anyone to a sub-human status. Given that truism, regardless of their social status, he and his family would never stoop to a disgraceful position nor violate the laws of the land. Likewise, they would never disregard the rights and dignity of other people, not even the littlest children in society. "I may add that animals too have rights and such rights should not be violated. This is precisely why we frown on the maltreatment of dogs and other domesticated animals," he concluded.

Sayzay nodded as he listened keenly to his father's words. Then he said, "Papa, I agree; no one can take away our dignity. I am grateful to you for teaching me the laws of the land, insisting on character, dignity, and respect for self and others." He disclosed that, in actuality, a considerable number of girls in Fasawoba, in the region and around the country had expressed interest in him but he was not interested in any except Kolu. Sayzay ran to his room and quickly returned with a big brown envelope. He pulled out pictures of gorgeous girls, which he showed his father to add credibility to his words.

"So, she is not the only girl in the world. Right?"

"No Papa but she is the only girl in the world whom I love, I mean truly and deeply love."

Sayzay's father informed that since Fahpeh's visit to his house, several friends had warned him. He said that although they spoke to him at different times, they said the same thing. They told him Fahpeh had become vicious, vindictive, and incredibly cruel. For instance, one person said, "Fahpeh lacks caution or compunction when it comes to exacting revenge or getting rid of rivals, real or imaginary. Worse still, Fahpeh could get away with anything because of his wealth and influence in the region and throughout the nation." A female leader stated that because of Fahpeh's dirty deeds, arrogance, and disregard for others and laws of the land, he had no friends and no one respected him regardless of his riches. "No one cares for his money," the respectable lady emphasized. "Believe me," another person said, "Fahpeh sees himself like a mini god and therefore acts accordingly. He disrespects everyone and totally disregards the laws of the land. He violates people's rights with impunity and worse, he has personally been involved in, or directed the elimination of others in society." The person therefore appealed to Mr. Kargbo to warn his son strictly. "Only God knows Fahpeh's future," the kind friend concluded.

"In addition to what people have told me, I know Fahpeh and have had my own experiences with him. I am aware of his activities in the community, "Sayzay's father stressed. He therefore strongly encouraged Sayzay to rethink his love for Kolu.

Without remembering his conversation with Uncle Gayvlor, Sayzay's face dropped when he heard of Mr. Fahpeh's alleged infamy. Nonetheless, he said in a soft husky voice, "But Papa, Kolu is the only girl I love, no one else. Why should I stop loving Kolu because you, her father, or anyone else opposes the pursuit of the only jewel in my life? I'm sorry to hear her father is allegedly infamous but that's no reason for me to stop wooing Kolu. I love her deeply and sincerely."

Mr. Kargbo struggled strenuously to maintain his composure. He stood up from his armchair, reached over a shelf and grabbed a kola nut. Sitting back down, he informed his son that whatever was said of Fahpeh was not mere allegation; it was all true. Yes, it was also true that nothing was proven against Fahpeh in court but that was because there had been no court trial; Fahpeh's cases never went to court. "Besides," Mr. Kargbo went on, "I'm not trying to prevent you from taking a wife; of course I would like nothing more than see you married to a lady of your choice but in this case, I fear for your life and the lives of other members of your family. I know, and others have confirmed that Fahpeh has grown tyrannically vicious. Don't you see the facts my dear one?" Mr. Kargbo said he had lived long enough to see strange and horrible things happen without investigation, not to mention indictment, trial and subsequent sentencing of vicious culprits. "That's the society we live in Sayzay. Don't you see the facts? Haven't you heard of houses being burned down, people brutally murdered, and more but with no investigations?"

"But I always hear the police vowing to investigate thoroughly."

"True, but then what happens after that? Nothing," Mr. Kargbo lamented. He reminded Sayzay that under such circumstances, the police put out serious but bogus statements and thereafter did nothing. This was unfortunate as poor people lost their properties, rights, and even lives with impunity. In frustration, Mr. Kargbo said it was not fair but that was the world, in which they lived. In other words, people committed crimes and hurt others as if there was neither an earthly body nor a Supreme Being to whom the perpetrators were accountable.

"What am I to do?" Sayzay asked in frustration.

"Listen to us," Sayzay's father replied laconically. He reminded his son that God did not come down from His throne to warn people on earth. Rather, He spoke to people through other people. It therefore behooved humans to listen to one another, at least occasionally.

Sayzay took a deep breath. "Of course Papa I care for my life and the lives of members of my family. However, as I have said repeatedly, I love Kolu deeply. I love her so much so that I can give up the entire world to get her; in fact, she is worth dying for and if I die in pursuing her, it will be a worthwhile death."

"And if members of your family die too?"

"I would not want that Papa and therefore pray that never happens."

"But it's possible if you do not stop wooing Kolu."

"I'm sorry to hear that Papa but even that will not stop me from wooing Kolu. Some things are so precious, some feelings are so deep and genuine that they are worth dying for and for me, this is it."

Sayzay's dad sighed heavily as he looked directly at his son. "Oh love, love, love unrestrained. Are your life and the lives of your loved ones dispensable because of your love?"

Sayzay said he did not want anyone to lose a fingernail because of him. For him, if he had to die for Kolu, it would be a worthwhile death. "I'm not sure how many times I have said that Papa but I truly mean it. Did you not love my mother in similar fashion, I mean at similar depth?"

"Different time, completely different situations," his father briefly replied.

"But you loved her deeply; didn't you?"

"I did and still do; I always will. She's everything to me."

"Please Papa, tell me. How did you meet and woo her? Neither you nor Mom ever talked about that; I'm dying to know."

Sayzay was right. In his culture, in general, for there are always exceptions. For example, romance is not discussed and definitely not demonstrated, in the presence of children. Of course, this does not include deeply rooted erotic looks that convey "I love you" messages a million times in a quick glance. Mr. Kargbo therefore laughed. "As I have said, those were different times and completely different circumstances. You will not understand, let alone appreciate what we did in those days."

"But Papa, I beg once more. Please tell me how you wooed her," Sayzay pressed on.

Mr. Kargbo laughed again. Giving into his son's demands, he explained that he and his wife were borned and grew up in Fasawoba. At one time, he noticed her incredible beauty and wanted to court her.

"What did you do?" Sayzay was anxious to know. Smiling broadly, Mr. Kargbo explained that when he was sure he wanted this beautiful one, he asked an elderly aunt to approach her for him.

"I find this difficult to understand let alone believe. You mean you did not go to the lady yourself? I know you could not write her for neither of you could read or write but why didn't you talk to her directly? If for some reason you could not talk to her yourself, what did your aunt do?" Sayzay could not wait to hear the rest of the story.

"As I said, those were different times," his father reiterated. Explaining further, Mr. Kargbo said his elderly aunt approached the young lady and presented her with a keyyi[5], but, as expected, it was a firm denial. However, the aunt did not give up easily. She went back to the young lady every day for two weeks explaining why the proposed relationship was not only right and necessary but sanctioned by the kinship and above all, by the ancestors.

"How did your aunt know that the relationship she was trying to establish was sanctioned by the ancestors?" Sayzay asked.

"I think that was her way of encouraging the young lady to consider the matter seriously. I'll bet she narrated history to show connections between the two households and hence, an approval by the ancestors."

"What happened next?" Sayzay probed again.

---

[5]A keyyi is a headtie or large handkerchief that is presented to the prospective girlfriend who is being wooed as a token of sincerity.

Mr. Kargbo relayed that finally, the lady said, "It's tied up," meaning, the matter is in suspense. In other words, the young lady was saying either let me think about it or I will consider the matter seriously. This was an encouraging improvement. The aunt went back for another two or three weeks before the lady finally said, "My hand is under it," meaning, "I agree."

Sayzay screamed with excitement. "So what did you do next?"

His father laughed again. "The next day," he said, "I took a huge bundle of firewood to the lady's house."

"For what? You did not even know the lady yet. Why did you take firewood to her house?" Sayzay did not understand.

"To show my appreciation and delight especially since she had accepted the keyyi," his father explained. Mr. Kargbo further stated that, in return, the lady cooked him a nice meal, the meal usually referred to as 'the girlfriend rice'. "When someone brought that bowl of rice, I was on cloud ninety-nine," he narrated excitedly. He said, after that, he did favors for the young lady for a month or so before finally asking the elderly aunt again to ask the lady to spend a night with him. As usual, it was a firm denial but eventually, she did. Soon, they were talking about marriage.

"So, is it from that experience you have always talked about a dogged denial at first and a solid submission later?" Sayzay asked.

"Absolutely," his father agreed. "Since then, she has been the lady of my life and will always be," he emphasized pounding on the bench on which he sat.

"Wow! That was exciting," Sayzay exclaimed. He hoped that his father's experience would be a basis for understanding his pursuit of Kolu. He vowed to do anything to get Kolu. To that end, he prayed to God she eventually became his and his alone, regardless of what her father, mother, brother, or anyone else said or did. In so many words, he said he could care less if people branded him as obsessive or maniacal. "I will listen to my heart, nothing else," he concluded.

Sayzay's dad sat quietly thinking but Sayzay had no idea of what. After a while, Mr. Kargbo said, "I still advise you strongly to rethink this thing over. I know how strong love can be; yes, it's a driving force but it ought not drown one's wisdom and obscure logic." In his own words, Mr. Kargbo counseled that there was a difference between reason and insanity, between persistence and indifference to reality, between confidence and arrogance, between prudence and imprudence, between tenacity and Sisyphean effort, between determination and self- destruction, and between fruitful versus futile or frivolous pursuits. He prayed to God to give his son the right frame of mind.

Sayzay appreciated the advice but tried to convince his father from another perspective. "But Papa," Sayzay said, "you just told me you met my mother at a completely different time and under different circumstances. Why then don't you want to accept that our time is different from yours and therefore, we see things differently? Why don't you want to allow me to live in line with our time?"

"No matter the time," Mr. Kargbo responded, "there is always common sense; there is always reason and logic; and there is always a need to embrace reality as opposed to fighting a frivolous battle."

"But you agree that our times are different, isn't it Papa?"

"Absolutely," Mr. Kargbo concurred. Yet, he reiterated the point that certain invaluable characteristics of humans largely remained stagnant from generation to generation. Sayzay was not convinced. Perhaps he was just reluctant to see the reality of the matter. Conversely, he frowned on his father's failure to see the reality of the matter or at least strive for a balanced perspective.

CHAPTER SIX

As Sayzay talked with his father, there was a knock at the door. Golo and Gayduobah, two of Sayzay's teammates and close friends, both wearing very casual clothes, stopped by to see him. "Go talk with your friends," his father demanded.

"Welcome gentlemen," Sayzay, also in casual clothes and slippers, greeted his guests. "Let's talk in my room."

In his room, Sayzay offered his friends soft drinks, which they took with pleasure. "Thank God none of you drink anything alcoholic because, as I do not touch that stuff myself, I do not have anything here like that," Sayzay informed his guests. Everyone laughed. Of course, the youngsters would not do anything without a few teases here and there. These were followed by hearty laughters. Meanwhile, Sayzay retrieved some fresh corns. He pealed them and lined them up near the fireplace in his father's room for them to enjoy later. There was nothing like nicely roasted corn during this time of year.

When they settled down, Sayzay's friends cut directly to the chase. They disclosed that they were at hand to advise Sayzay against wooing Kolu. They reminded him that he had not spent lengthy time in Fasawoba but they did and therefore knew Mr. Fahpeh's vicious and vindictive character. "So my brother," said Golo, "look around for another girl to befriend; and believe me, there are gorgeous ones around. Along with our girlfriends, we will be delighted to help you." Gayduobah concurred. "Golo is right. There are many beautiful girls around and I know that quite a number of them admire you very much. Consider one of them and not lose your life pursuing someone who does not love you; worse, she does not think you are a befitting human being." He reminded Sayzay of the insults from Kolu's father and worse, his open threats. "We know that man and fully understand that he is capable of doing what he says without remorse or regrets," Gayduobah concluded.

Golo chimed in. "Think of what our wise old people say. 'It's better to marry someone who loves you than one you love'. I think that says it all."

Sayzay thanked his buddies but reiterated his unbending love for Kolu. "Gentlemen," he articulated carefully, "my love for Kolu is genuine; therefore, nothing and no one can change it. I also know that wooing Kolu is difficult, even dangerous, given all I have heard about her father but nothing good comes easily. If I'm to get Kolu's love, I must be willing to work hard for it and if necessary, pay a price or two."

"Knowing that Kolu's father can kill in cold blood, what if that price is your life?" Golo asked.

"So be it," Sayzay came back forcefully. "I'm sorry if this disappoints you and please do not think I'm downplaying your advice. I am not; rather, I appreciate it highly as I know you are seeking my best interest and welfare. I also understand the dangers involved here but if my love for Kolu is true, and it is nothing less, then, I must pursue her regardless of any threats or oppositions, including her resentment and insults."

"Wow Sayzay," Gayduobah declared, trying to control not only his disappointment but fiery fury. "I have never seen anyone blinded by love to this extent. We are talking about your life Sayzay! Don't you understand? Can't you see the glaring facts?"

Rising up, Golo said Sayzay probably was downplaying the threat from Mr. Fahpeh because he had not personally experienced any of Mr. Fahpeh's cruel acts. He therefore excused himself shortly. In a few minutes, Golo was back with an older gentleman. "Do you know Mr. Kezeli," he asked Sayzay.

"Of course I do," Sayzay replied. "However, although we live in the same neighborhood, it's been a while since I saw him. Actually, I do not think I have seen him since I returned to Fasawoba," Sayzay explained. "How are you Mr. Kezeli and may I offer you a soft drink?" The older man accepted Sayzay's offer, shook hands with him, and took a seat. He said he remembered when Sayzay was born. He also remembered Sayzay growing up because his house was not far   from Mr. Kargbo's but he too had not seen the youngster for a while. "But why did you ask me to come here?" Mr. Kezeli asked Golo.

"Well Mr. Kezeli, I would like you to please tell Sayzay about your daughter Seeapulu."

Mr. Kezeli sat a while. His demeanor changed to a melancholy one. In a husky voice, he slowly explained that Mr. Fahpeh's son, Akoei, was interested in his beautiful daughter. However, given the reputation of the Fahpehs, the young lady had no interest in Akoei although Akoei offered money and expensive gifts. In fact, Seeapulu did not accept any of his presents.

"Did you know about Akoei's advances toward your daughter?" Gayduobah asked. "No I did not," Mr. Kezeli answered. "If I did, I would have stepped in in one way or another." He explained further that when Akoei could not get his way with Seeapulu, the young man threatened her. Beyond that, Mr. Fahpeh himself threatened the young lady stating that, as poor as she was, she ought to have felt lucky that Akoei was interested in her. He said if she did not go out with Akoei, she would be in for the worst.

"Did she report this threat to you?" Golo asked.

"Yes she did and that's when I went to see Mr. Fahpeh but he would not allow me into his house. He said I was too filthy to enter his house." Mr. Kezeli said he therefore waited for an opportunity to confront Fahpeh in public. When he did, he warned Fahpeh that if anything happened to his daughter, He, Fahpeh, would be held responsible.

"What was his response?" Sayzay asked.

Mr. Kezeli was almost in tears. "He said my daughter's life was not worth the price of his lunch; therefore, he would eliminate her if he wanted to and nothing would come out of it. Before getting into his car, and in the presence of others, he told me if I cherished my daughter's life, I better advise her to go out with his son otherwise,

... That's when I challenged him; I mean, I dared him do anything to my daughter." Mr. Kezeli assumed that to Fahpeh, this public challenge was an insult and therefore, to prove he could do whatever he wanted, in less than a week, Seeapulu's tortured body was found behind a house at the edge of town. "I have never felt such a horrible pain regarding my young daughter's death; I have not gotten over it and do not think I ever will," Mr. Kezeli stated sadly.

"My God!" Sayzay exclaimed. "Did you tell the police and the elders of the town?"

Mr. Kezeli said he did. More than that, knowing that with Fahpeh, nothing would come out of this barbaric act, he was determined to take the law into his hands. He therefore borrowed a gun, bought a few single-barrel bullets but, knowing his dirty deeds, Fahpeh left town for days and when in town, was holed up in his gated home. Mr. Kezeli said after many attempts and with the elders of the community advising him, he eventually gave up and left his with God. "The God who made us is a just God; He will settle this sooner or later. Believe me; Kolubah Fahpeh will pay for my beautiful daughter's innocent blood he shed with impunity."

Golo asked if Mr. Kezeli knew of any other gruesome act by Mr. Fahpeh. "Yes I do," replied Mr. Kezeli. "In fact, there are several that are not hidden in the community." He cited two instances where Mr. Fahpeh himself was interested in a couple of young ladies (at different times) but each time, he was rebuffed. This tore his ego apart. Consequently, both ladies were found dead at different times. "That's the kind of satanic beast you are talking about," Mr. Kezeli concluded.

The youngsters thanked Mr. Kezeli for his time. They gave him a few coins in appreciation. When he left, Golo turned to Sayzay and said, "Need I say more? Do you now understand the nature of the beast you are messing with in the name of love?"

"Believe me, I do," Sayzay assured his bosom friends. "I still maintain nonetheless that a true and genuine love is worth dying for." Upon saying that, he once more ran to his father's room to look at the corns, which he had been turning back and forth. As they now seemed roasted, he took them back to his room in a small plate.

As the young men enjoyed freshly roasted corns, Golo asked, "If you die without marrying Kolu, most likely, another man will. Have you thought about that?"

"Yes! If I die in her pursuit, I will die a satisfactory death so anyone else may marry her."

Gayduobah was grossly irritated but fought hard again to control his emotions. "Are you hearing yourself Sayzay or have you lost your mind? Is dying in the pursuit really worth it?" Pleading with Sayzay to heed their warning, he reminded him of an old adage: "An animal destined to die never hears the hunter's whistle."

"Is it worthwhile to die in a cause?" Sayzay redirected the question. He said some causes were so valuable that they were worth dying for and wooing Kolu was one such cause. In fact, he could not see anything more valuable, not even life itself. "Forgive me gentlemen," he pleaded, "whether Kolu knows it or not and whether she detests or appreciates my suit, she is everything to me and I will do anything to marry her." He was convinced the marriage would occur regardless of who approved or disapproved.

"Sayzay, let me inform you," said Golo. "This is no cause but a senseless pursuit. If Kolu were in love with you, I would have said she made a juju[6] with your name." Golo added that, conversely, if this was Sayzay's way of deviating from the norm, it was a futile radical venture.

"No Golo," Sayzay rejected rising from his seat. He walked to his small table, pulled out a sheet of paper. "Although this is the kind of stuff some call bombastic language, listen nonetheless to what someone wrote about being radical. 'Radicality without rhyme or reason reflects and reinforces rigidity of imbecility.' So, Golo, my dear friend and brother, this is not a matter of mad radicality."

---

[6] A juju is an African medicinal charm people believe is capable of inflicting harm or disease and, in other instances; making a person do something, he or she would not have done otherwise.

"I do not understand those big words but I still maintain that it seems you are either out of your mind or someone made a juju with your name.

Sayzay said he was guilty as charged. He added, "Indeed, my love for Kolu has charmed and mesmerized me completely and only one so deeply in love, I mean genuinely in love will understand. Trust me Gentlemen on this one; I'm not mad, only in love so much so that not even life itself surpasses my love."

"Sorry Sayzay but that sounds like madness to me," Gayduobah stated in a frustrated tune.

"Like I've said, it may seem so to someone who does not fully understand genuine and deep love. Look gentlemen, I'm not pursuing Kolu for her beauty although that's appreciated highly, nor for her potential riches (for her father currently owns everything). I love Kolu because I love Kolu and nothing else. If she lived in a palace, I would love her. If she lived in a cottage or a shack, I would love her. If she were in prison, I would love her. If she were on a hospital bed, I would love her. What else can I say gentlemen?"

Golo tried his luck one more time. "What if, after your long and tireless pursuit, someone else marries Kolu? What will you do? Will you say, 'had I known'? Or will you say 'What a fool I made of myself?' Honestly, what will you do or say?"

"I certainly hope that will not happen," Sayzay replied. "However, it's very possible and if it happens and that's what makes Kolu happy, I will rejoice for her but live a single man till I die."

"So you will not marry anyone but Kolu," Gayduobah, still angry, questioned as if seeking to confirm Sayzay's position.

"No one else," Sayzay reiterated. "Only god knows the future but let's say, and god forbid, Kolu dies tomorrow. I just cannot see myself ever falling in love with another lady anywhere near as I love Kolu now. As a result, I will live a bachelor till I die." Sayzay sat quietly looking at his guests as if trying to fish some answer or answers from their demeanors.

The two visitors did not present changed emotions but seemed helpless in their effort to persuade Sayzay and possibly save his life. They stood up simultaneously, shook his hand and encouraged him to rethink his position. "We are here to help in anyway Sayzay; that's what friends are for," Golo declared and Gayduobah concurred.

∞ ∞ ∞

As usual, end of dinner at the Fahpeh residence meant every plate had half to two-thirds of food untouched and yet, the food had to be put in the garbage along with everything left unserved on the table. Yet, servants dared not touch any left-overs except those they could hide in the most secretive manner.

At the end of another family dinner, as a maid cleared the table, Mr. Fahpeh, taking advantage of a rare occasion when they did not have business guests, changed the conversation. "I went to that dog's house today," he informed the family. He explained that he had warned Sayzay and his father strongly about his daughter.

As Mr. Fahpeh spoke, a male worker stood patiently for he dared not interrupt the boss to ask whether he wanted coffee or not. When Mr. Fahpeh noticed him, he signaled for coffee and the worker took off. Then Mrs. Fahpeh asked. "What did they say?"

"What could they say?" Mr. Fahpeh replied. He clarified that he warned Sayzay's dad that if he, Mr. Fahpeh or anyone, including Kolu herself caught Sayzay even looking at Kolu, let alone write her a letter, Sayzay and his wretched family would endure heavy consequences. Raising his voice slightly higher, he spoke as if making a vow to his family. "If they dare challenge me, they will pay a heavy price for their stupidity. I have not taken any nonsense from anyone and Siefa and his stupid family will be the last I will spare." As her father spoke, Kolu's face turned to a serious one. It got worse when her father addressed her directly. "Now Kolu, I know you still do your voluntary work although I do not see any sense in it because I think people ought to provide for themselves as we do. Those same people pray to their God daily and yet that God does not provide them with anything. They will languish in poverty until they die. It is therefore beyond me that they continue to pray to a God who does not care about them? That is, if he exists at all—something I seriously doubt.

This is why I think that, if they are that dumb, they should be left alone to fend for themselves. I'm sure however that even when they die, they will remain dirt poor. If they make it to Heaven, and that is if there's one, there must be a ghetto part of Heaven where they will languish in eternity." Mr. Fahpeh gave up one of his rare laughs. He gulped a half-full glass of wine before reaching for his coffee cup.

Unlike her father, Kolu was not amused. She was not bemused for either she had heard this double dose of blasphemy and diatribe on numerous occasions but her facial features changed drastically when he said, "Anyway, if you have to visit them, from now on, you must go with at least one other person and one of my bodyguards. I will not allow you to go into that filthy town alone. People born in that town are destined for doom and destruction; my dear daughter will not be a part of that damned destiny."

Kolu lifted her head and looked slightly at her father. She was careful not to frown for that would imply a disagreement with her father. Mr. Fahpeh was intolerant of disagreements with him, not even from his daughter. Kolu therefore spoke softly but clearly in a disappointed tune. "But Dad, I work with little children and visit the elderly. What can they possibly do to me? She struggled to fight back tears and did a wonderful job masking her emotions.

"Like I have said, those so-called elderly need to provide for themselves but I'm not concerned about them. I am concerned about other people in the town who will see you going from one elder to another. I do not want them to harm you because of what I have told sick, stupid, and senseless Siefa Kargbo or what might befall him and his family if his dirty dog son does not stop harassing my daughter. Who do they think they are?" Making no reference to other things he had done (or was suspected of doing) in the community, region, and throughout the country, he shook his fist up and down like a dog wags his tail when preparing for battle.

Kolu was in severe pain although she was not sure if it showed. She tried to conceal her agony as much as she could. Somehow, she was succeeding although in true terms, she was burning deeply within. She just could not understand her   father.

She therefore said nothing.

"What will you do Dad?" Akoei asked.

"Well, I am not sure exactly what. I can take court action against them but believe me, if all fails, I will crack that dog's head and pay for it myself; I am prepared to do so and I honestly mean it. There's much distance between him and my daughter for him to even look at her. A dirty peasant's son? No way!"

Kolu could no longer hold her emotions. When her tears ran, she excused herself from the table. Her brother and parents continued drinking and talking about Sayzay and his family, a family they described as dirt poor, ignorant, an incredibly backward. Worse, according to them, Sayzay, his family, and similar families in Fasawoba were permanently stuck in that lowly position and would never ever escape from that stagnation, a position they deserved because of their ignorance and filthy lives. According to Mr. Fahpeh, their poverty condition would continue even into Heaven if there was one. Conversely, the Fahpeh family would never ever stoop to that lowly position, not with the money and property Mr. Fahpeh had and continued to accumulate. Without an iota of doubt, they were set for life even if Mr. Fahpeh lost half, indeed three quarters of his wealth, an enviable position for any family. Hence, he often said, "I do not know if there's a heaven but here on earth, I'm my own god. Therefore, no one and nothing can touch me."

CHAPTER SEVEN

At the Fahpeh residence, Saturday mornings were different from any other day of the week. The Fahpehs individually crawled out of bed at different times and dragged themselves to the breakfast table while servants worked frantically throughout the house.

The day following Mr. Fahpeh's imposition of restrictions on Kolu's voluntary work was a Saturday; it was even more different from other Saturdays. Up to noon, Kolu had not gotten out of bed. Unlike her brother and parents, she often did not shower in her private bathroom but preferred the big bathroom because of its huge mirrors. Late morning or early that afternoon, she was not in the big bathroom either. She had not even left her room. Her mother therefore went to her door because, mindful of threats from her parents, none of the domestic workers dared wake her up.

"Are you going to get something to eat?" Kolu's mother shouted as she knocked on the door. She knocked a few times before Kolu rolled over in bed.

"Who is it?" Kolu asked in a shrill sleepy voice. "Your mother!"

"I do not want to eat anything," Kolu's shrill voice once more came through.

"Are you alright?" her mother's curiosity swelled. "Open the door."

It took another minute or two before Kolu crawled out of bed, opened the door, and fell back into the bed. Her eyes looked reddish than usual. "What's wrong with you? Have you been crying? Are you O.K.? Can you talk? What's the problem?" Mrs. Kebbeh Fahpeh threw out a stream of questions without waiting for answers. Quietly, she prayed her daughter was not doing drugs. She could not fathom the thought of her two children into that mess. Kolu couldn't, good Heavens no, she thought. "I'm sure she doesn't," Mrs. Fahpeh whispered. She grew more convinced of that when she remembered Kolu did not even drink. She breathed a sigh of relief and looked curiously at her daughter.

As her mother stood there and threw a series of questions, Kolu was in no talking mood, which made her mother even more curious. "Please tell me Kolu; what's bothering you? Is it that Sayzay business?"

Kolu remained quiet but her mother pressed on. Finally, out of respect for her mother, Kolu said, "Yes, I am sick and tired of that Sayzay business. Dad is punishing me because of what Sayzay is doing and saying but I have done all I can to discourage Sayzay. Why is Dad punishing me? I cannot visit the children and my dear elderly friends without a bodyguard. That's not fair. No, it is not fair for me to be deprived of the things that mean the world to me." Addressing her mother audaciously, she said she knew that luxury, fame, money, and the like mattered to her parents and brother but to her, interacting with, and serving others was the most satisfying thing in life. She broke down and wept bitterly as her mother looked   on.

Mrs. Fahpeh sat at the edge of the bed and moved closer to her daughter. She put her left hand on Kolu's chest as the latter lay in bed. "You know your father loves you dearly. He is just concerned about you. He's looking out for your safety."

Kolu still was in no talking mood. She lay quiet for a while before she spoke in an angry voice. "But I have been going to those people since I was twelve years old and nothing has happened to me. What could possibly happen now?"

Kolu's mother removed her hand from her daughter's chest, stood up and walked out the door. In minutes, she was back with her husband who was still in his pajamas although it was past noon. "What's the problem Dear?" Mr. Fahpeh inquired. "Are you alright Darling?" He rambled on and on promising to solve whatever problems, Kolu had regardless of how much money was required. "Just tell me Darling and the money will be available in minutes. Believe me no money is too much to satisfy your needs; that's how much you mean to me."

Again, Kolu, who had changed position on the bed, took a minute or two before she answered. Clearly, her problem was not about money; therefore, unlike her brother who would have made up some ridiculous story to get a large sum of money, she was not looking for money. Instead, she repeated what she had said to her mother. "Dad, those people mean a lot to me. You have no idea how much I gain by visiting them. They thank me for helping them but frankly, although for whatever reason you see them differently, they help me far more than I help them. Now, I cannot visit those lovely people without a bodyguard? Why?"

Going further, Kolu boldly confronted her father, stating that she could not do what was pleasing or satisfying to her, but what pleased her father. Pointing fingers directly at her father, she said, "You are the only person who can determine what is good or bad. You are the only person who is right, no one else. Why Dad? Why? For once, please tell me."

As Mr. Fahpeh looked on and listened in disbelief, his daughter teared up again.

He leaned over Kolu who was lying on her stomach with her face turned toward the wall as if she did not want to look at her parents. "Kolu my sweet darling; please look at me."

Not wanting to disrespect or disobey her father, Kolu slowly turned her head in the direction of her parents. She looked terrible. No doubt, she had been crying.

"My goodness Darling, I did not know how much visiting those people meant to you," Mr. Fahpeh confessed. He asked her to cheer up. He said she could visit poor children and the elderly any time without a bodyguard and as always, a vehicle would be available to take her. He suggested nonetheless she took a friend or two but if she did not want to do that either, she was free to go alone. "What's important to me is your happiness, and I can do anything to get it," he concluded.

Kolu sat up in bed. "Thank you Dad," she said. I truly appreciate that; and yes, visiting those people means a lot to me, a lot more than money and material things."

"If those visits are so important to you, do you mind if I come along once in a while?" Mrs. Fahpeh asked. Kolu hesitated. Her mother pressed on. "Do you?"

I do not mind. I wish you had done so long ago. Believe me, you will learn a lot from those   people."

"I do not think I will come every time; maybe just once in a while. As you know, your father and I were born here and grew up here so I am not sure how much more I can learn from them but we'll see."

Kolu did not respond nor did she read much into her mother's remark. She finally got out of bed, visited her private bathroom to freshen up before going to the dining table to eat something. While her father took several shots of hard liquor in another room, her mother sat with her and wanted to converse with her but Kolu was in no talking mood.

It seemed Kolu was not in a mood for food either. She took a bite or two and gave the food back to the maid and returned to her room. She assured her mother she would be all right; she just needed a little more time to recover.

Shortly after Kolu crawled back in bed, there was a knock on her door. "Who is it?"

"Your one and only dynamic, modest, talented, incredibly handsome, inimitable, and absolutely awesome brother. May I come in?" although in a beautiful nightgown, Kolu pulled a blanket over herself and replied affirmatively and Akoei entered the room wearing a pair of expensive sneakers, short pants, a designer t-shirt, and a huge gold chain with matching bracelets. "My goodness; why are you in bed this late?"

"Nothing."

Obviously, Kolu did not want to talk much but that did not deter her brother. "I know it's that stupid Sayzay stuff. That's precisely why I came to talk to you about." He took a seat on the chair next to Kolu's bed and crossed his legs.

"I don't want to talk and especially about that," Kolu was very clear not looking at her brother.

"But can I just tell you what I think about the whole thing?"

"No," Kolu said. "Now let me get some sleep. See you later."

"I do not believe this. My little sister is kicking me out of her room. O.K... I get the message but honestly, promise me this; can we talk later?"

Kolu once more unequivocally rejected the offer. When Akoei pressed his luck, she blew up. "I told you I do not want to talk about it. Now get out and leave me alone!"

"Sorry, sorry, sorry!" Akoei apologized. "Goodness, I have never seen you in such a horrible mood; something must be terribly wrong. For sure, it cannot be that stupid Sayzay business. I promise you Sis; if it is Sayzay, I will take care of him before Dad does." He disclosed that with small money here and there, and with the right sources, he had handled several people and nothing happened; he knew exactly what to do. Kolu did not respond nor did she fully understand what her brother meant.

For days, even weeks, Akoei sought an opportunity to talk with his sister regarding Sayzay. Fed up with his pestering, she gave in. "O.k., Akoei, when do you want to talk?"

"Sunday afternoon when Mom and Dad are resting and most of the servants are out of the house."

"What's so secretive about this?" Kolu seemed baffled. "I'm not interested in Sayzay and will never be. Everyone knows that."

This was music to Akoei's ear but he wanted to be doubly sure. Therefore, Sunday afternoon, he suggested meeting in one of the small studies next to the living room. "We are here now. What do you want to talk about? I'm all ears," Kolu got the ball rolling.

The study, like every room in the house was laced with expensive furniture, artwork, rare rugs, and exquisite wall decorations. Something exuded an inviting fragrance. If they wanted anything to eat or drink, they only had to push, a little button and a servant would be at their beckon call. Knowing this, Kolu was sure Akoei would soon order a drink or two.

"No Sis," Akoei rejected. "If I do take something, it will be much later. This discussion is too important to ruin it with drinks. On second thought, maybe I will just have a drink to keep me going." He pushed a button and a servant came over. "Double shot of my usual stuff," he ordered. The servant nodded politely and ran off.

"Oh my dear brother; you know that alcoholic drinks ruin your life and yet cannot leave it alone? Why?" Kolu asked.

"Please do not change the subject," Akoei pleaded. "This is not time for an Alcoholic Anonymous type of counselling; we are here for a serious matter."

"Serious matter?" Kolu repeated her brother's words. "What's so important about this discussion? I'm really dying to know."

Akoei took a deep breath, cleared his throat, and jumped into the matter. "Well, I really do not have anything new to say because that stupid Sayzay's pestering behavior is not new. However, I want to know exactly where you stand on the matter."

"I'm surprised at you Akoei," Kolu reprimanded mildly. She said she had told Akoei and her parents repeatedly that she had no interest in Sayzay. In fact, she resented his wooing so much so that she refused to see him play football or even look at him. However, she stressed that her decision had nothing to do with her social status. Just then, the servant knocked the door lightly.

"Come in," Akoei ordered. The young man set a small table in front of Akoei, ran back to the cart he was pulling, and returned with drinks. He poured the drinks into Akoei's glass before leaving.

When the servant left, Akoei took a long sip of his drink before pressing his sister to clarify her last point. She did not equivocate. "Look Akoei, as I do not want to offend our parents, I do not say it openly but for me, social status really does not matter; I therefore disagree strongly with Mom and Dad on the matter. Instead, I believe in the humanity and oneness of people far beyond each person's social status."

Akoei still was baffled. "I do not understand where you are coming from," he confessed.

Kolu looked around the nicely decorated study as if searching for the right words. "Akoei," she said, "you will not understand as long as you live within the walls of our parents' house. When I do voluntary work with poor children or visit the elderly who live alone, I learn a lot. They may not have money or material things but they have a lot, I mean a lot we do not have and truly need.

"You must be kidding. Like what? What could those sick, ignorant, and dirt-poor peasants have that we could possibly want, let alone need? Like I say, you must be truly joking Kolu. Besides, what does this have to do with Sayzay?"

Kolu aspired to be as clear as possible. "Those people may not have money or material things but they have love, character, integrity, moral values, care, concern, and respect for others, as well as respect for the laws of the land. These are precious commodities money cannot buy." To clarify further, she pointed out that it was very refreshing to know that the people in town deeply loved and cared for one another. Above all, they loved and feared God. In her view, there was no doubt the Fahpeh family truly needed to think and behave similarly.

"And what do those have to do with Sayzay? Are you saying Sayzay has a chance to date you even those he does not have money or material things?"

Kolu rejected the thought. "No, no, no! Beyond social status, there are major differences between Sayzay and me. Besides, I do not have any feelings for him or anyone else for that matter, not at this time." Akoei said he was glad to hear that and hoped Kolu's decision remained unchanged because that was the main thing he wanted to talk about. He said going out with Sayzay or anyone else at that low peasant level would definitely bring shame and disgrace on the family. "Kolu," he stated with emphasis, "I hope you never dream of doing such a thing to Mom, Dad, and me because if you ever do, you will see the wrong and cruel side of your brother."

Kolu was taken aback. She thought a minute or two before addressing her brother. "Honestly Akoei, what will you do? Do you think you can threaten me? Forget it! This is precisely why you must get out of the walls of this house for all you hear here is social status, income, wealth, rich friends, luxurious materials, expensive trips, expensive liquor, expensive clothes, on and on."

"And what's wrong with those?" Akoei chuckled. "Those are the things everyone wishes to have and we not only have them in abundance but we have them for life. So, why not celebrate and enjoy them to the fullest?"

"Sad thing is that richness makes us blind, insensitive, and even suicidal."

"What in the world do you mean? You must be out of your mind," Akoei screamed.

"Well, for one thing, have you ever thought of the fact that indulging in those 'rich habits' of ours can be harmful to health? For you, Mom, and Dad, for example, don't you know that excessive drinking can ruin your health and shorten your life? I'm sure you will not deny the fact that it's Dad's riches that make us insensitive to, and disrespectful of others. In addition, have you ever thought of others who do not have even a fraction of what we have and yet are happier?"

Akoei disagreed strongly. He did not want to comment on Kolu's points about drinking and being insensitive to others but he was sure poor people could not be happier. Quite the contrary, he was sure poor folks were always miserably sad. Besides, whether sad or happy, if they did not have much, that was none of anyone's business. "If they want to change their poor pitiful situations," Akoei lectured his sister, "they ought to play smart as our dad did and find money, food, and material things on their own. They should not expect handouts because we did not get rich by getting handouts from anyone and definitely not by foul means."

Kolu shook her head in disgust and disagreement. She regretted that her dear brother was not only holed up in the walls of their parents' house but even worse, limited by mental and psychological walls that prevented him from knowing and appreciating the worth of other people and the realities of life. In frustration, she raised her hand and pointed. "Look at the expensive furniture and paintings in this little room alone. Life is far more than such things. Believe it or not, it's a pity to think of life only in terms of these mundane things."

"Mundane? What does that mean?"

Kolu smiled lightly feeling victorious for having one edge over her boastful brother. "I mean these worldly things or more correctly, these worthless worldly things, as I see them."

Akoei felt a slight sense of defeat but overcame it quickly to return to his main issue. "Little sis, I am not kidding," he emphasized. "If you ever consider bringing shame and disgrace upon our family, I will be the first to prevent you. I will not allow any behavior of yours to break our parents' hearts and thereby shorten their lives." He then reminded Kolu about what their dad had said repeatedly; that is, they were not allowed to associate with, let alone accept people from other ethnic groups, not even people who spoke their language but different dialects. Going father, he underscored that people from other religions were out and so were ugly people.

Kolu was visibly angry. "You ought to be ashamed of yourself. In this day and age, you still talk about ethnic differences and all of that nonsense just because Dad says?"

"That's what Dad says Kolu and that's what we do. Remember, it is from him we will get our life-long income. Only a person out of his or her mind would disrespect such a person especially when he is your dad."

Even in her anger, Kolu let out a faint smile. "By God's command and by the mandates of our culture, I will never disobey my parents or any elders regardless of their status but you, of all people, you talk of ugly people?"

"Yes, ugly people are not welcome either," Akoei reiterated. "Ugly people, stupid people, mean people, unreasonable people, greedy people, narrow-minded people, materialistic people, and any other misfits should be avoided at all times."

Kolu's smile turned into a giggle. "Many of us need to look into the mirror daily." Akoei looked slightly angry. "I just mean, as we are taught in Sunday school, it's better not to judge so we ourselves will not be judged."

Akoei knew what his sister was talking about for he was not the best-looking gentleman on the block. However, he was not about to be defeated a second time.

"Do not be jealous of my looks dear Sis but this is not about me but you."

"Jealous?" Kolu laughed lightly. "Do you really mean jealous?"

"Yes, jealous; and I still insist that, as Dad says, we must avoid at all cost the slightest possibility of our family being polluted by misfits. I for one will not go an inch against Dad's words for I do not want to miss a penny of inheritance money."

Kolu found her brother's words intriguing. She informed him that with or without money, in less than two years, she would turn eighteen and shortly after, be a high school graduate. Then, she would expect her brother and parents to respect her decision as a young lady.

"We will as long as such a decision does not include dating, or, God forbid, marrying an idiot like Sayzay or anyone of a lowly peasant status or from another ethnic group. No one will stain the purity of our family. I swear Kolu if you dare pollute our family with a lowly person or an idiot, I will show my resentment in more terrible ways than you can ever imagine."

Kolu was livid. "Akoei, I'm sick and tired of your empty threats; in actuality, you cannot do me a thing, and you very well know it. Stop making yourself a powerful person when you are not." She said she could not emphasize the point enough but sincerely wished her brother would get out of the house and learn the realities of life as she had learned from her elderly friends and precious children. She looked at him directly and said, "Akoei, humanity is what counts, not your dumbbell differences. That's the truth regardless of what you say or think." Kolu appealed to her brother to get out of his shell, for goodness sake, and join the rest of thoughtful and logical humanity. Stated differently, she encouraged him to be a part of the human family and enjoy all the benefits of being an open-minded, accepting, and nonjudgmental human being.

Akoei did not seem to be listening to his sister's words. Instead, he shocked her when he said, "Like Dad says, and as I have reemphasized here, those peasant elders ought to fend for themselves. I for one resent you taking things out of this house to them; I do not call that generosity but thievery."

"I, a thief? Akoei, you have blown below the belt and ought to be doubly ashamed of yourself." She said unlike her brother who not only boozed every penny he got but also stole money and drinks from the house, she saved whatever allowance Dad gave her and bought things for her friends. Most definitely, she did not steal things from the house. She could not even fathom the thought of lying to her parents to get money. She said while she appreciated the critical life's values and even the tutoring she received in the home, she gained morally, ethically, and spiritually by venturing out among the elderly and poor children. "This is why I am absolutely convinced you need to get out there and see other people so as to understand various values of life."

"First, for your information, Dad knows I do drink and ..."

"Does he know you do steal too?" Kolu cut in.

"I help myself with my father's drinks and that's no one's business."

"And the money you always take without our parents' knowledge or permission, in other words, steal?"

"I have never been accused, let alone indicted." Giggling, Akoei said a thief was a thief only when caught. Beyond that, he vowed not to stoop to the level of peasants. Rather, he would remain in his parents' luxurious mansion, enjoy himself to the fullest, and not play the idiotic game of going into smelly peasant houses.

"Kolu," he called his sister's attention, "those people are disgusting in every way." He said the people's houses had fireplaces in their bedrooms and therefore breathed smoke all day and all night. Their ceilings, clothes, and everything else was dirty. With a mocking giggle, he said he could not believe that the people ate their dirty food in those dirty rooms. Hence, he had no doubt that the people lived miserable lives. "No wonder they do not live long but again, who cares for the loss of such miserable lives?"

Kolu could not be more disgusted with her brother. "I am sure you do not realize that in fact, you have stooped far below those poor but very respectable people. Because of their high ethical standards, they do not steal their peasantry notwithstanding. This is why, unlike us, they do not lock their doors."

Akoei laughed. "Kolu," he said, "first of all, those people do not have doors. They hang some silly bamboo stuff in front of their houses. Secondly, they have nothing worthy of stealing; so why would they bother to lock their doors if indeed they had doors? Besides, of all people, you ought to know that we lock our doors because if we did not, those uncivilized and unruly peasants would steal every pin in this house. You know it, Kolu, you know it! They are worse than wolves, no, worse than hungry lions," Akoei emphasized shaking his fist in the air to dramatize his resentment. He pushed a button for more drinks and was served immediately.

Kolu shook her head in disgust and amazement, probably for both her brother's words and incessant drinking but Akoei paid no attention to his sister's mood. Rather, he once more stressed that anyone going into smelly homes of peasants was idiotic. "Quite frankly," he went on, one who does so is either a hypocrite, trying to cover his or her evil deeds by attempting to do a good deed or such a person does not have a clear brain. Why would anyone leave this beautiful home and go to smelly peasant houses? Kolu, can you give me one clear and logical reason? Akoei challenged.

Kolu made no attempt to address Akoei's challenge which she termed as ludicrous. Rather, she was disgusted with him. "It is absolutely mind-boggling that you do not know a thing beyond this house and yet you look down on other people and insult your sister. I imagine the next people you will insult will be your parents and who knows, maybe next will be God?"

"I have told you that, like Dad, I do not believe in that God business. You and Mom may go to your church and get an earful of nonsense. Besides, I think you and Mom are hypocritical because you refuse to attend church in town. You rather drive to the regional capital to attend church with rich people. If God is everywhere, as you claim, why Mom will not allow you to worship Him in Fasawoba?"

"I have to hand it to you; you have a point there. Personally, I do not mind going to church here but as you said correctly, Mom says she will not go to church with those people."

"Mom may have a point. I just do not think God is everywhere. I do not even think He exists and if He does, He is not as powerful as you claim. Why, for example, didn't He stop Dad from becoming rich when Dad does not believe in Him? No Sis, there's nothing like a God. It's all in your imagination."

"May God forgive and bless you Akoei," Kolu prayed. "You truly are a lost soul. How could you not be? You look down on humanity and do not believe God. I just do not know what can save you. Believe me, neither money nor your booze will. Therefore my dear brother, while you still have time, I hope you will not only join the rest of humanity but that you will also repent."

Akoei found his sister's remarks amusing. After a quick giggle, he rebutted.

"Everyone knows Dad is rich and therefore you and I will inherit very good money. Moreover, as the elder, I will be fully in charge. With that and my extraordinary, I mean super-marvelous looks, what girl in her right mind would not want to marry me? Trust me, I will marry a gorgeous lady and live happily ever after."

It seemed Kolu's turn to laugh. "Only dreamers live in fairy tale land. When you come back from that dream land, you will join the rest of humanity and the realities of life."

"Fairy tale?" Akoei was shocked. "I'm talking about big bucks and you talk of fairy tale?"

"Your dad's big bucks, not yours. You have no idea how long it will take for you to inherit a penny. In case you do not know, both parents have to die before anything comes to us and by then, who knows what will be left? Who knows what liens and other encumbrances may have to be cleared? If you had half a brain Akoei, you would stop your boozing and boastful talks and prepare yourself, not rely on money that's not yours, money that's uncertain."

"You are out of your mind. I'm talking about money in the bank."

"True, money in the bank, but in whose account?" Kolu laughed.

Before Akoei could utter another word, there was a knock on the door. "Come in," he said confident it was one of the domestic workers. Their dad opened the door.

"Oh hello children. What are you talking about?"

"Just talking," Akoei refused to answer the question directly and earnestly.

"Indeed, we are talking Dad," Kolu concurred without saying what they were talking about. "But now that you are here, I have a question for you about something that has been on my mind for a while."

"What is that Dear?" Mr. Fahpeh asked as he took a step into the study.

Kolu said from her visits to elders and children in town, she noticed that, based on culture, children in the town called their parents by the parents' first names although a few were beginning to call 'papa' and 'Mama'. "Why do you insist we call you Dad and our mother, Mom?"

"Oh Kolu, I hope you are not losing your mind," Mr. Fahpeh answered. He said his family and the people in town were far apart in terms of socio-economic status and education; in fact, the people were not educated at all. "So my dear, why compare them to us? It's like night and day, and I am absolutely confident it will remain that way forever."

Kolu had doubts, perhaps more questions but did not ask. Akoei smiled from ear to ear. Stepping out the door, Mr. Fahpeh asked the siblings to freshen up and appear at dinner in formal clothes as he was expecting three business friends for dinner.

The discussion with Akoei lingered for days in Kolu's mind. She resented Akoei's threat and intimidation, vowing never to given into them. She repeated the point that Akoei could not do her a thing and he himself knew so. "How dare he threaten me? The nerve of him!" she stated angrily. On the other hand, she truly felt sorry for him. She had no doubt that Akoei knew nothing about other people and yet looked down on everyone or almost everyone. Kolu therefore wished her brother would learn because, she was sure again, the bulk of his problem sprang from failing to interact with other people. Other than brief interactions with other students in school, he was stuck mainly in the Fahpeh home. When he ventured out, he only looked for people of similar social status. In frustration, Kolu continued, "He really needs to interact with people of different ethnic groups, socio-economic strata, religions and more. He will learn that we are more similar than different. Ultimately,

I hope he learns that it's humanity that counts, not any other differences."

Kolu also thought over her father's characterization of the people in Fasawoba as not educated at all. "How could Dad say that?" she wondered. She said the people developed themselves in various ways, had a governance system based on an incredible traditional bureaucracy, built their own homes, sewed their own clothes, had superb farming and hunting skills, raised their children ingeniously, and performed various ceremonies with skills and accuracy. With these and more, true, they were not literate but that truism notwithstanding, how could Dad say they were not educated? The only answer she could find to her own question was, "Ah yah, that's Dad for you!"

CHAPTER EIGHT

When Kolu got angry, she often calmed herself by reading poetry. One day, she read and reread John Donne's poem, No Man Is an Island. After reading, she thought deeply about her discussion with her brother and the nagging Sayzay issue. She decided to discuss both issues with Fahzie, her older sister.

"Sis Fahzie," Kolu said at the rear of the store, "I would like to discuss a couple of issues with you."

Wearing a long dress and looking very smart, Fahzie drew two chairs close and sat in one. "Sure," she said. "I'm all ears."

Kolu angrily discussed Akoei's threats but mainly zeroed in on Sayzay's relentless pursuit. "This man and I have nothing in common but I do not know how to get rid of him. I do not want him today, tomorrow, or ever; it will never never happen."

Fahzie briefly commented on Akoei's threat toward his sister. Regarding Sayzay, she said, "I can only talk about that if you promise never to tell Mom and Dad how I feel about the matter." She waited for Kolu's response not knowing what to   expect.

Kolu sat quietly for a while wondering why her sister did not want her to reveal the gist of their discussion with their parents. Surely, Fahzie must have had a reason but what could that be? Without speculating further, she promised. "I give you my word on my honors Sis Fahzie; I will not tell anyone about our discussion here. Please tell me what you honestly think."

"Have you read the poem by John Donne that says, No man is an island entire of itself?"

"That's one of my favorite poems," Kolu revealed excitedly. "I read and reread it this morning."

"Great!" Fahzie jubilated mildly. She plunged into the heart of the matter, getting everything or almost everything off her chest in a direct and honest manner. "Kolu, my little sister, you know I love you dearly. I will never say or do anything to harm you nor will I lie to you." She looked directly at Kolu as if to say, "I sincerely mean every word."

Kolu nodded also as if to say she believed her sister. Kolu therefore listened intently and as she did, Fahzie talked at length about their parents. She pointed out what Kolu already knew; that is, their parents had everything or so it seemed but they did not fear God and this was especially true of Dad. Without fearing a Supreme Being, it was no surprise that they had no respect for anyone or that they disregarded every cultural guideline and every law of the land. The only thing important to them were their money and social status which they used in many and varied ways. Fahzie accepted the fact that money and social status were important but insisted that life was far more important.

Kolu moved her chair a bit closer in a bid not to miss a word. Fahzie leaned forward slightly to ensure her sister heard her clearly. She continued her scathing criticism of their parents.

"But what does this have to do with my resentment of Sayzay?" Kolu wondered aloud.

"Everything," Fahzie stated tersely. She explained that their parents' opulent lifestyle and extreme emphasis on social status were the bases for Kolu's stance.

"No Sis Fahzie!" Kolu rejected strongly. "I do not have any feelings for Sayzay or anyone else; social status has nothing to do with it. Although I do not preach a sermon about it especially at home with Mom, Dad and that Akoei, to me, humanity counts, not social status or anything else. As I believe in God, I have no doubt that every human being is a child of God and should be treated as such." She said income and social status were blessings and she wished her parents saw it that way.

Fahzie was doubtful and yet pleased. She wondered if Kolu's stance would have been the same if Sayzay were from a higher social class. In other words, Kolu said she and Sayzay grew up differently; this implied that if they did not, she would consider him. On the other hand, Fahzie was both surprised and pleased that her little sister emphasized humanity more than social class. Kolu easily noticed her sister's facial expression.

"You seem surprised Sis Fahzie. Why?"

Without answering Kolu, Fahzie excused herself briefly to get a cup of juice. "Would you like some?" she asked Kolu. Kolu nodded and her sister poured her a cup too and returned to her original seat. Although older than Kolu by ten or more years, she was an attractive young woman too. "Now what were you saying?" she tried to get back on track with their conversation.

Before Kolu could respond, Fahzie's little boys came running into the living room. "Mom," Sopo, the younger called, "Sumo took my toy and hit me."

"You tell story," Sumo denied the allegation. "See Auntie Kolu, this is mine," showing a toy car to his aunt. It was not clear why he directed his response to the allegation to Kolu instead of his mother. "I will get you another car Sopo," Mom resolved the problem. She did and the boys ran off. "Now where were we?" Fahzie asked.

Kolu said she wanted to know why Fahzie seemed surprised about Kolu's stance on the issue of social class. "Oh that one," Fahzie remembered. "Frankly, I am but ought not to be, knowing you visit the elderly and play with poor children and yet, I was a little surprised. Forgive me Little Sis."

"That's alright but what were you about to say?"

"I was about to say that is normal, a mature and open-minded way of thinking."

"What's normal?" Kolu pushed her sister.

Fahzie explicated that it was normal, absolutely normal and acceptable for Kolu or anyone else for that matter, to reject someone because of a lack of feeling for that person. On the other hand, Fahzie thought it was unacceptable for a person to reject another because of differences in social status, ethnicity, nationality, race, or any other 'external difference'.

Kolu shook her head. "People have preferences Sis and so people make decisions based on their preferences, tastes, etc..." She said in like manner, various things attracted people and for different reasons; there was no one-fit-all criterion.

Fahzie said she understood and accepted that. She nonetheless was appalled by rejections not based on personal particularities and character traits but group affiliations and other external factors. "Love is a natural thing. When it is genuine, it knows no bounds," she underscored.

Kolu agreed. "But even if I had any feelings for Sayzay or anyone else, my parents will not accept that person if he is not within our so-called social status, ethnic group, and things like that. I do not understand especially in this day and age."

"Precisely my point," Fahzie emphasized. She referred to Sayzay as a considerably handsome and talented young man who loved Kolu with all his heart and soul but was being rejected for one and only one thing, his social status. Nothing was said about his manners, respect for others, adherence to the laws of the land, work ethic, belief in God, and above all, sincerity and depth of his feelings toward Kolu. Fahzie paused as if searching for the right words to utter. Continuing, she explained that she had two children for a man she loved very much and thought he loved her too but ultimately, she was left with two children to raise by herself. The experience left a bitter taste in her mouth regarding relationships but she would not allow that one experience to ruin her life. "I will date for sure but now, I will be very careful," she vowed.

"That's another point, Sis Fahzie. It's not only that I do not have feelings for anyone at present but if I were to date anyone in or out of my social status, how would I know if that person had genuine feelings toward me. Will the person not be interested because of my modest looks or the possibility that I may gain money from my father now or later? How would I know?"

My dear Little Sis, first, it is very humble of you to refer to yourself as having 'a modest look' because you are incredibly gorgeous. Second, while it is advisable to be careful, one ought to know also that life is a gambling ground; it is rare, if ever, that one is sure of anything especially when it comes to the future. However, there can be convincing signs. For example, from what you tell me, this young man says if he does not marry you, he will live a bachelor for the rest of his life. How many men can say that and sincerely mean it?"

"Yes, he has said and written something like that," Kolu assented. "But sis Fahzie, I do not know how to say it any more. I do not have feelings for this man and even if I did, my parents would kill me. I just told you what my brother has said."

"Akoei is not crazy and believe me, our parents will not throw you under the bus, no matter what," Fahzie was sure.

Kolu was not so sure. In fact, she wondered if her sister truly understood her parents. Without paying attention to Kolu's doubtful looks, Fahzie lectured her sister mildly, stressing that Kolu's happiness in life was far more important than pleasing her parents or living in an ivory tower. "This is precisely why I prefer to live here than back home with our parents. Here, I'm free and do not have to walk on eggshells. I prefer happiness and health with little than misery and consequent ail health in abundance."

This time, Kolu agreed. "That makes a lot of sense to me Sis Fahzie," she commended. Kolu further confessed that often, she grew sick and tired of the opulent life, missing out on nice family discussions but rather dressing up for dinner because so-and-so was coming to dinner, and on and on. In addition, she disclosed that when she returned home from visiting her elderly friends, she often felt guilty when a maid or man servant waited on her. Other times, she wished she could get on her knees and work with the servants but Heaven forbid; her parents would kill her if she tried. Tired of being driven, she wanted to learn how to drive but her parents said there was no need for that when drivers were available at all times. She therefore had to hide to learn how to drive and thanks to God, Jimmy, her driver was willing to oblige especially since he got very good tips for the driving lessons. Kolu said nonetheless that she totally detested such form of dominance and worse, total lack of preparation for the future. Instead, her family swam in a pool of certainty that life was a bed of roses, nothing would change and the future would only be brighter, fruit bearing, and beautiful, never bleak. "What if that pool dries up?" She snapped her fingers in disgust.

"You get my point," Fahzie complimented. She appealed to Kolu not to misunderstand her. As far as she knew, their parents were good people. Moreover, she was grateful to them for giving her a high school education and giving her an opportunity to run her own store. Nonetheless, she found it regrettable that her parents' riches had transformed them into mini gods and so they behaved as if they owned the world and all the people in it. "This is particularly true of Dad," Fahzie went on. She hoped her parents would come down from the ivory tower and teach their children the realities of life. "They know the realities of life for they did not start out rich," Fahzie was sure.

Kolu concurred. She revealed that occasionally, her father talked about his young days when he had nothing. Unfortunately, he had now come to believe that in the same way he struggled to make it, everyone should do the same. He therefore saw no reason to help others. In other words, he bled to succeed and others should do the same or drown. "Quite frankly Sis Fahzie, and I am telling you this in strict confidence," Kolu stated once more in disgust, "it bothers me when dad does not care for anyone, not even the people who work for him. Mom is not that extreme but she goes along or pretends to do so for fear of offending her husband."

"That's a real pity," Fahzie lamented. "As you and I have read in John Donne's writing, 'No one is an island'. Everyone needs someone at one time or another and Dad ought to know that."

Kolu nodded in agreement. She thought it was a blessing that her father was well-off but, on the other hand, it was a real pity that he refused to help anyone. Similarly, she regretted her parents' horrible treatment of their workers and, once more, this was especially true of her dad. "Sometimes I am afraid to eat at home," She divulged. "It does not make sense to maltreat people who prepare your food and drive you; they hold your life in their hands but that does not seem to cross Dad's mind. All he knows is he is very rich and therefore can do anything. He does not think he is answerable to anyone, not even to God whose existence he doubts. May that same God bless him!" Kolu concluded her windy remark.

Fahzie ironically thanked God for the Sayzay episode because prior to it, she had not talked in depth with her little sister and so knew not what Kolu thought especially with regard to matters at home. She agreed with Kolu. "That's regrettable indeed. Someone must have helped him to be where he is; he likewise ought to help others. Life is a matter of give and take. When up today, help those who are down so when down, others may help as well. This is precisely what's portrayed in the parable of the unjust steward."

Kolu agreed. It seemed she could not overemphasize her parents' indifference toward others. "They love their children dearly but care for no one else. I find that difficult to understand. Likewise, although I appreciate the manner and extent to which they provide for Akoei and me, I do not think it's right to allow children to do whatever they please." She provided a number of glaring examples. For instance, at seventeen, and even before that age, Akoei was allowed to drink heavily and do whatever he wanted. When he did horrible things or got in trouble, and that was more often than acknowledged, they cover everything up by hook or crook, never reprimanding him. "If I am blessed with children, I would not want them to grow up in such an atmosphere," Kolu stated sternly.

Fahzie agreed too. "This is why I indicated earlier that I rather live in this modest place than in our parents' house, the upper social class amenities notwithstanding." She reiterated the point that life was more than riches. "Do not get me wrong. It's a good thing to have money but, take it from me Little Sis, while money provides comfort and whatever luxury one can afford, money does not make people happy; people do." She explained that the people who made one happy did not include hypocrites and gravy seekers, the pretentious ones and those who masked their true characters to get what they pleased. "Rather," she went on, "the people who make you happy are those God allows you to help or those with whom you share gift, talents, or time. They are people who come whether you have money or not, those who are willing to offer you their last, those who forget their own needs and give you their time any time you need them, and those who are absolutely genuine in their dealings with you." She looked at Kolu and was pleased the young lady was listening intently. "Yes, people make people happy and there's no happiness greater than giving to others. In other words, giving is the best way of living."

"That's right sis Fahzie. I'll bet you teach that to your children."

"I do."

Kolu was silent for a moment before saying, "That's good, very good. They will grow up as very good children. But Sis Fahzie, let me ask you about the points you made earlier regarding different people in our lives. Aren't those the same ideas and qualities to consider when one is seeking a lifetime   partner?"

"Absolutely!" Fahzie could not hide her excitement. She said choosing a lifetime partner on pretentious grounds was an open invitation to disaster. Likewise, choosing a lifetime partner to please others was a plunge into misery. Instead, one had to go with his or her heart and soul. "You must listen to the inner voice, the intuition that shapes and propels your inner thoughts." Then she laughed lightly and asked, "Haven't you read about King Cophetua who married a beggar maid?"

"No I have not," Kolu fell over laughing.

Fahzie explained that King Cophetua and the Beggar Maid was a famous legend about an African king who shunned all women until he fell in love with a beggar maid on first sight. "The legend is alluded to in various Shakespearian plays and relatively modern works, including the works of Alfred Lord Tennyson," Fahzie lectured. "Look it up," she encouraged her little sister.

"I will," Kolu promised. Just then, she glimpsed at her gold watch. "Well Sis Fahzie," she said, "thank you very much for the discussion. Once more, on my honors, my lips are sealed but I have to get back home in time for dinner." She said it was another dress-up dinner as the family was expecting two of her dad's business partners for dinner. She regretted that this was the case most of the time; nothing like casual clothes and nice family discussions at dinner.

Fahzie agreed that the monotony of formal life during normal family times had to be boring. She expressed her thanks and gratitude to Kolu for coming and trusting her enough to reveal her major concerns to an older sister. "I'm truly pleased for the confidence you reposed in me. As big sister, I'm here any time you need me. You know you will get nothing but the truth from me. So, let me give you my last two-cent words. First, it pays to be oneself than being pretentious; it equally pays to fear God, respect others, and serve humanity to the best of your ability. Secondly, the word 'never' belongs to God alone." Upon saying that, Fahzie walked with her little sister to the front of the store where a waiting car drove Kolu away.

For inexplicable reasons, the journey back home seemed much farther than it usually was. Nonetheless, Kolu did not say a word to Jimmy, her driver, until she reached home. At dinner, she barely ate anything but excused herself early to go to her room. Permitted to do so, she closed the door and went to bed. While her brother and parents continued drinking, she tossed and turned in bed thinking about her sister's words. Eventually, she fell into a deep sleep.

CHAPTER NINE

Late on a Saturday afternoon, domestic workers in the Fahpeh home were busy cleaning up and preparing dinner when Akoei walked in with a stranger.

"Where's Kolu? Where are Mom and Dad?" he inquired with authority.

"In the garden," a manservant replied, pointing to the garden as if Akoei did not know where it was.

Akoei hesitated whether to go to his room before going out to the garden. On second thought, he led his friend into a beautiful courtyard with meticulously manicured lawn, colorful flowers, especially rows and rows of beautiful roses, nicely trimmed trees, painted poles, luxurious seats, and more. The Fahpehs were sitting beneath a shelter that looked like a backyard umbrella except that it was bigger, higher than an umbrella, and not easily removable. Regardless of its size and height, if the family preferred to fold it to enjoy a mild sunshine, they simply pushed a button. To open it up again when the sun was too hot, the same button did the trick. The umbrella was so huge that they could sit under it through a heavy rainstorm if they chose.

The Fahpehs were dressed casually but their casual outfits were good enough for many people's formal wears. Mr. Fahpeh was on his fourth triple shot of mixed drinks, Mrs. Fahpeh on her third glass of red wine, and Kolu, sipping on a glass of ice tea with cheese and crackers.

"Greetings Mom, Dad, and my beloved sister Kolu. How are you all today?" Akoei greeted with a sense of exuberance. When his family returned the greeting, he straightened his seemingly expensive dress pants and said, "I want you all to meet my dear dear friend Zawu."

He turned to his friend and said, "Zawu, this is my wonderful family— my dynamic parents and of course, my gorgeous sister, Kolu.

These people made me into what I am. They are the kindest, most humane, considerate, and wisest people I know on planet Earth." Wearing what looked like expensive clothes too, Zawu greeted the family and smiled broadly at Kolu. He and Akoei sat close to one another.

Mr. Fahpeh welcomed Zawu warmly and then asked, "Where are you from and who is your dad?"

"I am from Gizisu."

"Oh that's only five miles from here," Mr. Fahpeh interrupted. Zawu nodded.

Akoei did not wait for his friend to respond to the question his father posed earlier. Rather, in an attempt to either show off his friend or rescue him from talking about himself, Akoei explained, "His father, Mr. Kokulo Subah is the General Manager and CEO of a multi-million dollar company although he has a large company of his own. I tell you, the man is loaded. I know it first-hand and I kid you not!"

"That's wonderful," Mrs. Fahpeh approved. "How long are you here?"

"Just visiting Akoei, Mam. I return home tonight."

"Are you driving?" Mr. Fahpeh inquired.

"No Sir. I am using my same experienced driver who has served me since I was fourteen when Dad said then I could have my own car and driver."

"And how old are you now?" Mrs. Fahpeh appeared to be taking turns with her husband in asking questions of their son's friend.

"Nineteen Mam. I have graduated from high school and already have spent one semester in college. I believe in a sound education. I am therefore thankful my parents encourage me to pursue same. Now I know that there is nothing like sound education, nothing comes close."

"That's good," Mrs. Fahpeh approved once more.

Regarding Zawu's emphasis on education, Mr. Fahpeh appeared doubtful, if not in total disagreement. He also was not sure about Zawu's father. Without commenting on either point directly, he asked, "Does your father live in Gizisu?"

"I have not heard of him."

"No Sir," Zawu replied. "He lives in Coastal City, our capital but is originally from Gizisu." He explained further that his parents returned to their small birth town regularly and wanted their children to know their true origin.

"I thought that may be the case," Mr. Fahpeh said in a relief tune. "I have gone through Gizisu many times and did not notice anything impressive, certainly nothing remotely resembling a company headquarter." He admitted that it had been years since he stopped in the town but again, Gizisu was not a big town. If anything stood out above the ordinary, it would be noticed easily.

Zawu nodded politely and explained further that, while his parents owned a fabulous mansion in Coastal City, they built a very modest home in Gizisu as they did not want their residence in their home village to appear strikingly different from other dwellings in the village. However, their home in Gizisu was furnished with the most modern furniture and gadgets as they had become accustomed to such a modern lifestyle.

"Do your parents enjoy visiting Gizisu and if so, how often do they come back?" Mrs. Fahpeh asked.

Zawu said his parents were in Gizisu frequently although their work schedules kept them away more than they would otherwise prefer. "My parents really believe in associating and identifying with their people, regardless of their level of education, and no matter who they are or how much they own," he said. Kolu's father caught her smiling. When she made eye contact with her father, she reduced her broad smile and looked at her brother instead.

Zawu continued. "When Mom and Dad are back in their little village, they do not speak a word of English unless absolutely necessary. Moreover, they are always learning about the culture so they may pass on same to us, their lovely children."

Without any prompting, Zawu aspired to relate other valuable teachings by his parents. Unfortunately, he was not typically articulate probably because of the excitement of meeting new people. Essentially, however, he intended to reiterate some of the valuable teachings of his parents. For example, he stated in so many words that his parents often said, "Prejudice, bigotry, and any form of degrading others blinden people and hinder their interpersonal relationships." They also said, "Egocentrism, ethnocentrism, and elitism are asinine for they not only solidify a spurious sense of superiority but they also symbolized a lack of self-confidence and self-esteem."

Whether she understood Zawu's drift or not, Mrs. Fahpeh not only concurred but praised the young man. "That's very nice,"she said as her approval statements were beginning to sound like a broken record. "But will you have dinner with us? It's getting kind of late."

"Thank you Mam but I must be going in another hour. Mom andDad are expecting me but I truly appreciate the invitation."

"Very well" Mrs. Fahpeh accepted the rejection of her offer. "In that case, we will leave you young people to yourselves. If you change your mind about dinner, just know it's an open invitation." She added that if Zawu wanted to spend the night, he could be accommodated easily as her home had several guest rooms.

"Thanks again Mam," Zawu said politely before Mr. and Mrs. Fahpeh left. As soon as they did, Akoei ordered drinks for himself and Zawu.

"So, I understand you are in high school. What year are you in?" Zawu asked Kolu as he smiled from ear to ear, looking at the beautiful teenager.

Kolu straightened herself in her chair and set down her cup of tea. "This is my junior year," she said somewhat sheepishly.

"Do you plan to go to college?" Zawu tried to force a conversation. "Maybe," Kolu said not wanting to discuss her plans with a complete stranger. She was beginning to resent the streamof questions but at the same time tried to be polite.

Akoei noticed his sister's demeanor and so jumped in. "My buddy here plays the guitar and sings well," he informed his sister knowing she loved music. He took a sip of his drink, clear his throat and set down his glass, which seemed like a luxurious vessel designed for a king. "I tell you Sis, he's good in many ways. As you know, I do not make many friends. When I choose one, he must be among the best and I cannot find a friend better than Zawu. I can do anything for him even if my life depended on it and I have no doubt he can do the same for me." He turned to Zawu and asked, "Right Buddy?" Zawu affirmed exuberantly. The two laughed and slapped hands together.

"What kind of songs do you sing," Kolu asked.

"Almost anything," Zawu preferred to be somewhat neutral since he did not know Kolu's taste in music. He took a risk by asking, "What kind of music do you like?"

Kolu smiled sweetly. "Well, almost anything too but if I have to choose, I prefer contemporary Gospel music as well as poetic and romantic songs."

That's your cup of tea Buddy," Akoei laughed. He straightened his pants and picked up his glass again. He pushed a little button and a man servant ran from the house. He ordered more drinks.

"Yes indeed," Zawu confirmed. "I love to play and sing romantic songs. "Would you like to hear me play Kolu? I'd love to sing to you. I mean, it will be a real pleasure."

"Sure," Kolu consented. "When?" Zawu probed.

"Any time after school or during the weekend."

"Shall we say next Saturday then?" Zawu tried his luck.

"That will be fine," Kolu agreed.

"Where?" Zawu asked as he lifted up his glass once more. It seemed he and Akoei could not get enough of the booze.

Kolu was beginning to wonder how much hard liquor this gentleman could handle. She hoped he was not as bad as her brother was. She did not think Akoei had any match when it came to drinking probably with the exception of their old man himself. She then answered Zawu. "This back garden will be fine. The cooks will prepare wonderful munchies for us. I'm sure Akoei will handle the drinks. He has no problem in that arena."

Akoei shook his head in disagreement without articulating his reason for disagreeing.

"You do not seem to agree with me," Kolu probed. "Certainly it cannot be with regard to your unmatched ability in the drinking arena."

"No sis. I disagree with your suggestion. No, no, I do not like the sound of that at all."

"Akoei, make yourself clear please," Kolu demanded. "You do not like the sound of what?"

Akoei said he was referring to Kolu's suggestion regarding where Zawu was to play for her. He turned to his sister and said, "The three of us will go somewhere. I know just the right place. Believe me, you will like it, not to mention Zawu's incredible   musical talent."

In the house, Mr. Fahpeh pressed a button and a nicely dressed maid ran over. He made sure all the domestic workers dressed appropriately, regardless of their tasks.

"At your service Sir!" the maid said humbly.

"More drinks for the Mrs. And me," Mr. Fahpeh ordered. Clearly, he and Mrs. Fahpeh were not through with the drinks for the night. In fact, they had just begun, as they still had not had dinner.

"Yes Sir!" the maid said as she ran off. In minutes, she was pushing a special cart with all kinds of drinks. She knew exactly what to serve the Mr. and Mrs. She carefully poured in each luxurious glass, as she could not afford to make any mistakes. She knew without a doubt that even a slight mistake could result in a back-hand slap or worse, cause her a job. The boss was uncompromisingly strict. After her diligent service, she quickly left the living room. None of the domestic workers was allowed to linger for long in the presence of the boss and members of the family.

"That is an interesting young man Darling," Mrs. Fahpeh said. Her husband nodded without saying anything. "I hope Kolu gets to know him or better still, he gets to know Kolu." Mr. Fahpeh nodded again. "Aren't you going to say anything Darling?" Mrs. Fahpeh asked.

"Not much Dear," Mr. Fahpeh said. "I certainly would like to know his dad. Maybe   can do business with him." Then he switched gears and reiterated his determination to silence Sayzay if the young man ever looked at his daughter, let alone write her. "No useless man or woman, and certainly no dog will come into this family. No, we will not stoop that low," he stressed with a serious face. "I swear Darling; I will eliminate that dog in a moment if he ever comes near my daughter."

Mrs. Fahpeh nodded in agreement. "The nerve of him to think that, as lowly and wretched as he is, he can come close to our daughter, not to even think of dating her. He is definitely out of his mind and if he does not get back into his doghouse, I agree with you; he should be eliminated. What? Such a bottom-of-the-barrel peasant? What does he have and what does he know about proper etiquettes? How will such a wretch know how to accompany our daughter to a formal gathering let alone how to behave when he gets there? Oh no! God forbid. Kolu rather die unmarried than stoop that low." Mr. Fahpeh nodded too before picking up his glass.

As the Fahpehs continued their conversation, the young people entered the living room. "Are you leaving?" Mrs. Fahpeh asked Zawu. Zawu nodded. "But it's almost dinner time. Are you sure, you do not want to stay for dinner? Our chefs are wonderful cooks," Mrs. Fahpeh enticed Zawu.

"Thanks again Mam but I really should be going. Mom and Dad are expecting me as we have special guests tonight. I never disappoint my parents; that's just how I was raised and am grateful for it." Mrs. Fahpeh smiled agreeably and Akoei walked with his friend out the door.

"What do you think of him?" Mrs. Fahpeh asked Kolu.

"Just another guy Mom," Kolu responded after taking a seat across the room from her parents.

"Just another guy?" Mrs. Fahpeh reechoed her daughter's words, looking somewhat doubtful, even bewildered.

"Just another guy," Kolu repeated herself without paying any attention to her mother's looks. Rather, she wondered why this line of interrogation. Did Zawu impress her mother that much? Was she aware of the extent to which he drank? Did she know the number of boys Kolu had rejected on grounds that she did not have any feelings for them? Kolu wandered on and on.

"Does that mean you will never consider dating him? He is well groomed, properly mannered and not only looks like a nice guy but more importantly, from a very good family," Mrs. Fahpeh continued. She avoided making any comparison to Sayzay but that's exactly what she meant.

Kolu was a little surprised at her mother's words but knowing her mother, almost nothing from her surprised Kolu. "I do not know Mom and you do not know either if he would like to date me."

"What if he does?"

"Well Mom, I do not know. As I have said, I have no feelings for anyone, at least not now."

"But you have to date at some point and eventually get married," Mrs. Fahpeh pressed on in an unrelenting manner. Obviously, she wanted to get a commitment from Kolu regardless of how long the young lady had known Zawu. The key was he was from a good family and, in this case, 'good' meant rich and consequently in a high social class.

"I know," Kolu said "but the decision is not an easy one. I must avoid guys Dad calls vagabonds."

"How about Zawu? He looks like a perfectly nice gentleman, certainly nothing like a vagabond. You heard him say he has his own driver and has had one since he was fourteen. His father is not only a CEO but owns a big company; no doubt, they are doing very well."

Kolu was somewhat indignant but tried not to show it. "Mom," she exclaimed, "you just met him today. Why do you think he is perfectly a nice guy? For starters, I'm concerned about his drinking which does not surprise me as he hangs out with my   brother."

Mr. Fahpeh broke his silence. "There is no Mr. or Miss Perfect out there; they all have their pluses and minuses."

"Precisely," Mrs. Fahpeh concurred. "Get to know him a little. You might like him."

"I do not believe you are asking me to know this man whom neither you nor I know," Kolu did not hide her disbelief. "I do not hate him, I do not hate anyone but you have not known this man for more than ten minutes and you are asking your daughter to date him? That's weird to me Mom."

"Go where and how your heart directs you Darling and you will have my blessings," Kolu's dad surprised his daughter because of what he said and because he almost never used a sacred word like 'blessing'.

"Wow! Do you mean that Dad?"

"Of course I do," Mr. Fahpeh assured his daughter as he sipped on his drink and pressed a button for another. He made it clear that Kolu's desire was not only his delight but his absolute delight. "If there's a God, although I definitely doubt that, you will have your wishes in life. I know I will live to see it." Yet, he made it clear that he would not accept a wretched person in the family; he had made that clear to his children on multiple occasions.

Kolu was all smiles although she was not surprised by her father's blasphemy. He's playing God again, Kolu thought to herself before speaking up. "Thank you Dad but I hope you remember that. I say so because I would like to prepare myself for the future. I would like to go to college someday as no one knows the future." Her parents nodded somewhat indifferently. Before she could say another word, her brother reentered the living room.

Akoei was exuberant, perhaps too exuberant thanks to the few drinks he had. "So, what do you all think of my buddy? He is just a great guy, I mean absolutely awesome." Giving no one a chance to respond, he went on. "Sis Kolu, that's the kind of guy to go with, not that idiotic Sayzay." Akoei's parents looked at one another for he had said what they were thinking.

"When I decide to date, it will be my decision as to when I date and whom I date," Kolu was emphatic.

"But as I have told you, do not bring any stupid person into this family; believe me, I will not stand for it."

"Again Akoei, my dating life will not be subject to your likes and dislikes in the same way I will not dictate to you as to who to date or not date."

Akoei laughed while his parents remained silent, paying attention to every word between their children. "Don't worry about me dear Sis," Akoei advised. He said he did not date idiots nor would he ever put the family to shame by doing anything stupid like bringing in an idiot or different person. His reason for not doing so was supposed   to be clear to everyone; that is, the Fahpeh family was not only well off forever but was intact and unique. No one, and yes, absolutely no one could ruin that, not even God. Akoei paused to sip on his drink, which had been refilled.

"May God forgive you for your blasphemy," Kolu prayed for her brother and she knew this would not be the last time for such a prayer. Yet, she repeated her point that Akoei's dating life rested on his decision, not Kolu's. In like manner, only Kolu and no one else, certainly not Akoei, decided as to whom she dated. "I hope that settles it," Kolu concluded. Still saying nothing, Mr. and Mrs. Fahpeh simply smiled as the servants set the table for dinner.

CHAPTER TEN

The Fasawoba High School football team had spent the entire afternoon at the coach's home discussing strategies. With the help of Sayzay, the team once more made it to the regional championship. Unfortunately, it would be a rematch of the previous year's game when they went up against the boys of Suo-mee-lazu. This was unfortunate because knowing the talents of the boys of Suo-mee-lazu dampened their hopes of winning. After dinner, the coach called in the team for a final discussion.

"The last thing we want is for you to defeat yourselves before the battle begins," the coach stressed. "This as never been your propensity and should not be now. You are as talented, if not more, as the boys from Suo-mee-lazu."

A number of the young men looked at one another, not knowing what 'propensity' meant. Golo caught Sayzay smiling lightly but no one asked the coach. It seemed however, the coach noticed why a number of the boys seemed stunned. "I mean," he said, "this has never been your preferred behavior, tendency, or leaning and it should not be now, no, not at this critical juncture. Rather, you must believe in yourselves as I believe in you." The coach further emphasized the importance of playing defense but at the same time, underscored the importance of smart offensive plays. "We will not win if we do not score," he pointed out the obvious.

The team members agreed with the coach and vowed to play as best as they could. Before they left, the coach reminded them of the practice schedule in preparation for the big game which always coincided with the end of the school year.

As the players left, the coach beckoned Golo, Sayzay, and Gayduobah, his top players. The three waited for the others to leave. "Now, great players," the coach began. "I depend on every player on the team but especially on the three of you. So, no matter how badly the others play, and God forbid, no matter how far behind we fall, I do not want the three of you to lose your cool; you must be calm at all times. When you lose your cool and allow yourself to be angry,you lose your ability to think and act swiftly and smartly. As you know, this is a game of patience, skill, swiftness, and stamina; he who lacks those qualities will not play, let alone win." The coach assured the trio that the opposing team would do anything to get them disqualified so they had to be on their guards. This was especially true of Golo and Gayduobah who were at mid-field. "On the other hand," the coach chuckled, "if you do to them what they want to do to you, the better but be smart about it so you do not get a whistle or worse, a red card[7].n the process." The three did not laugh but took the coach's words seriously. They felt a certain degree of pressure but were determined to live up to the task.

∞ ∞ ∞

On another Saturday, Zawu's driver pulled up in front of the Fahpeh residence where Kolu and her brother were waiting. He beckoned them to get into his car but Kolu insisted on using one of her father's vehicles. Akoei, on the other hand, wasted no time in jumping into the card with his buddy. "On our way back," his sister told him earlier, "you will ride with me," and he accepted that.

Kolu and her driver drove behind Zawu's car. Akoei directed the driver to a nice building not far from Fahzie's store. The three got out of their cars and Akoei led the way to a basement room that was already

---

[7] In football, which some call soccer, a yellow card pointed to a player means severe warning. A red card indicates ejection from the game; that is removal without replacement thereby leaving only ten players for one's team on the field.

set up for them. "Dad has already paid for the evening," he informed the two. "Eat and drink to your heart's pleasure."

"I thought I was going to pay for this," protested Zawu. "My dad gave me enough money to cover the check and tips here especially when I told him who would be my company tonight."

"That's alright," Akoei assured his buddy. "It's really no big deal and Dad does not mind at all. As he has huge shares in this restaurant, we can come back as often as we wish and he will pay. The management here is aware of that arrangement and will do all it can to accommodate us most appropriately. Believe me; they will not do anything stupid to anger Dad. They know that if he pulls his shares out of this restaurant that will be the end of this business. So, enjoy yourselves."

The three sat around a nice round table. Zawu's driver brought in the guitar and left. "After eating and having a drink or two, I will sing and play what you prefer Kolu," Zawu declared with a grin. "I will try to be at my very best."

"I will take a glass of juice but do not feel like eating," said Kolu. She said nothing about watching her weight, the reason behind her reluctance to eat anything.

"Come on Sis; you must eat something small. After all, both of us are in for a treat tonight," Akoei predicted. The next time both of you come here, I am sure you will order a glass of wine or something stronger; Zawu will make sure of that." Kolu shook her head in disagreement. It was not clear as to which proposition she rejected, coming back with Zawu alone or taking a drink. She did not clarify and no one asked.

"I agree with Akoei, you need to eat something small," Zawu insisted.

"O.K., I will have a small sandwich," Kolu capitulated. She looked over the menu and placed her order. She said she could not eat the entire sandwich. Her brother gladly volunteered to eat whatever she could not handle. He said he was not watching his weight. Besides, since his drinks did not get him to put on weight, he did not think anything would make him fat.

Although only the three were in the exclusively reserved room, the waitress waited on them and it seemed she was assigned to them for the entire evening. Evidently, it was not cheap to reserve this private room in an exclusive restaurant but they paid no attention to prices on the menu. As Akoei said, they ordered whatever they wanted.

Zawu and Akoei ordered their first two drinks when Kolu inquired as to when Zawu would start playing. "That's the reason we are here. Isn't it?"

"Well, I guess you are right," Zawu agreed picking up his guitar.

"Now, what do you want to hear?" He strummed the guitar, drummed lightly on the back of it and sat up straight. He cleared his throat as if ready for an outstanding performance. Kolu's anticipation was palpable.

"Whatever you can play," Kolu left the door wide open for Zawu as she looked directly at the musician.

Zawu strummed the guitar again. He leaned forward and started. "Skip, skip, skip to my Kolu, skip, skip, skip to my Kolu!" Akoei clapped and screamed but Kolu sat still. Although not a musician, she knew the original song to notice easily that the singing and guitar were both out of tune, far out of tune. Zawu did not notice. He kept singing at the top of his lungs. At one time, Akoei jumped out of his chair and started dancing. When Zawu finally noticed that Kolu showed no emotions, he stopped and asked, "Is the music O.K.?"

"Go on," Kolu commanded. "Can you play something else?"

"Of course, of course." Zawu strummed the guitar again and started, "My lovely Ko—lu!" Kolu also knew the original song. This was far worse than the first song Zawu tried to sing. After the two songs, he put the guitar down and ordered more drinks. He and Akoei drank a glass after another until they were inebriated.

"Time to go folks," Kolu announced. Without waiting for the guys, she stood up and grabbed her purse as her beautiful, huge, and luxurious gold chain swung back and forth.

"Wait!" cried Zawu. "Let me play one more song, my favorite." Kolu could only say she had heard enough as she headed for the exit door. The guys followed.

As planned, Kolu and her brother rode back together. In a horrible voice, he tried to explain one thing or another but Kolu was in no talking mood, as she knew her brother was too drunk to discuss anything reasonably.

At the Fahpeh residence, Kolu quickly ran to her room while the driver helped Akoei into his. The driver was accustomed to doing so and did not mind it a bit. This was because he often used the occasion to help himself with money hanging out Akoei's pocket or lying around his room. Sometimes the driver reached into Akoei's pocket, pulled out his wallet, and helped himself to a good sum. However, not once did Akoei mention a missing money.

Early Sunday morning, Akoei was at his sister's door. "Sorry Sis we made a fool of ourselves last night; it was all my fault. I earnestly apologize for I blame it all on me."

"How come?" Kolu could not understand. Her brother said if he had not arranged for many drinks to be served; maybe everything would have gone right. "Zawu is a nice guy and I honestly hope you go out with him, just once."

"To be honest Akoei, I think I like the guy. I'm only concerned about his drinking. He is no musician. I think he ought to play on two occasions: when his neighbors are away or when he wants to send his neighbors away." Akoei could not hold his laughter. He nonetheless reiterated his plea for Kolu to go out with his buddy. She agreed somewhat begrudgingly.

The following Saturday, Zawu was back to pick up Kolu. His driver drove them to their familiar spot. Kolu ordered a meal and so did Zawu. The evening was going well until Zawu started drinking again. Kolu stopped him. "If you want me to come back here with you, you must not drink yourself to death," she stressed in a no nonsense tune. "For goodness sake; you need to moderate your drinking otherwise your throat will dig your early grave, and believe me, I will not be at the funeral."

"Sorry, sorry, Kolu; that's enough drink for me," Zawu apologized. He kept his word and they had a fine evening. Kolu also kept her word for in another week, they were back in the same place. Kolu began to like Zawu, even overlooking his drinking at times.

∞∞∞∞

Sayzay and his teammates continued practicing for the big game. One day, Akoei showed up for practice. After watching the boys through a long work-out, he asked to talk with Sayzay. "About what?" Sayzay could not mask his surprise.

"About my sister, of course," Akoei stated as if Sayzay should have known. As Sayzay listened intently, Akoei spilled the beans. "My sister is deeply in love with a fellow named Zawu. He is from a rich family like ours. His father might be richer than mine although I somewhat doubt that."

Sayzay stood still wondering why Akoei felt compelled to reveal this information. Paying no attention to Sayzay's long face, Akoei explained excitedly that, whatever the case might be, Zawu and Kolu were not only going out strongly but planned to announce their engagement soon. "My, my, my," Akoei chuckled. "That will be a huge party. I will make sure to invite you to the party so for once, and I'm definitely sure for the last time, in your pitiful peasant life, you may have a really good time.

Akoei stressed his points for he was sure, after all, there was no dodging the fact that, what he and his family considered crumbs and left-overs would be more than enough for a feast for Sayzay and his family. Worse, Sayzay and his family would live such a life to their death. "So, if and when I invite you, you better come and enjoy for once in your life," Akoei said giggling.

Sayzay stood speechless for a while. "Don't you have anything to say? I told you. You and Kolu are nowhere socially compatible. Now, she has found someone of our social class." He boasted that the kind and intelligent gentleman was not only an amazingly talented musician but he was in college. Akoei grinned mockingly and stated matter-of-factly that Sayzay would never ever make it to college because of his peasant status. "that lowly status," he said, "keeps you ignorant thereby making it impossible for you to go to college. Besides, even if you could cheat on the exam to be admitted into college, you would never afford proper clothing for college, let alone books, tuition, room and board. I will not even mention entertainment for that's something you do not know anything about. Your best entertainment is drinking smelly palm wine." Akoei paused a minute as he was absolutely enjoying the moment. He laughed again but Sayzay was not amused.

"Akoei," Sayzay said, "I do not drink, not even what you call smelly palm wine. Yet, if you invite me to the party, I will come not to have a good time but ..."

"To spoil the party?" Akoei jumped in. Without allowing Sayzay to respond one way or another, he said, "We will kill you on the spot. Don't forget, you are talking about two very rich families. I swear Sayzay, we will kill you and nothing, I mean nothing will come out of it for no one will investigate the loss of your useless life; both families will make sure of that with small handouts here and there to the police. If your poor father makes any effort to ensure investigation of the matter, he too will be a goner. So, do not dream of it if you care for your ever-miserable and useless life."

Sayzay seemed amused. "No, I will never spoil Kolu's party. I will come to support Kolu and celebrate with her for her new life."

"You mean you will not be angry? If so, you do not love my sister as you claim."

"I do love her and that's precisely why I will support her for her happiness means a lot to me. Also, I will support her because no matter where she goes, and no matter whom she marries, she is my wife and always will be. I know I will marry that woman before I die or I will die a bachelor. So, if your aim is to ruin my day and week, you have failed miserably. Kolu is my love now and forever."

"You are absolutely crazy," Akoei scolded. "What does it take for you to understand that you and my family are not in the same social class, nothing close? In fact, "something close," is an insult to my family for you are not even worth to be one of our servants, not even the toilet boy. So, dumbbell Sayzay, knowing all these things, tell me one thing;

what does it take to get into your skull that you will never never marry my sister?"

Sayzay looked at Akoei as if feeling sorry for him. He said Akoei would never understand because Akoei was locked up in a sheltered world, which left him narrow-minded and oblivious to reality. "I truly pity your condition," Sayzay pronounced.

Akoei exploded. "Nonsense Sayzay! You pity my condition? A lowly peasant like you? How could you?" Walking around in circles as if he owned the world, Akoei said he had everything he wanted and more. Better still, he could get more if he wished and that would be his status till he died. On the other hand, Sayzay was poor, dirt poor and would remain so till he died. How then could Sayzay pity his condition? "Listen blockhead," Akoei pointed at Sayzay. "It's the other way around. In your only world of abject poverty, you live a pitiful and miserable life and worse, it's a stagnant position which will never change." To exemplify, Akoei stated that his lunch was good enough to be Sayzay's feast and what he spent on drinks for one evening could easily be Sayzay's annual salary if he were ever employed. "That's the truth fathead and that's how it will always be," Akoei giggled mockingly.

Sayzay was not even slightly intimidated. Instead, he shook his head in disagreement. He said only God knew the future. "If He exists, I hope He knows," Akoei continued his mocking laughter. He said he and Sayzay had unchangeable futures. "The difference is mine is a bright and rich future while yours is the opposite. You will die dirt poor Sayzay and nothing will change that!" Akoei added that, worse still, there was no one willing to rescue Sayzay from his misery, certainly not Akoei. To underscore his point, Akoei stated that if he had money to waste, he would rather burn it or flush it down the toilet than give Sayzay a penny; Sayzay just did not deserve it. He therefore encouraged Sayzay to continue wallowing in perpetual poverty. Akoei then laughed interminably. It seemed he could not control his amusement and self-adulation.

As Sayzay looked at Akoei in amazement, the latter wanted to be sure that the former truly understood his plight. "Let me ask you honestly,"

Akoei stated seriously. "Do you have any idea, or do you harbor any hopes of getting out of your present miserable lifestyle given that your great grandfather and your grandfather were poor, very poor and your father is the same? Honestly, do you?"

Sayzay thought over the matter for a moment. Maybe he has a point, he thought to himself. But by a miracle of god, he truly had no means of getting out of poverty.

"Answer me honestly," Akoei demanded. "Frankly, I do not," admitted Sayzay.

"There you go," Akoei mocked. "For once in your miserable life, you have given me a true and logical response. Why then should my sister waste her precious time on a poor one like you? What do you have to offer her or anyone for that matter?"

"I do not know Akoei except that I am sure I will marry Kolu or no one else."

"I do not blame you," Akoei said. "As I have stated repeatedly, your poverty has robbed you of common sense, reasoning power, and not to mention logic. Keep wallowing in that dream while my sister prepares for her wedding."

Sayzay stood speechlessly as Akoei walked away. For the first time, he was convinced Akoei had overpowered him in both truth and logic. Yet, he remained resolute in his determination to marry Kolu.

****

Increasingly, Kolu was getting involved with Zawu much to the delight of her family. She and Zawu had exchanged several letters and expressed feelings for one another. No doubt, Zawu was sure the relationship was bound to be stronger and stronger. He started to think of marriage. That will be a huge wedding day, he thought. On the other hand, he had some fears and concerns.

As Zawu's feelings swelled, so did Kolu's concerns. She therefore decided to visit Fahzie one more time. She knew she could get nothing but straight talk from her older sister.

Fahzie was outside her store when her sister's car pulled up. It probably goes without saying that she was excited to see her little sister.

Kolu ran out of the car and gave her sister the biggest hug ever. "Great to see you Sis Fahzie. As always, you look good, very good indeed. Each time I see you, it seems you are getting   younger."

Fahzie laughed. "Well thank you but flattery will get you nowhere."

Kolu laughed too. "But I mean it Sis Fahzie. You really look beautiful."

"Thanks again but if I could, I would give my left hand and foot to be half as beautiful as you. Honestly, Little Sis, you are gorgeous. I always boast of your beauty."

"Now, now, who talked about flattery? If I ever heard of flattery that must be it."

The two laughed and entered the store. Fahzie headed for the rear of the store knowing Kolu was on hand for another discussion. "So, what brings you here apart from saying, 'Hello'?"

Kolu cut to the chase. She revealed her relationship with Zawu, which was much to the delight of her family. She disclosed that she had gone out with the young man several times and found some things appealing about him but other things, a real turn-off.

"Do you like him?" Fahzie asked. "Kind of."

"No, tell me the truth. Do you like him?" Fahzie restated her question. "I know it's too early, or so I think, to talk about love."

"It is," Kolu admitted "but I really think I like him."

"Let me ask you again my darling sister. "Do you like him because Akoei, Mom, and Dad do?"

"I really think that has something to do with it but even on my own, I kind of like him. I just wish he did not drink so much.

Fahzie said no one was perfect. "We all have our strengths and weaknesses; some of us have made our mistakes but …" she hesitated. "Do you like him because of his professed social status which, most likely, is the reason why Mom and Dad approve? Are you even sure that what he professes is true? Have you or any member of the family visited his home to see what it is like? Did he tell you from what high school he graduated and which college he attends?"

The stream of questions threw Kolu into a deep thought. Clearly, she had not thought of these things. "That's why I like to come to you Sis Fahzie; you make me think. You force me to face reality and believe me, I appreciate it although quite frankly, I sometimes resent the truth, especially when it is not in my favor," Kolu admitted unashamedly.

Fahzie recalled an old saying that the truth hurt but assured her little sister that she was not trying to hurt her. Quite the contrary, she was trying to guide her into making the right decision so she was not hurt in the end. Fahzie said she knew how it felt for she had experienced it firsthand. "Take it from an older sister who loves you dearly," she concluded.

Kolu fell in deep thoughts while Fahzie sat quietly watching her little sister. "Well sis Fahzie," she said, "I really think I would like to know this gentleman for a while. I have not dated anyone; I therefore want to give it a try."

Fahzie agreed, even encouraged Kolu to do so. However, Fahzie said she was afraid Kolu was playing the social class game. She said Kolu was saying one thing but doing another. For instance, she was sure Kolu was interested in Zawu only because of his social class. In addition, Kolu wanted to please her brother and parents.

Kolu jumped in quickly. "But Sis Fahzie, love does not happen at once; it comes gradually. Isn't it?"

"That's true. I have heard people talk of love at first sight but do not know if that's possible; frankly, I do not think so. But my concern is you dating someone because of his social class or in an attempt to please others; that will only lead to disaster sooner or later. On the other hand, if you truly are convinced that there is a possibility you will have a relationship with this gentleman, by all means, go for it but do it for yourself and from your heart."

"I will do just that Sis Fahzie and thanks for the advice. I know I will come back again and again." Kolu stood up to leave and Fahzie walked her to the door.

"You know you are welcome day and night," she patted her sister on the back as Kolu jumped in the car. When the driver drove off, Fahzie murmured, "I have to pray for my little sister. I pray God guides her into making the right decision." Fahzie closed her store and put her children to bed.

"My goodness," Sayzay's father said. "What is this horrible dressing about with fake beards and all?"

Sayzay laughed. "Well Papa, we have a funny program tonight and I am to appear like a grandfather." He did not want even his father to know of his mission. I know I can pull this off, Sayzay thought to himself.

"Good luck for you truly look like one," Mr. Siefa Kargbo said with a chuckle.

Sayzay made his way around town to Fahzie's store. He knocked lightly at her window. She grabbed a flashlight and went to the window. "Who is it?"

"Sayzay," the stranger whispered. "Please let me in."

Fahzie opened the door and fell over laughing when she saw Sayzay although she kept the laughter down not to awake the children. "What brings you here? She asked.

Sayzay took a while to catch his breath. "I understand Kolu is deeply in love with a man named Zawu. Do you know anything about it?"

"Deeply in love?" Fahzie repeated as if she had not heard the words correctly.

"Yes," Sayzay said softly. "I just want to know if it's true although I know that if true, there's nothing I can do about it other than going into my shells and lamenting for the rest of my life."

"I tell you the truth Sayzay, Kolu is dating Zawu; they have gone out several times." Sayzay's breathing increased but Fahzie encouraged him to calm down. She assured him that Kolu was not in love, at least not yet. However, Fahzie truthfully revealed that Kolu seemed to like the gentleman but had a number of reservations, even doubts. Fahzie paused for a moment before adding, "I am praying fervently that God guides her into the right direction."

"I will join you in prayers," Sayzay promised. "Believe me, I will give myself a week to prepare but will do a seven day fast. Whether it's me or anyone else, I will pray for her to make the right decision and be happy in a relationship. I love her deeply but her happiness is paramount to me."

Fahzie looked at Sayzay somewhat strangely as if to say she could not believe her ears. "You are a very nice man Sayzay. I also pray for your happiness."

Sayzay thanked Fahzie and said he felt relieved. "We have a big game coming up so I need to be at my best. When Akoei first told me the news, it rolled off like water on duck's back but as it sank in, it affected my practice seriously. Now, knowing the truth, I will go out there and, believe it or not, for Kolu, I will play my hardest. After the game, as I have said, I will do my seven day fast."

"Please play your best," Fahzie pleaded. "Akoei told you a lie. Kolu has not brought herself to love the guy, let alone engage him. I tell you the truth, she is struggling with the decision as to whether to continue dating him or not."

Sayzay sighed again. "Again, we will pray, I mean pray really hard," he said softly before leaving.

The regional championship game started with a bang. Less than ten minutes into the game, a penalty was called against Fasawoba. Sayzay looked around the crowd but did not see Kolu and her parents. Because of Zawu, they refused to attend the game. However, Sayzay was not discouraged. Rather, he set his mind on Kolu and Kolu alone.

With his mind fixed on Kolu, Sayzay was ready. When the referee blew his whistle, the captain for Suo-mee-lazu put his foot into the ball. "Saved!" the crowd shouted as they did a year earlier. However, this was too early for a huge celebration.

The first half ended in a scoreless game. The coaches called their boys to strategize. The Fasawoba coach pulled out a small chalkboard on which he sketched what he thought were the game plans for the opposing team. Quickly, he mapped out a counter strategy. Next, he sketched two familiar formations that would enable them to defend on one hand and, on the other, score. By the time he finished, it was time to return to the game. He encouraged the players to remain focused and calm. "This victory is ours. I know it is because I believe in each of you."

The second half was tougher than the first but both sides kept up the pressure. When Gayduobah stole the ball from an opposing player three or four yards into the opposing territory, he signaled a play to his teammates. In response, two players ran right and two went left. Gayduobah faked a rush toward the opposing goal. Quickly three opposing players rushed on him in an attempt not only to stop him but crush him. Skillfully, he landed the ball at the feet of Golo who was one of two players who ran right. Golo dribbled the ball past one person, a second, and a third before releasing the ball smartly. "Goal!" the crowd shouted in jubilation.

It took a while to clear the football pitch. When the game resumed, the Suo-mee-lazu boys were more aggressive than ever but Sayzay was up to the task. They made several substitutions to equalize and possibly win but Sayzay would have none of it. He made incredible saves. The game ran into injury time and soon, the final whistle blew. The crowd flooded the field. Sayzay, Golo and Gayduobah were lifted up high. Fasawoba High School was regional champion. Its players were headed to the capital, Coastal City to compete for the national championship and that's all the crowd sang: "Coastal City here we come! Coastal City here we come! Coastal City, here we come!"

Kolu and her family were not at the game so Sayzay could not expect a hug from her. Instead, unexpectedly, an incredibly beautiful lady hugged Sayzay to pieces and did not want to let go. She whispered in his ear that he was a great guy, an amazing fellow. She said she, the coaches, fans and everyone in the region owed the victory to him. He politely smiled and wondered about the stunning beauty in his arms.

CHAPTER ELEVEN

News about Fasawoba's sensational victory went viral nationwide. Every release featured Sayzay extensively. Newspaper, radio, and television personnel visited Fasawoba to interview the coach, players, and parents. The town had not seen anything like it.

As teachers, parents, and well-wishers in Fasawoba celebrated, the coach and his players only thought of the national championship which was to involve the four cardinal regions of the country; those were the Northern, Southern, Eastern, and Western regions. It was arranged that the Northern Region, in which Fasawoba sat, would play the Southern region first and the Eastern Region would go against the Western Region. Winners of those games would play for the national championship. Sayzay and his teammates therefore had their works cut out for them.

As Sayzay and his teammates prepared for the national championship game, his mind was set on Kolu. Would she come to Coastal City to see him play? Would she give him another hug after the game? Like a hungry eagle, his mind wondered back and forth seeking a landing spot. For now, there was none but that did not discourage him for a moment. Kolu was his love; now, that thought was enough.

As Sayzay wondered about Kolu, he was the last person on her mind. Instead, she thought more and more about Zawu. She requested, and her family gladly consented to invite Zawu to dinner. Zawu showed up for dinner like a nice gentleman. He was dressed remarkably. He brought a dozen roses for Kolu and an expensive bottle of wine for the Fahpehs. The Fahpehs were impressed. While Mr. Fahpeh suppressed his emotions, Mrs. Fahpeh did not; she was all smiles and sometimes the smiles gave way to hearty laughs. "You are a true gentleman Zawu and I hope you get to know my daughter better," she said. This was music to Zawu's ears.

At the Fahpeh residence, every meal was a feast with exquisite dishes prepared by a team of experienced chefs and served by specially trained domestic workers. The dinner with Zawu was no exception; if anything else, it was more exquisite and formal than usual. Everyone was enjoying the meal with wine and laughter. Jumping from one conversation topic to another, Zawu said, "I almost forgot to congratulate you all from Fasawoba for a wonderful regional victory; that was incredible." He said he could not admire Sayzay more. "The gentleman was unbelievably sharp between the poles; I have never seen a goalkeeper like him and have no idea when I will see another even close to his caliber. Doubtless, the man is in a category by himself, untouched, and unmatched." The Fahpehs nodded and Zawu went on and on praising Sayzay. He did not notice that people at the table suddenly went quiet.

"I do not understand much of that football stuff," Mrs. Fahpeh finally spoke up, resorting to falsehood in an attempt to change the topic.

"But Mrs., you should have seen the gentleman," Zawu returned to his praises of Sayzay. "He was awesome. He saved one penalty and many goals. But for him, the other team would have won by no less than ten goals but no, that great and wonderful goalie would have none of it. I sincerely hope he plays beyond Fasawoba although I would not recommend him for the national team which not only pays next to nothing but treats players like trash."

Zawu fervently wished an outstanding professional team drafted Sayzay for Sayzay truly deserves such an opportunity to make a huge amount of money. He further admired the fact that Sayzay was not only a brilliant goalie, a nice looking gentleman but, from his interviews, it was easy to tell he was raised well. Without noticing that people at the table continued to be very quiet and in fact, some people were rolling their eyes, Zawu said he liked the fact that Sayzay always commended his teammates and gave thanks to God. Then he added, "That's the kind of guy everyone with half a brain could kill to be his friend. One girl will be lucky, indeed blessed to be his girlfriend. If I had a sister, I would do anything to have her date Sayzay."

"Coming from Fasawoba, he has absolutely no chance of being drafted by a professional football club," Mr. Fahpeh predicted. "Let's face it; what professional team will come this far to recruit a peasant village boy? It's never going to happen."

Politely but sternly, Zawu countered that he had never seen a goalie as sharp as Sayzay. He disclosed that he was a big football fan who had watched national and international matches as well as professional teams. He reemphasized that after seeing various matches, he was yet to see a goalie as sharp and smart as Sayzay regardless of the fact that Sayzay was just a high school player.

"I play once in a while and have seen many who are far better than Sayzay," Akoei murmured softly. "Dad is right; I am sure he will never make it to the pros; the national team is out for him," Akoei also predicted although he was never good enough to make the sixth string team of his high school.

Zawu was tempted to ask Akoei for an example of a goalkeeper better than Sayzay but he resisted the temptation, as he did not want to take his friend to task especially since he knew Akoei was dead wrong. Yet, he added, "I'm not sure if we are talking about the same Sayzay. This goalkeeper is unsurpassed on every count in my book; he's just awesome."

As Zawu completed his fourth drink while digging into his second serving, he said time would prove him right because he had no doubt Sayzay would be drafted sooner or later by a professional team with which he would make mind-boggling sums of money annually. He prayed for same as he reiterated that Sayzay certainly deserved such a reward for his incredible talent.

Mr. Fahpeh had had enough of the Sayzay talk. Also working on his second serving and fifth drink, he too resorted to falsehood to change the topic. "Look Son," he said, "we are not a football family and so are not interested in the topic."

"Now I understand," Zawu relented, reaching for his drink. "Please excuse me; I am a big football fan. If you are not, let's talk about something else."

Following Zawu's capitulation, the meal continued with jokes and laughters. It seemed the more drinks, the louder the laughters. The only person calm at the table was Kolu but she was used to that.

After the meal, the family and its visitor talked for a while; of course, more drinks flowed. Afterwards, Kolu and Zawu left for their usual spot. When they were seated at their regular table, Zawu ordered drinks. When the drinks arrived, a glass of juice for Kolu and a potent mixed drink for Zawu, Kolu explained why the family was avoiding a discussion centered on Sayzay. "He has said he is deeply in love with me and will marry me or no one else."

"What!" Zawu exclaimed, putting down his drink. He was visibly shaken up. "That lowly Sayzay? That good-for-nothing peasant? You mean Sayzay? Sayzay?" He repeated himself in total disbelief.

"Yes, Sayzay," Kolu assured. "My dad has gone to his father's house and threatened them but it has made no difference. He continues to insist on marrying me. He even repeated that after my brother told him I was dating you. I mean, the man will not give up for anything or anyone."

"What! Sayzay?" He could not believe his ears. "But the two of you are nowhere close in social class," Zawu opined. "Nowhere   close!"

"Well, that may be true but that's not my reason for not dating him. We grew up differently and do not have much in common. More importantly, at the time, I did not have feelings for him or anyone else." Kolu further explained that she was not heavy on social class, ethnic, or other differences. "To me, the oneness of our humanity is what counts most; all, or almost all other differences are insignificant, I mean absolutely immaterial. Besides, we are all children of one God and therefore should treat one another as equals."

Zawu refused to comment on Kolu's allusion to God for he did not go to church. Likewise, he was not interested in getting in an intellectual discussion with Kolu. His concern was their relationship. "Do you have feelings for me?" he put his luck to a test.

Kolu hesitated and this was scary for Zawu. After all, he was not used to being rejected by girls; that is, until they found out about his drinking. Now that Kolu had found that out and yet went out with him convinced him of a solid relationship; but, was he right or was he living in an illusory world? What did the angel seated in front of him think of him? Was she true to the words she expressed in her letters or were those meant to make him feel good and no more? He did not know for sure but hoped for the best.

"Well, Zawu," Kolu finally spoke much to the delight of Zawu although he wished he did not get any bad news. "I do like you; you come across as a very brilliant man and I like that, among other qualities of yours. Frankly, I'm afraid I may be falling in love. However, as I have told you in my letters, my main concern is centered on your excessive drinking. I have seen my father and brother drink and know what alcohol does to people."

In addition, Kolu expressed concerns about the fact that she did not know Zawu. She knew nothing about his background, his parents, nor what he did. The only thing she knew was what he said; that is, he was a college student. She did not know from which high school he graduated or what college he attended.

Zawu had a serious look on his face. Clearly, something bothered him and he looked it. In fact, he looked as guilty as a little boy caught with his hands in the cookie jar. He set down his drink and looked at Kolu. "Kolu, my dear, I am already in love with you; who would not fall in love with an angel like you?" He revealed that he had told his parents about her and they were elated. As such, they were willing to spend whatever it took him to date Kolu. He said his family's prayers were that their relationship blossomed into marriage but before that, he would make efforts for Kolu to know him and his family better. However, he stressed that, from the onset, he wanted to make it clear that he was not a perfect person; like everyone else, he had his pluses and minuses. Of course, he did not mention his parents' wish; that is, they prayed that, if the relationship worked out, Kolu's reputation and influence would change him for the better.

Naturally unmindful of Zawu's parents' wish, Kolu endorsed Zawu's statement. "That's right; we all have our strengths and weaknesses. We therefore have to learn to deal with one another's limitations. I am not perfect either; in fact, no one is," she said in fact.

Kolu's understanding of the matter pleased Zawu tremendously although he knew, without a doubt, Kolu was not aware of the extent of his limitations and drawbacks. As such, on his honors, he promised to cut down on the drinking and that pleased Kolu. She smiled broadly. "If you could do that, I will appreciate it highly. I know Mom and Dad already like you very much, not to mention my brother but the excessive drinking really turns me off." Zawu nodded in agreement. Kolu then excused herself to visit the ladies'.

Zawu watched lustfully as Kolu made her way to a door just a few feet from the table at which they sat. Looking at her nicely shaped butt and smooth thighs protruding from her short beautiful dress was irresistibly tempting. Her nicely brayed hair that fell in the back beyond her shoulders did not help matters. He watched her closely as she opened the door and walked down a narrow hallway to the ladies'. He stood up and waited by the door. When he heard her coming back, he jerked the door open, went in, and closed the door behind him. "Going to the bathroom too?" Kolu asked.

"No, coming for you."

Kolu laughed. "I'm alright. Do you think I need some protection or something like that?"

"No," Zawu's response was barely audible. He grabbed her and pulled her to himself.

"What are you doing?"

"Just want to hug you to pieces. Gush, I could not take my eyes off you as you walked to the bathroom. You are incredibly beautiful. Has anyone told you that?" Without waiting for an answer, he added, "I hope I'm the first to tell you and I mean it. You turn me on in every way."

He hugged her repeatedly and she seemed to enjoy every minute of it. "Have you ever kissed anyone?"

"Ehn ehn," Kolu shook her head.

"Are you sure?" he whispered.

"Positive!" She was right for she had not affectionately hugged any male. In fact, beyond greeting and celebratory hugs, she had never hugged a man beside her brother and father. She was in for a treat. Zawu, who obviously was very experienced, hugged her harder and kissed her passionately. He ran his hand in her hair and around her neck. With the fragrance of her expensive cologne, urging him on, he pushed her again toward himself and she cooperated like a drowning man who needed to be saved. He pushed her toward the wall, rested his back on it, and turned her around so her butt rested directly on his front. He pushed her toward him and held both of her breasts while kissing her neck repeatedly.

"Ahhh! She groaned softly. "You are too much Zawu."

"You ain't seen nothing yet Darling." He pushed her closer to himself and ran his fingers down her stomach, touching every inch   of her expensive dress. Then he turned her toward him and held tighter. Although he had been with many girls, he could not describe the feeling he had when her soft body lay in his chest. He began to run his hands on her back. He slowly made his way down to her butt, pressed on and pushed her toward himself.

"No, no," she protested. "Let's go back to the table." He hugged her more but she insisted. He kissed her repeatedly but she said once more that she wanted to return to the table. He reluctantly gave in and led her back to the table.

CHAPTER TWELVE

Fasawoba took no chances in celebrating the high school's regional victory. The Town Council passed a special ordinance to celebrate the town's victory and a parade was planned and well attended. The Fahpeh family did not attend.

Following the parade, which included congratulatory speeches, the Fasawoba High School coach was very strict regarding practices in preparation for the big game. Besides, Sayzay spent hours practicing one-on-one with the coach or with one or two players sending shots his way from various angles.

After another intensive team drill, Golo and Gayduobah said they wanted to cool off at Sayzay's house. "No problem," Sayzay accepted the proposition. He said he had soft drinks but, as he told them before, he did not drink beer, wine, or definitely hard liquor. If this was acceptable, his friends were more than welcome to spend the evening with him.

"We will be there immediately after a quick bath," Golo assured. "You know we do not drink either," he reminded his friend.

"I do not want to surprise you Buddy, but there is a stranger in town who will be coming with us," Gayduobah divulged.

"Stranger?" Sayzay repeated the word.

"Yes, stranger," Gayduobah confirmed. "The stranger is presently with my girlfriend, Yongorwelay who will be coming with us to your house. Deddeh, Golo's girlfriend is coming too; I'm sure you remember her."

"Mmm" Sayzay said neither rejecting nor jubilantly accepting; he just did not know what to make of the proposition. Maybe it was another journalist who wanted to interview him but if that was the case, why would the stranger be with Yongorwelay? Who was this stranger? Not getting any answers to his own questions, Sayzay forgot the stranger and straightened up his room to accommodate six or seven persons. He took a quick bath before informing his father of his friends' visit.

"Do you have enough soft drinks or do you think you need to run out and buy some more? I do have a small amount of money here."

"Thanks Papa, but that will not be necessary. I already have told them that I have soft drinks but do not drink wine, beer and definitely not hard liquor. Fortunately, they do not drink either."

"How about something to eat?" Mr. Kargbo inquired. "Do you have any munchies?"

"No papa, I do not. They know my mother is not well so I do not think they expect to eat when they get here." Sayzay said he was dying to receive his guests but did not tell his father the reason for his anxiety.

Sayzay did not wait long when his guests arrived. They included his buddies Golo and Gayduobah and their girlfriends along with a stunningly beautiful young lady. "This is my friend Tayzu," Yongorwelay said. She is an admirer of yours." Then it dawned on Sayzay. This was the same young lady who hugged him to pieces after the regional championship game and would not let go.

"Yes I am," Tayzu admitted. Then she shocked Sayzay. "I am from Biahlaw, the regional capital but I came here specifically to meet you and congratulate you for your heroic football performance. You are awesome. I told you so after the regional championship game and meant it."

"Wow! Thanks a million," Sayzay said. "I'm truly flattered. You went through the trouble of coming here just to congratulate me? Indeed, it's flattering but I hope you congratulate my teammates to. Without them, there would be no victory. As they say, 'one tree cannot make a forest'. In the same way, one player cannot make a football team. But again, I thank you from the bottom of my heart for coming; it's a real pleasure."

"No, no, no," Tayzu rejected. "The pleasure is mine. To meet you in person is more than a pleasure and a delight; it's a dream come true. And I agree; your teammates were awesome too."

"Well gentlemen," Yongorwelay announced, pulling to herself a small basket she was carrying. "The three of us cooked small food and prepared some munchies for you guys. I must say, Tayzu provided almost everything." She opened the basket and then looked back and forth at Tayzu and Sayzay and blushed. She herself was a very fair complexion beauty and so appropriately named Yongorwelay, meaning, the bright or light-skinned Yongor, an adult female name.

"Thanks ladies," Golo complimented. "Although we ate something small at home, we dearly need this after a long practice session." He dug in as the ladies served.

"I do have soft drinks if anyone is interested," Sayzay informed his guests. When everyone took a bottle of soft drink, he turned to Tayzu. "How long are you with us here in Fasawoba?" He chewed on awaiting her response. The food did not only exude a tantalizing aroma but it tasted incredibly good.

As she watched Sayzay chew, Tayzu blushed. She wondered whether to answer the question truthfully or stretch the truth. If she had a choice, she would spend the rest of her life with Sayzay in Fasawoba but this certainly was not the time to reveal that truth for it would make her appear desperate and foolish.

"Did you hear my question?" Sayzay asked.

"Yes, I did," Tayzu replied. "I think I will be in town for a few days with my dear friend and sister here." Then she went a little farther. "I won't be surprised if I came back to visit a few more times." Then she thought to herself. A few more times? No, many times. No again, only once but to stay forever. Her thoughts rolled on and on as she dreamt of spending her life with Sayzay, her only love.

The evening conversations went from one topic to another. Not surprisingly, football was a leading point of discussion although no one made any predictions. How could anyone predict anything but victory for Fasawoba? At the same time, given the talents of the boys from the other three regions, the possibility of winning seemed remote while the thought of losing was frightening. Yet, everyone remained optimistic.

As the evening dragged on, it was evident that the visitors would soon leave. After all, another tough practice session was planned the next day. Yongorwelay therefore whispered something to Sayzay before she and the others headed for the door. Sayzay and Tayzu were left alone.

"Sayzay, do you remember me at the game?" Sayzay nodded in agreement. As if this was not enough, Tayzu reminded him. "I was the lady who hugged you over and over after the game. Sayzay," she paused shortly and thereafter chose her words carefully. "Please excuse my boldness but, from the bottom of my heart, I want you to know that you are the apple of my eye and I came here to let you know. Quite frankly, words cannot express adequately my deep and sincere feelings for you."

For a moment, Sayzay thought of his father's words that they were in completely different times. Most probably, this would not have happened during his father's young days.

"Did you hear what I said Sayzay? I mean it most sincerely."

"Yes I did and truly appreciate that but ..."

"I know about Kolu," Tayzu cut in. "You are in love with her I understand."

"The only lady I have ever loved romantically," Sayzay did not mince his words.

"That's wonderful. You are taking a risk on her and I am taking one on you; God will settle all in the end and I pray He does so in my favor, as selfish as that may sound."

Sayzay was lost in thoughts. What did she mean? What risks were they both taking?

Tayzu did not bother clarifying her statement. She had a more important mission, one that could not wait. She was direct about it.

"Once more, please excuse me for being bold," she said "but before I go, may I get another hug?"

Sayzay thought quickly. If she came this far to see him and express her feelings for him, the least he could do was to give her a desired hug but certainly no more. He therefore consented by saying, "Sure." He gave her a big hug but refused her attempt to kiss him. He preferred to kiss Kolu than any other girl. Nonetheless, she melted deeper and deeper in his arms with tears running down her cheeks. Melting in her only love's arms truly was Heaven on earth for her. Eventually, he let go and led her to her friends.

"How was it?" Yongorwelay asked.

Although she noticed that Sayzay had returned to his room, Tayzu was not sure what to explain. She was speechless as she reveled in the precious moments with Sayzay. She had to, for she had thought of Sayzay over and over, dreaming dreams and hoping hopes. Like a child hoping for a good Christmas, she had wished wishes and prayed prayers about Sayzay. She finally remembered she had not answered

Yongorwelay's question. She therefore whispered, "It was alright. No, it was not all right; it was excellent, nothing less than Heaven on earth. Thank you my sister for making this possible. God be praised for that's the one and only love of my life." Golo and Gayduobah listened to the exchange without comments. They only hoped finally, their buddy would shift his attention to this beautiful queen who was wooing him like a hungry lion. In fact, as much as they could, they would make sure of that, and knowing how close they were to Sayzay, they did not think they would fail.

The next day, Tayzu and the girls wen to the football field to watch Sayzay and the other boys practice. After the practice session, Golo requested that they met at his house. Again, the three ladies prepared food and everyone had a very good time. Tayzu insisted on sitting next to Sayzay the entire evening and when she did, she grinned from ear to ear. Eventually, everyone left to prepare for another practice session.

"You really need to think about Tayzu," Golo told Sayzay. "She is not only incredibly beautiful but she is deeply in love with you and sincerely so."

"Thank you my brother but as you and Tayzu know, and indeed as everyone knows, I am in love with Kolu and no one else. However, I also believe in God; whatever He says goes. You know what the Good Book says; 'In their hearts, humans plan their course but the Lord establishes their steps'."[8]

"Does that mean you will rethink your position and seriously consider Tayzu as a girlfriend?" Golo inquired.

"Most certainly," Sayzay pleasantly shocked his friend. "I love Kolu and Heaven knows my love for her is deep and sincere. However, if I cannot get her, I will consider another who shows me true love." He reiterated the line Golo cited earlier to the effect that it's better to marry one who loves you than the one you love.

"I'm glad to hear that; I mean, exceedingly glad to note that you are not only overwhelmed by emotion but you are injecting some logic into that emotion. We praise God for you," Golo rejoiced and Gayduobah supported reservedly.

Kolu's driver moved somewhat quietly in front of Fahzie's store. Two men and a lady were leaving the store with merchandise. Good, Kolu thought. My sister is doing business today. Unknown to Kolu, one of the men stopped and stared at her. When she finally caught the man staring, she jumped out of the car and quickly headed for her sister's store.

---

[8] Prov. 16:9

Fahzie was at the rear of the store when Kolu walked in. Thinking it was another customer, Fahzie ran to the counter. She fell over laughing. "Hello Customer. What would you like to buy today?"

Kolu laughed too. This customer cannot afford what she wants to buy."

"Then she will get it free of charge," Fahzie continued the silly conversation.

"What would she like?"

"She actually needs a pound of love, an ounce of truth, a dose of open-mindedness, a huge dose of faith, a cup of self-confidence, a gallon of independent thinking, ten measures of humility, a drum of health, and a heap of happiness."

Fahzie laughed. "Well, money cannot buy those precious commodities. We will give them free of charge today." The two laughed and headed for the rear of the store.

"Sis Fahzie, I need your honest opinion because ..."

"No reason necessary," Fahzie cut off her sister. "You know you will get my help at anytime, anywhere, and anyhow. Moreover, you will get nothing but honesty at its best. So, shoot!"

Kolu sat thinking; she did not know how or where to start. Her sister nudged. "Go on Kolu. 'Lay it on me,' as you young people say. Tell me what's on your mind."

"Sis Fahzie, it's getting serious."

"Do you mean between you and Zawu?"

"Exactly," Kolu smiled broadly and the smile turned to laughter. "He gave me a hug that made me think I was in Heaven. I have heard girls in school say one is not to kiss and tell but I must tell you the truth. When he kissed me, I almost passed out.

Wow! It was wonderful; my first kiss ever!"

"Tell me something," Fahzie encouraged.

Kolu could not stop smiling. She explained, as much as she could, the close encounter between Zawu and her. It made Fahzie curious. "You know you can tell me everything. Did he go farther?"

Kolu laughed again. Her momentary silence seemed like centuries. Fahzie did not know what to expect although she hoped for an answer in the negative. If in the positive, what could she do? She looked up and down as if searching for the right answer somewhere. Still not hearing anything from Kolu, she pressed on. "Did he?"

"No, no," Kolu stated emphatically. "He tried but I refused. After our close encounter at the restaurant, he wanted to stop that night at a friend's house but I insisted on going home." She paused, smiled broadly and said softly, "But I think I have found the love of my life; it can't get better than this."

"Take it easy sweet Little Sis; take it easy. However, whether he is the love of your life or not, for now, I'm just glad to hear that Kolu; I really am. I pray God guides you in every way. As you know, His way is the best."

"To hear what and why are you glad Sis Fahzie?"

Fahzie was not sure whether to explain in intimate details or just state the obvious. She elected to do the latter. "I am glad to hear he did not go farther. I say so because my dear Sis, it's neither good nor a self-respectable thing for a woman to give into a man quickly or easily, no matter how much you care about him. It is always advisable to know the man a little, gain his respect, and be assured of everything or almost everything before dropping your pants for him. After all, most men these days want only that."

"What Sis Fahzie," Kolu thought she knew what her sister meant but wanted to be sure.

Fahzie did not beat around the bush. "To get into your panties and after that, they are finished with you as you have just become another statistic."

"Do all men think and behave that way?"

Fahzie knew her little sister was indirectly making efforts to protect Zawu or, at the very least, hoped Zawu would be an exception. Either way, Fahzie was not about to generalize for she knew that would be false and misleading. "No," she said.

"There really are caring men out there. It's just that ..."

"What again?" Kolu could not wait.

"It's just that there is no easy way to tell. Most of them will say what you want to hear and do whatever it takes to get what they want. But," she threw in the familiar conjunction, "there are men who care sincerely. They treasure a relationship ahead of anything and everything else. Unfortunately," she went on, "more often than not, those are the ones that are maltreated by women. That is truly regrettable because, I tell you the truth, such men are the smart ones because once one has a solid relationship, and everything else falls in place in an amazing way, sometimes far more than one expected. Don't get me wrong; there are also men who maltreat women and I'm a living witness."

"So shall we reword that Scriptural verse and say 'Seek ye first the kingdom of a relationship and all the other things shall be added onto you'?" Kolu chuckled.

"You can say that," Fahzie said, remaining serious. "But," and there was that familiar word again, "it ought to be a genuine relationship because knowing the sincerity of the quest for a relationship is the ten million dollar question. Again my dear Sis, do not get me wrong; there are sincere men out there; it's just difficult to know." Fahzie explained further that she did not expect Kolu to fold her hands and sit perpetually in doubt as to which man was sincere and which one was not. "This was why I told you some time ago that life was a gambling ground; you have to use your instinct and pray hard." She disclosed further that it was precisely on that ground that she did not stop dating after her first real love broke her heart and left her with two children. Fortunately, she was happy with her boyfriend, once a regular customer, she hoped to marry.

"Do you think Zawu is sincere? Sis Fahzie, please tell me the truth."

Fahzie knew exactly why her sister was asking. In response, she could not afford to give Kolu false hopes nor could she afford to scare her sister away from a possibly promising relationship. The truth of the matter was she did not know and she said nothing less. "To be honest with you dear Sis, I do not know the man and so cannot judge him. I will only continue to pray for you. As you know, when you rely on God, you cannot go wrong."

"We will be glad to stop by one day so you may meet him. He is delightful in many ways except …"

"I told you; we all have our strengths and weaknesses. However, meeting him for a few minutes or even an entire day is not enough for me to form an opinion for he might be on his best behavior during that time. This is where prayers come in."

"So you have no opposition to me dating him; do you?"

"Of course not. As always, I only advise that you be careful and don't allow him to move too fast until you know him fairly well." Fahzie pleaded with her sister not to be carried away by outward shows. She cautioned Kolu not to give in easily to a man whose only intention was to get into her pants. She emphasized that Kolu's body was the most precious thing Kolu had and giving it to anyone ought not to be an easy decision. In sum, Fahzie advised, "Whoever gets your body must be worth your person."

Kolu was grateful for such a wonderful older sister. She thanked Fahzie before leaving the store. Fahzie stood and watched her sister move away. She once more renewed her determination to pray for Kolu.

CHAPTER THIRTEEN

Sayzay and his teammates along with their coaches rode to Coastal City in a special van provided by the provincial government. The same government arranged accommodations and practice facilities. The only thing they had to do was to play well. Of course, players were under the strict supervision of their coaching staff. Fortunately, the boys were incrediblydisciplined. The coaches therefore focused more on coaching than supervising.

It probably comes as no surprise that many people from Northern Region paid their own ways to see the Fasawoba boys play in Coastal City. Among the many fans were Golo and Gayduobah's girlfriends as well as Tayzu. Fortunately, the three girls traveled in a chauffeur-driven private car provided by Tayzu's parents. This gave them easy and free movement in Coastal City. Nonetheless, chances of socializing with the players prior to or during the games were slim. This was because the players' high discipline standards notwithstanding, the coach made sure there was no socializing until the final game was over. All the Fasawoba players knew that and none expected anything less.

As previously, arranged, Northern Region was to play Southern Region. This was expected to be a tough game but most sport commentators gave the edge to Northern Region, meaning, Fasawoba probably because of Sayzay's incredible talent between the poles. Nonetheless, the coach and players prepared as if this was the final game of their lives. They paid absolutely no attention to polls and pundits. Upon arriving in the capital city, their coach worked out an arrangement for them to practice secretly on a high school field thirty miles from the city. They arrived at the site early in the morning, did various exercises and practiced football until noon. They broke off for lunch, rest and relaxation until two o'clock in the afternoon. From two until four o'clock, the coach mentally and psychologically prepared the players by giving lectures and showing films of breath-taking international matches. At four o'clock, they were back on the pitch until sundown. They returned to Coastal City for dinner and a nice evening rest. They followed this routine for the entire week preceding the big game. The coach wanted to keep himself, and definitely his players away from the public especially from news media agencies. In that regard, fact that the players were extremely disciplined was a huge help.

On the day of the game, the coach returned to his mental preparation of his players. He did so by showing films of various famous players demonstrating mental toughness when the game was at stick. In addition, he lectured his players on topics such as mental toughness, discipline, unselfish plays, and supporting one another even if someone messed up. "If we are to win, and we must, we will win as a team, not as individuals," the coach stressed. To exemplify, he said if a player had a twenty percent chance of scoring but realized that another player had an eighty percent chance, for sure, the ball was to be passed to the teammate with a higher chance of scoring. "While I want each of you to score a dozen times, nevertheless, do not take unnecessary risk in a bid to become a leading scorer and thereby gain praise and admiration. No, pass the ball and let another score with the understanding that the praise and admiration go to the team, not to an individual. At all times, avoid the dual malady of showing off for the crowd and trying to impress me or anyone else at the expense of the game."

After a lengthy lecture on teamwork, playing unselfishly, focusing on winning, not showing off for the crowd, being patient and even tempered, etc., points players had heard a thousand times, the coach could tell easily that his boys got the message and were prepared. Satisfied, he allowed them to rest for most of the day and get a nice meal. There would be a very light workout session just before the game. He said he was 'holding to his chest' the treat and entertainment he had reserved for them after the victory.

The game between the Northern and Southern regions was carried live by national radio and television stations. The game started with each team testing the waters of the opposing team. For almost five minutes, neither team could get the ball into the other's goal. Finally, a dynamite shot flew from Gayduobah's legs into the opposing goal but the goalkeeper collected it like a piece of cake. No doubt, this was bound to be a tough match.

The game continued for another five minutes with each side exchanging jabs and skillful kicks. Then the coach of Fasawoba ran up and down the sideline screaming, "Hiba-hiba low, hiba-hiba low!" No one knew what that meant but the Fasawoba players definitely did and they went to work. In a few minutes, the ball from the Fasawoba boys flew from the mid-field to the left out who rushed toward the Southern Region goal. When everyone ran toward him, he passed the ball across the field to the right out where Golo was waiting. He trapped the ball skillfully before passing it to Gayduobah. Gayduobah faked once, twice and let the ball fly. "Goal!" the crowd shouted.

After the Northern region first "pulled blood," the Fasawoba fans attempted to flood the field but thanks to the tight security, no one reached the pitch. As such, a delay in the game was avoided, much to the delight of players and coaches.

When the game resumed, each side had near misses but to Sayzay, this was a routine matter. However, routine or not, near misses gave each side hope and optimism for victory. The game continued in that manner until the end of the first half.

As soon as the whistle blew ending the half, coaches called their players for a quick strategy session, which was not to be disturbed by fans. In no time, the whistle blew for the resumption of the game.

The Southern Region players had regrouped and were prepared for Fasawoba, or more correctly, the Northern Region. They pressed hard but only a few balls were sent Sayzay's way, which he collected easily. Even with the near misses, the crowd had not really seen his talent as a goalkeeper.

As the second half progressed, there were signs that the Southern Region boys were growing tired. Gayduobah once more took the ball past mid-field, dribbled a little and dropped it to Dorbor, a 'dangerous' leftist. Dorbor did not disappoint anyone. He moved the ball forward a few feet and skillfully sent off one of his best shots. "Goal!" the crowd roared. This second goal seemed to have angered, or perhaps invigorated, the Southern Region boys. They pressed harder and rushed fiercely toward the Northern region goal but Sayzay displayed his magic masterfully. No seat in the stadium was occupied; fans were on their feet, most cheering Sayzay.

Despite the renewed vigor of the Southern Region boys, their wings were finally clipped. Ten minutes to the end of the game, Zayzay, an incredible striker, showed his juice. From twenty yards out, he aimed for the net. "Goal!" the crowd   exploded. This sealed the fate of Southern Region as the game ended three-zero. The Northern Region was a finalist.

When the final whistle blew, girlfriends, families, and well-wishers of the Northern Region players took to the field. The coach was lifted up high but he was not too keen on celebrating as his mind was set on the final game.

Among the people running on the pitch was Tayzu. She had to fight off a number of girls but succeeded in running into Sayzay's arms and hugging him repeatedly. "Thank you Darling; you were awesome as usual." For the first time, Sayzay was not uncomfortable with Tayzu addressing him as "Darling" especially since this was a time for celebration. On her part, Tayzu knew eventually, that title would stick for good. She had no doubt about it and was sure in due course, her beautiful wedding ceremony would prove her right. She could not wait.

After the game, Tayzu, Deddeh, and Yongorwelay wanted to have dinner with Sayzay, Gayduobah, and Golo but they could not. Knowing that the coach would not even listen to a request toward that end, the young men did not bother to ask. They plainly told the young ladies that they were not permitted to leave the team at any time until the final game was played. Although disappointed, the young ladies understood. They too wanted nothing but national victory for the Northern Region.

∞ ∞ ∞

In Fasawoba, Maa Gaamai was sitting outside her house warming herself under a beautiful afternoon sun when Fahzie showed up. "Maa Gaamai, Ya na?" she greeted.

Maa Gaamai did not distinguish the voice nor could she identify the speaker because of her failing eyesight. "Who is that?"

"Your granddaughter Fahzie," the visitor identified herself. "Oh!" the old lady said. "Is that Fahzie, Fawkpa's daughter?"

"Yes Maa," Fahzie replied. "This is your granddaughter."

"There's seat for you, my granddaughter," the old lady said which was a welcoming statement. "I have not seen you for a while. Is your body well?"

"By God's grace, I'm well," Fahzie replied. "I brought you small food and some fresh juice." The old mom was delighted. As she ate, she plunged into a long lecture about Fahzie's parents. She remembered their wedding and relayed how she assisted Fahzie's mother, Wenwu, on many occasions. "Oh she was a lovely lady," the old mom recalled.

Fahzie nodded politely and appreciated the history lesson although she had heard it on numerous occasions. When Maa Gaamai finished her food and drank her juice, she once more thanked Fahzie for her thoughtfulness. Before she returned to another long history lesson, Fahzie said she wanted to talk with the old Maa but not outdoors; she preferred to go inside. Maa Gaamai agreed and both headed for the house, with the elderly lady taking baby steps to avoid any accidents. Fahzie patiently walked besides her watching carefully for anything in the way that might trip the kind elderly lady.

Once in the house and seated comfortably, the old ma first said a blessing, which Fahzie appreciated very much and for that, she gave the old ma a few coins. Then Maa Gaamai said, "So, what's on your mind my beautiful granddaughter?"

First, Fahzie once more thanked Maa Gaamai for the sweet words of blessing. She said the old Ma's blessing truly touched her. The elderly lady appreciated the young lady's realization that blessings from elders were important. "Now-a-days," the old Ma said, "many young people do not appreciate the importance of a blessing. This is one of the reasons for their many misfortunes, failures, and setbacks. They do not know that the God of the Heavens releases blessings through the elderly as well as young people specially anointed. This is true my dear little one," Ma Gaamai stated with unshakable conviction.

"I absolutely agree," said Fahzie. "I have no doubt that a blessing from the elderly is a blessing from God." Then, turning to the matter at hand, she explained that her little sister, Kolu, who visited the old lady regularly was facing a problem most young ladies faced; she was not sure if the man she was dating was the right one or was it the man she was avoiding. "Kolu is a beautiful and wonderful young lady. I cannot find adequate words to praise her because, unlike my wayward grandson, she supports me generously. She has been visiting me since she was twelve years old and I always appreciate her visit," the old Maa said. She added that she appreciated and loved Kolu dearly not only because of the young lady's visitation but she brought gifts and, above all, she made the old lady laugh. "When she makes me laugh, I forget all my problems; that makes me feel better as well as joyful. I really like that because, given all I have experienced, I do not have many reasons for mirth and laughter." Maa Gaamai therefore vowed that if she could do anything to help Kolu, she most definitely would for that was the least she could do in her old age. Unfortunately, Kolu was so self-sufficient that the old mom did not think she could do anything for her. She did not think she could do anything for anyone.

"Of course there are many things you can do for Kolu, me, and many others" Fahzie assured the old lady. "As I stated earlier, your blessings are priceless." When the old Ma nodded in appreciation, Fahzie explained the situations her sister was facing with both Sayzay and

Zawu. She explicated that she did not know Zawu; therefore, in all fairness, she could not judge him. She similarly informed the elderly lady that she did not know Sayzay very well either but had met him on two or three occasions. Besides, since Sayzay was from Fasawoba, she heard about him all the time and knew his family. But regardless of how much she knew both men, she said she was afraid her little sister was making a decision based on social class. "This is why I'm here Ma Gaamai." Fahzie asked the elderly lady to join her in praying for Kolu to make the right decision. "To me," Fahzie stated earnestly, "it does not matter which of the two men she chooses as long as God directs her. Therefore, I am praying that indeed, God will direct her."

"Isn't Sayzay's Grandma Luopu Taapulu?"

"Yes Mam," Fahzie answered. "He is very attached to his grandmother. He is equally attached to his parents and uncle. From what I know, he is just a well-rounded, decent, respectful, and hard-working young man." Maa Gaamai paused for a brief moment without saying a word. It seemed she was collecting her thoughts or trying to remember the past. She then spoke in a soft voice. She informed Fahzie that she knew Luopu Taapulu well. Moreover, she knew Luopu helped raise Kolu's mother. As this made Maa Luopu a great source, Maa Gaamai promised to talk with her. Likewise, the old ma promised to talk with Kolu although she said she had to be careful in doing so. Specifically, with Kolu, she would not raise the issue directly. Laughing lightly, she added, "One has to be careful with young people when it comes to their love lives. Often, they

let their emotions, perhaps infatuations, blinden them to the truth."

The old Maa was grateful to God Kolu was not such a person. She emphasized that she knew Kolu well and knew the young lady to have a good head on her shoulders. Nonetheless, she promised not only to pray about the matter but encouraged Fahzie to pray along with her. "There is nothing the God of the skies cannot do. Whatever He says goes and whatever He denies goes nowhere."

Fahzie was pleased with the old lady's promise. Before she returned to her store, she gave the old lady a small present. In return, she received additional words of blessing.

* * * * * * * * * *

The semi-final match between the Western and Eastern Regions was tough but, as the pundits predicted, the Western Region won easily. This pitted the Western Region against Sayzay's team. Most Northern regioners feared this combination for the capital, Coastal City, sat in the Western Region and so had some of the best high school players in the nation. However, the Fasawoba coach never gave up on his boys; not for a second did he doubt them. "We may be going up against a powerful Goliath but we are victorious David; we will win," he told them. "You only need to trust yourselves as I trust you. If you do, and I pray you do, we will put the so-called sport pundits to shame." He said more than putting pundits to shame, the boys would take a national trophy back to the Northern Region and thereby make everyone in the region proud. "You have no idea how much joy you will bring our people if, no, I mean when we win the final. Moreover, each one of you will achieve a milestone to be remembered for life."

The players were energized by the coach's words. They had a meeting among themselves to think of the coach's words, come up with their own strategies without ignoring the coach's. Moreover, they made a commitment to one another to play well, avoid selfishness, but rather cooperate with one another, knowing that a victory would not belong to anyone but to the team. They also vowed not to be angry with anyone who made a mistake, no matter how dearly that mistake cost them as a team. With that, they were prepared for the final.

The huge stadium was packed to the max in anticipation of the national high school championship game. For at least three hours prior to the game, bands played and fans jubilated. People who were sure their team would emerge victorious, no matter what, held placards and shouted slogans. Not surprisingly, the Northern Region supporters were outnumbered overwhelmingly, nothing less than seventy to thirty ratio and that was a conservative estimate. Yet, the huge difference in the number of supporters did not deter the northerners, including northerners who lived and worked in Coastal City and nearby towns. On the other hand, to their utmost delight, licensed venders were having a field day selling whatever they brought. It seemed their first loyalty was to their merchandise and maybe secondly, to one of the competing teams. Others could care less who won as long as they sold their goods.

About ten minutes to the game, the two captains joined the referee and the linesmen in the middle of the field to the applause of the huge crowd. After the familiar rules and regulations were discussed, Gayduobah jogged off to join his teammates. In minutes, the Fasawoba boys, led by their coach, jogged on to the field. On average, they looked smaller than the Western Region boys but looked remarkably sharp in their specially designed jerseys.

The Western Region boys were fast players. Within the first five minutes of the game, they penetrated the Fasawoba defense three times and twice almost landed the ball at the back of the net if Sayzay were not incredibly skillful. Fifteen minutes after the game started, the Fasawoba boys had not crossed the mid-field line; their backs were against the rope, so to speak, constantly defending. Indeed, the D in defense was from Sayzay; he saved goal after goal to the applause of the crowd. Radio announcers however predicted that, if the first fifteen minutes were any indications, the Western Region was bound to win easily. "We know Sayzay Kargbo is an outstanding goalie," said one announcer, "but he can only defend so much. Sooner or later, the Western Region boys will find the back of Sayzay's goal."

The game grew hotter and hotter but no goals were scored to the end of the first half. Both teams ran off to their respective coaching staffs. The Fasawoba coach once more pulled out his small chalkboard and sketched both offensive and defensive formations; none of them was new. Before he continued, the whistle sounded for the resumption of the game.

The second half was more balanced than the first. On a number of occasions, Fasawoba penetrated the opposing team's defense but failed to capitalize. This was truly to the shock and amazement of the pundits. By this time, they thought, the Western Region would have been leading by no less than three goals.

As the game drew close to an end, both coaches made desperate moves. The Fasawoba coach ran up and down the sidelines screaming, "woko- woko yea, woko-woko yea!" His boys got the message and went to work but were unable to capitalize. Before anyone knew it, the whistle was blown for injury time. Again, neither side scored.

When the final whistle blew, the huge stadium was quiet; it was a draw game. However, this was the national championship and there could not be two champions. So, without determining a winner on the basis of points as done at the regional level, the game turned to five penalty kicks by each team. Sayzay was prepared and no doubt, so was the opposing goalie. They had no choice. Sayzay only wished Kolu was on hand to see him play. For sure, that would have energized him. However, even in her absence, he would put his mind on her and therefore play as if she were in the stands watching him.

To begin the penalty kicks, a coin was tossed to determine who went first. Western Region won the toss and elected to kick. The ball was placed ahead of Sayzay as he watched carefully. Shouts of encouragement rang from the stadium but, as he had promised to do, he set his mind on Kolu and focused on the ball. The whistle blew and an opposing player hit the ball. "Saved!" the crowd screamed. There was dancing in the stadium but it was too early to rejoice.

The ball moved to the opposing goal. There was high expectation in the stadium. The whistle blew and Yekeh, a talented Fasawoba player, put his foot into the ball. "Saved!" the crowd roared. The referee signaled for the ball to be moved quickly from one goal to another.

Sayzay stood still once more watching the ball. The captain of the Western Region skillfully kicked the ball into the left corner. "Goal!" the crowd shouted and the dancing began. This was, or at least seemed to be a definite sign that the Western Region boys would win easily. A number of experienced sport analysts explained as to why there was no way Northern Region could defeat the talented boys of the Western Region. Quickly, the ball was moved to the opposing goal. When the whistle blew, Dorbor put his left foot into it. "Saved!" the crowd roared and the dancing intensified. No doubt, the victory was the Western Region's. People in the region ran out to buy beer, Champaign, and whatever it took to celebrate a huge victory.

For the third time, the ball was placed once more in front of Sayzay. He watched the ball carefully. "As the coach said, this is no time to be discouraged or be nervous; we must win this one for Kolu," he whispered. As Sayzay thought intently, the whistle blew and an opposing player hit the ball as hard as he could. "Saved!" The crowd shouted with a roar that was not half as loud as the time when Western Region scored. Nonetheless, there was hope for the Western Region.

At the other end of the field, Gayduobah stood patiently awaiting the whistle. The stadium was relatively quiet. When the whistle blew, Gayduobah gave it his best shot. "Goal! The crowd became even more subdued. Suddenly, the Northern region boys had renewed hopes; of course, they had never lost hope.

Sayzay eyed the ball and the next kicker carefully. Inexplicably, the kicker hit the ball directly to Sayzay who collected it with minimal effort. The small Northern region group of supporters clapped continuously. "Go! Sayzay go!" the chanting continued until the ball was moved quickly to the other end of the field.

At one goal apiece and with one kick left against Sayzay and two against the opposing team, the stakes could not be higher but the coach had a glimmer of hope that possibly, just possibly, Fasawoba could win. This thought of a national championship was too much for the coach to bear; he therefore shifted his mind from that to the next kick. For now, wishes had to give way to fervent prayers.

Golo waited patiently for the whistle. His coach shouted, "Time to distinguish boys from men, and champions from losers; you are a champion Golo; go for it!" To say this was tremendous pressure for a young man would be a gross understatement but Golo only focused on the ball. He looked once at the ball and the open goal ahead and bowed his head. When the whistle blew, he dashed for the ball and let it fly. "Goal!" The Northern Region supporters could not be quieted.

The ball moved to the other end of the field; the Western Region's hopes were at stake. Sayzay once more put his mind on Kolu while focusing intently on the ball and the kicker. When the whistle blew, the kicker gave it a dynamic shot. Sayzay caught the ball incredibly but was pushed back. The crowd instinctively shouted, "Goal!" The Fasawoba coach disputed the call while unsurprisingly; the Western Region coach insisted it was a goal. The referee, who had not blown his whistle, and the first linesman agreed with the Fasawoba coach. The second linesman said it was a goal. However, when Sayzay was pushed backward, the first linesman ran quickly and dropped a handkerchief on the spot where Sayzay's heal stopped. Upon close examination, it was at least eight inches from the goal line. The referee therefore overruled the second linesman much to the annoyance of the Western Region coach and supporters. Supporters actually booed the referee but that meant nothing to the experienced and highly respected referee. He had heard many boos over his career but never cared as long as his conscience was clear about his calls.

After the hurly-burly died down, the ball was moved to the Western Region goal for one final kick, a pure formality. Many people in the stadium therefore were paying no attention but Zayzay took his turn seriously. When the whistle blew, he gave it one of his best kicks. "Goal!" The roaring from the Northern Region supporters increased and people flooded the pitch.

Wow! The boys from a small rural town were national high school champions; unbelievable. Undeniably, David had prevailed over Goliath.

When the fans mobbed the Fasawoba players, none was lifted higher than Sayzay. Tayzu and others rushed to him but could not reach him.

There was a real pandemonium. Radio and television announcers did not hide their amazement, joy, and admiration for the Northern Region's incredible victory.

While celebratory parties were put together quickly, in parts of Coastal City by business men and women, politicians, military personnel, and civilians who hailed from the Northern Region, back home in the region, every town and village was in uproar. People sang, danced, and drank to celebrate. A huge parade was planned in Biahlaw, the regional capital.

Following the huge victory, the senior senator treated the coach and the entire team to a very nice dinner from the Northern Region. Each player was allowed to come with guests. More than ten beautiful girls offered to be Sayzay's guest. Tayzu was sure of being asked. With support from Golo and Gayduobah, and their girlfriends, Sayzay asked Tayzu to go with him to the dinner; she was on cloud ninety-nine. "This is another step toward cementing my relationship with the love of my life," she whispered. "Prayer and patience are the words," she admonished herself, while her friends once more assured her confidently that her lasting union with Sayzay was just a matter of time. She could not wait.

The dinner was well attended. The senator and other dignitaries from the Northern Region praised the Fasawoba boys and their coach for a monumental achievement. With food and drinks in abundance, and melodious music to match, everyone had a great time.

Before the Fasawoba boys and their coaching staff left Coastal City, they had a humongous surprise. The President of the nation invited them to a celebratory dinner at his official residence. This was incredible. None of them had ever seen the president in person, let alone talk with him. Everyone was excited for a once-in-lifetime experience.

The President and First Lady did not disappoint the players and their coaches. His residence was nothing like they had ever seen. He gave each person an envelope with an undisclosed amount. As he embraced Sayzay repeatedly and incessantly sang the young man's praises, it was conjectured that Sayzay must have received a healthy purse. This would not be a far fetch guess for Sayzay's envelope was much larger than everyone else's.

Regardless of whatever they got, each player and coach was delighted to meet the President and First Lady in person and shake their hands. Each person took picture with the first couple and was given a copy to take home. For sure, each would treasure that picture for life. In fact, before they left Coastal City, they made copies of their pictures to ensure they did not lose such memorable pictures.

CHAPTER FOURTEEN

Sayzay and his teammates returned to the Northern Region to a hero's welcome. In Biahlaw, they were met on arrival by the provincial governor, paramount, clan and town chiefs as well as traditional leaders, organizations, and associations. They themselves could not believe the reception.

The governor declared a special day of celebration to allow people of the region to congratulate the team from the small town of Fasawoba. Parents of the players attended along with the town chief and entire Town Council of Fasawoba.

The program for the celebration of the Northern Region's victory was lavishly planned and executed. Speaker after speaker thanked the team and praised Sayzay as the MVP, most valuable player. At the end of his remarks, the governor said, "I have heard rumors of our MVP having an interest in Biahlaw. I hope that is true and if it is, I give my approval before he asks." The audience went wild.

As the audience cheered, Sayzay was not amused. Golo and Gayduobah tried to cheer him up. "Whether you want it or not, you are now a celebrity, and for celebrities, anything goes," Gayduobah told him.

"But I do not have an interest in Biahlaw or anywhere else except in Fasawoba," Sayzay muttered. Conversely, Tayzu was once more on cloud ninety-nine. Smiling from cheek to cheek, she was confident that in due course, she would have her love in her arms for life.

"Shut up and just enjoy this historic moment," Golo, scolded Sayzay. "I thought you had reconsidered Tayzu as your girlfriend. Are you going back on your words?"

"True, I had reconsidered Tayzu but deep down in my heart, I know without doubt that Kolu is my only love. I will marry her or no one else.

Golo was shocked. "I cannot believe you made a complete about-face in favor of Kolu."

"My dear brother," said Sayzay. "I did not make an about-face. Rather, I remained steadfast, focusing only on Kolu. Frankly, I tried to consider Tayzu but found out quickly that no one could come between Kolu and me. No one could take the place of Kolu in my heart. In other words, my love for Kolu was, and remains, so strong that I could not dampen, resist, avoid, ignore, or substitute it." In so many words, Sayzay elucidated that acting against one's feelings or, worse still, one's conscience was more than hypocritical; it was iniquitous, even murderous. Hence, he added, "That's why I resent the governor's statement about me having an interest in Biahlaw."

"Well, Mr. Flip-flapper, be that way," Golo rebuked. "We still support Tayzu. In fact, she has invited us to her house and we are going. Mr. Flip-flapper, I want you to know you are coming along and that's that." Sayzay shook his head violently but Golo did not relent.

After the program and sumptuous meal, Golo and Gayduobah and their girlfriends persuaded Sayzay to honor Tayzu's invitation. Begrudgingly, he went along. Regardless of his about-face decision, Golo, Gayduobah, and their girlfriends knew it was just a matter of time when they would get Sayzay and Tayzu together. Therefore they were all smiles when they headed toward Tayzu's home.

Tayzu and her parents were at the door when the visitors from Fasawoba arrived. Tayzu hugged each of them but when she reached Sayzay, it seemed she was determined to keep him in her arms forever. She would have kissed him but for now, she knew he would reject her again so she kept hugging him to pieces. Finally, he gently pushed her away to shake her parents' hands. "Welcome to our modest home," Tayzu's father said. "I have followed you young players during the last two years and I dare say, you make us very proud. Congratulations!" Tayzu's mother endorsed her husband's statement and the players thanked both of them.

When the visitors entered the living room, their jaws dropped. It was incredibly beautiful with extremely expensive furniture. "Before we go any further," Tayzu said, "let me introduce everybody. Well, these are my dynamic parents, Dr. Folomo and Dr. Mazu Koboiku. My dad is chief surgeon and Medical Director of Northern Regional Hospital and my mom is professor and department chair at Northern Regional University where I am currently studying." She then introduced the visitors to her parents.

"You are all welcome," said Professor Koboiku. "It's a real delight to have you all visit us before you return to Fasawoba." Two house workers, a lady and gentlemen entered the living room, greeted the visitors, and began to serve. The visitors had eaten so much that they had very little room for much food. However, they took soft drinks and helped themselves to munchies.

"My parents had a full meal prepared for you all," Tayzu informed her guests. "Ah well, maybe next time. As Mom said, I'm just very glad you all came by; believe me, I appreciate it highly." The visitors thanked Tayzu and her parents before departing for Fasawoba. Tayzu promised to visit them within a week or two.

The Fasawoba Town Council once more declared a day of celebration and planned a parade to honor the town's high school players and their coach. It was a beautiful program but once more, the Fahpehs did not attend.

The regional and national championship games were followed by end-of-school year ceremonies. Fasawoba High School organized a beautiful program, which included the graduation of the school's twelfth grade students. The faculty and staff paid special tributes to the school's three outstanding players, Sayzay, Golo and Gayduobah who were graduating. Each received a special award. In brief remarks on behalf of his colleagues, Gayduobah thanked the faculty, students, the Parent Teacher Association, and the Fasawoba Town Council. He paid tributes to the coaches, expressed appreciation for his teammates and thanked God for the victory.

With high school behind them, the graduates had to decide their next steps. Few could afford to go to college. Many therefore would be job searching or simply staying in Fasawoba to serve their families and community as best as they could.

****

It had become customary for Zawu to have dinner with the Fahpeh family once or twice a week. During the graduation weekend, he spent hours with his buddy but always went back to Gizisu which was not far away.

Following the graduation ceremonies, Zawu was having dinner with the family when Mrs. Fahpeh asked if her son was thinking about college. "No Mom, I have not thought of it and quite frankly, even if I am to go to college, I would like to wait at least a year. I just need to get out there and experience the world a little."

Everyone was briefly quiet at the table until Zawu spoke up. "I do not think you will regret that Buddy. As they say, 'Experience is the best teacher'."

"I will let you wander out there for a month or two but will not allow you to roam forever like a vagabond," Mr. Fahpeh's emphasis could not be mistaken. He made it clear that he was not crazy about college but whether Akoei went to college or not, he needed to be in Fasawoba so Mr. Fahpeh could take him beneath his fatherly wings. According to Mr. Fahpeh, the young man needed to learn the business, it's ins and outs. He needed to learn how to handle the banks. Specifically, Akoei needed to learn how to give the banks a good dose of their own medicine and get rich in the process. In the same way, it was imperative he learned how to handle the people with the revenue agency, people whom Mr. Fahpeh called stupid folks, some of the dumbest people with whom he had ever dealt. Although they were truly dumb, Mr. Fahpeh clarified; handling them required special tact and trick. Only he could skillfully teach same to his son. With a broad victorious smile, Mr. Fahpeh said his son also had to learn other secret deals and transactions, which regularly and consistently brought in huge sums. "As I am aging," Mr. Fahpeh said, "you need to learn these things for this is how you will become and remain rich for the rest of your life."

"Is it because of these various deals that you prefer to live here instead of living in Biahlaw or Coastal City?" Kolu inquired.

"You are very smart Darling," Mr. Fahpeh complimented. He said living in Fasawoba away from the limelight had advantages, including cost saving benefits.

Asked to clarify, he pointed out that for one thing, workers were paid much less in Fasawoba than in the capital city. Overall, the standard of living was far cheaper but the main reason was twofold, staying out of the limelight and being one of the wealthiest persons, if not the wealthiest   person, in the region. "Believe me, those are huge advantages," Mr. Fahpeh accentuated as if patting himself on the back for being a smart decision maker.

"Well Akcei, my buddy," Zawu averred, "Your great dad has wonderful plans for you. So, do not spend much time on your experience-seeking sojourn. You need to come back and learn from the master himself. After all, we are talking about your future, a future that is bound to be filled with big bucks. I'm grateful to God that I have a future like yours."

Mrs. Fahpeh smiled broadly and looked at Kolu who showed no emotions. Akoei also was full of smiles. Assurance of a bright future certainly made him happy. His mind ran to a thousand things he could do once he became rich and independent like his father. He could not wait.

Sayzay was dressed up again with his fake beard and all. He made his way to Fahzie's window and knocked. "Who is it?" Fahzie asked. "The same grandfather," Sayzay answered. Fahzie recognized the voice and so opened the door. Even though she expected to see what she saw, she still fell over laughing. "Grandpa greets you warmly," the visitor said. "How are you tonight?"

Fahzie was still laughing softly but led Sayzay to the living room, away from the children's room. "What brings you here? Before you answer, let me congratulate you for a great national victory. I never thought I would live to be a part of such a national notoriety."

"We did it as a team and owe everything to God; only He could make such a thing possible." Then he paused for a moment. "But Fahzie, please tell me; how is Kolu and how is her relationship with Zawu?"

Fahzie felt a sharp pain in her body. She did not want to lie to Sayzay but knew whatever she said would be like a dagger through the young man's heart. Her silence frightened Sayzay.

"That bad eh?"

"Well, maybe not but truthfully, not good either."

"Let me have it one way or another."

Sayzay's words reminded Fahzie of a Shakespearian character who, about to receive the worst news of his life said to the news-bearing messenger, "If it be mine, keep it not from me; quickly let me have it."[9] She therefore sat thinking and this silence frightened Sayzay further.

"Honestly Fahzie, give me the news, no matter how raw, harmful or painful it be; I'm armed and ready." He said no matter the nature or degree of the news; he knew Kolu would be his wife for life.

Fahzie finally broke the silence. "The bad news, as far as you are concerned is that, when I last spoke with Kolu, she said they were getting serious. I know they have exchanged several letters and he has been invited on more than one occasion to have dinner with the family." She was very careful not to mention anything about Zawu kissing Kolu. The last thing she wanted was a young man having a heart attack in her living room.

Sayzay sat quietly for a while. He thought of the many letters he sent Kolu but never got one juicy letter back. He thought how he could do anything to have dinner with Kolu and her parents. I could give up my national championship, my house, indeed my left hand to have dinner with that family but was never given the minutest of chance, he thought to himself. He had never even been allowed to go near the Fahpeh home, let alone enter it.

---

[9] Shakespeare's Macbeth, Act IV, Scene III.

"What are you thinking?" Fahzie asked. "Are you alright? I did not want to tell you a lie."

"You are an honorable lady. I needed nothing but the truth. I rather have the truth that hurts than the lie that kills," Sayzay said in a low groggy voice. Fahzie could feel the pain in his voice.

"Sayzay, I really care about you and have prayed very hard for you, Kolu and even Zawu." She said she had also prayed for her parents and her dear little Brother Akoei. Without doubting the prayers, she wondered if Sayzay was willing to look for another girlfriend as no one needed to remind him that, in wooing Kolu, he ran into one stonewall after another. She added, "While I truly admire your tenacity, maybe it's time to look elsewhere. After all, it's your happiness that counts." Sayzay groaned as if in deep pain. He had a huge lump in his throat and his eyes seemed teary. Fahzie could feel his pain but felt totally helpless as she was unable to do anything to help the young man.

"Good Fahzie," Sayzay finally spoke, "I do not think you understand. Kolu is my only love ..."

"Do you mean no other girl will go out with you? Give me little time to check around. There must be gorgeous girls of your age group who can kill to date you."

Sayzay looked at Fahzie once more as if to say, "If only you understood."

"No Fahzie, there are many girls who would like to go out with me but Kolu is my one and only love." He told Fahzie about Tayzu and the many letters and pictures of breath-taking beautiful girls he had received from girls throughout the nation.

It seemed Fahzie's turn to be speechless. She looked at Sayzay in total disbelief. "And you turned everyone down for Kolu though she has told you repeatedly that she will never date you? Even Tayzu?"

"Yes, even Tayzu but Fahzie, 'never' belongs to God alone. The only plan that works is one approved by God; everything else is only a proposal awaiting approval or disapproval." He paused as if gathering his thoughts. Then he added softly, "that's why people say God's time is the best time. I truly believe that and so agree with the Good Book when the writer says, 'My times are in your hands'."

Again, Fahzie was speechless. "So, seeing that Kolu is going out with Zawu and you just graduated from high school, what are your plans? I mean, do you intend to go to college?"

"No Fahzie, I do not intend to go to college, at least not right away."

"I understand; it's very expensive," Fahzie acknowledged.

Sayzay explain that the cost was a factor but not the only factor. He surprised Fahzie when he said he received money from the president and various well-wishers as tokens of appreciation for his athletic performance. "With this money, I can pay for one or possibly two years of college."

"Do it," Fahzie said with an emphasis on "it".

Sayzay waited for a few seconds to speak as if finding just the right word to utter. "Not now," he said slowly. "My mother is sick and I want to stay here until Kolu graduates from high school. Who knows what might happen between now and then? He further shocked Fahzie by revealing that, for those same reasons, he had turned down athletic scholarships to three colleges and two universities. "After a year, if those institutions still are interested, I might consider their offers. Meanwhile, I will continue practicing football to stay in top shape."

Fahzie seemed frustrated for lack of understanding of Sayzay's logic. "You know what our people say Sayzay?" Sayzay shook his head. "They say, 'hit the iron when it is hot,' a metaphor from blacksmithing. You must act when the time is not only ripe but also right. I mean, right now!"

"Not so hot please," Sayzay appealed. "I love Kolu and Mom; I will do anything for them."

"But by taking advantage of these golden opportunities, you will help them even more. Who knows, you might be drafted by some professional football club."

Sayzay was adamant. "I have discussed it with my parents, uncle and grandmother, and they disagree with me as you do but for now, the decision stands. Thank God I'm now a high school graduate who can make decisions on his own." Fahzie shook her head back and forth, as Sayzay stood up to leave. He put on his fake beard and headed for the back door.

When Sayzay left, Fahzie stood thinking for several minutes before she moved slowly toward her bedroom. "I do not understand; I just do not understand," she murmured to herself. She also promised to pray for everyone. "Only God can straighten this up and I do not have the faintest doubt that He will," she whispered with confidence.

CHAPTER FIFTEEN

A couple of days after Fahzie's conversation with Sayzay, she was thinking about their exchange when the door of the store swung open and in stepped one of Mr. Fahpeh's drivers carrying a suitcase. "What's this about?" Fahzie did not hide her curiosity.

"Kolu asked me to bring it in. She's out there gathering some more stuff."

Kolu briskly walked through the door carrying a few things in both hands. "Help Sis Fahzie," she called.

"What do you need?" Fahzie was totally confused. "Are you moving in or something?" Kolu, who was returning to the car stopped and laughed so hard that she almost fell to the floor.

"I am Sis Fahzie but I have no money for rent."

"You will be kicked out the next month," Fahzie threatened teasingly. "No landlord in town will take you in under those circumstances."

After they brought in everything, Fahzie demanded some explanation. "What's going on?"

"Let's go to the back," Kolu pleaded. When settled in the rear of the store, Kolu explained that in addition to the fact that Zawu's drinking was getting worse; he was becoming violent because she was not giving into his sexual overtures. "At one time, I was lucky to get away just in time for the chair he threw at me to miss."

"What?" screamed Fahzie. "That bad?"

"Yes," Kolu answered. She sat upright, straightened her dress and relayed tearfully that another time, Zawu knocked her to the floor of the private restaurant and would have hurt her if the waiter had not intervened. She was thankful to goodness they were in a private room.

More than that, she was grateful to God the restaurant had a waiter on duty that night who turned out to be a strong man. "That man saved my life," she teared up again. She said that was the last straw that broke the camel's back. "Sis Fahzie, I could not believe myself lying flat on the floor of a restaurant. Apart from the fact that my dress was messed up, my elbow was scraped and the back of my head hit the floor so hard that my head hurt for days. I can't take it anymore. I knew from the beginning that he was drinking but did not imagine him to be this bad."

"I do not believe my ears. Kolu, is this true?"

Kolu answered affirmatively. She said she was sure Zawu was not only drinking but also doing drugs. "His eyes do not turn red when he drinks but when he does drugs, it seems his two eyes have turned into blood and that's when he really gets violent. Believe me Sis Fahzie, I'm sick and tired of him and do not want to be alone with him anywhere."

"Have you said anything to Mom and Dad about this?

"I have but sadly, all they say is this young man is from such a rich family that we cannot afford to miss him in ours as if he is the only man on planet Earth." She said it really hurt when her parents stuck to their guns about Zawu even after she showed them the scars on her elbows.

"They did not think that was bad enough?" Fahzie was speechless. "No Sis Fahzie," Kolu replied tearfully. They continue to talk about social class." She relayed that her mother tried to encourage her by recalling the manner and extent to which her husband abused her when they were younger. Yet she stayed with him and now praises her God for doing so because, together, they made it into a high social class, implying that Kolu could, and should do the same.

Kolu teared up again. She stopped speaking to wipe her face and take hold of her emotions as Fahzie looked on helplessly. Then Kolu added softly, "Sis Fahzie, this blind focus on social class and social class alone is eating me alive."

As she continued sobbing quietly, Kolu wondered why her parents did not consider Zawu's horrible behavior, drunkenness, and drug use as bases for rejecting his pursuit of their daughter. Why did they not see that Zawu's true intentions were fake and shallow? Why did they not see all the horrible things about him? For instance, if he were truly in college, why hadn't he returned to school when colleges and universities were in session? "Why, why, why?" she sobbed on. Fahzie truly felt sorry for her little sister. As she wished she could do anything to ease Kolu's pains, a thousand thoughts flew around her mind. If only Kolu knew how much Sayzay really cared, she probably would change her mind about him. As Fahzie saw it, social class was not to be the be-all and end-all. No, there was much more to life than class, possessions, positions, and titles. Beyond those mundane designations, where was the true humanity? Why did people use those mundane designations to hurt others without the slightest fear of a Supreme Being? Why did those designations make some beings to turn into beasts? Fahzie thought on and on. "What are you thinking Sis Fahzie?"

"Lots of things; lot. I do not have time to explain and I'm sure you do not have time or patience to listen."

"Of course I do. Like what? You got me curious," Kolu seemed restless as she wiped her face. She twisted herself in her chair as if in pain and maybe she was.

"Never mind my dear Little Sis. I will continue to pray and pray really hard. But let me ask, why did you bring in these things?"

Kolu's serious face gave way to a jovial one. She smiled and then burst into laughter even while she was still wiping her tears away. "I told you, I'm moving in but cannot afford a rent."

"That's the joke. What's the truth?" Fahzie demanded.

Kolu explained that she had asked her parents, and if it was all right with Fahzie, for her to spend time in the store during the long summer break and even after school reopened. "Sis Fahzie, I just want to get out of that house and stay away as long as possible."

Kolu disclosed that she had told her parents that, after graduating from high school, she wanted to go to a four year nursing school. Straightening herself in her chair and looking directly at Fahzie, Kolu informed her sister that visiting her elderly friends and precious children taught her a lot. Consequently, she wanted to spend the rest of her life helping others.

As Fahzie listened patiently, she was sure their mother had to push Mr. Fahpeh to pay for Kolu's nursing school. He had no problem spending money on expensive liquor, clothes, furniture, and the like but when it came to education, he had to be pushed by his wife.

As if Kolu knew what her sister was thinking, she revealed that unbelievably, her father opted to pay the four-year tuition in full alongside rocm and board and the cost of books. In addition, thanks to Mom's insistence, he deposited a good sum of money in the college's account for Kolu in case she needed anything. Further, he offered to open a private account for her into which he would deposit money every month until she enrolled in nursing school. "By then, Kolu said with excitement, "I will have my own private account and additional funds in the college account. She clarified that, to keep track of the fund in the college account, she would sign off on every withdrawal to ensure that the college did not keep a penny of her money. There was a written agreement to that effect. "Nursing school here I come!" she shouted with excitement. She jumped up and did a little celebratory dance.

"Do you intend to attend nursing school in Biahlaw or Coastal City?"

"Absolutely in Coastal City. I will definitely be a big city girl. I hope you and the boys will visit me."

Fahzie was impressed, in fact, extremely touched and she did not hide it. She ran to Kolu and embraced her lovingly. "I am very proud of you Kolu. Beyond your present opulent lifestyle, you are looking at the future and the realities of life."

"But you need to hear more; perhaps you will change your mind about me."

"I doubt it," Fahzie stated firmly.

"Well, listen to this. I have told my parents that, more than just spending short terms here at the store, I would like to spend most of my time here with you and the boys." Before Fahzie could remind Kolu that she already had said so, Kolu explicated that prior to graduating from high school, she wanted to spend every weekend with her sister. When she went to nursing school, she wanted to spend longer terms at the store instead of staying at her parents'. "Believe it or not Sis Fahzie, that place gives me the creeps and that's why I brought a few things over here."

Fahzie was beaming with smiles. "Why would that make me change my mind about you? I love it. I need some company around here other than your two little ones and my boyfriend who is often out of town." She paused and then added, "But, as landlord, I have some restrictions."

"And what are those?"

Fahzie laughed. "Nothing terribly shocking but seriously, after all I have heard, I would not want Zawu visiting you here. If I can get a word to Sayzay, I will tell him the same although you have said you are not interested in him." Fahzie noticed with delight that, for the first time, Kolu did not emphasize her absolute reluctance to date Sayzay.

"That's fine with me," Kolu agreed. "As I told you, I'm doing anything and everything I can to stay away from Zawu. I have advised Mom and Dad to make sure that, given Zawu's drug use, bacchanalian propensities, and consequent violent behavior, Akoei should not hang out with him either but they swept my advice away as if from an idiot."

"My goodness Kolu; you have not even graduated from high school and already speak like a college graduate? What do those big words mean--bacchanalian propensities?"

Kolu could not stop laughing. "I just mean Zawu's drunken habits or tendencies."

"Wow! You really need to go to college. I do not know how you will sound when you complete college but, however you sound, and whoever you become, you will still be my little   sister."

"I say a big 'Amen' to that. Sis Fahzie, believe it or not, you are the best friend I have, honestly, more than Mom and Dad, and I will not even mention that Akoei. I am glad, indeed very blessed to have you as my big sister, chief counsel, and confidant."

"Flatter as you wish; say whatever you may but when you spend time here, you still will pay rent. Oh no, you will not sweet talk your way out of that," Fahzie said giggling. Kolu joined the laughter. "But did you say you intend to continue visiting your elderly friends?"

"Oh yes, nothing will change that. In fact, I have readjusted my schedule to visit twice a week instead of once. This is because I gain a lot by visiting my lovely children and wonderful elders."

As Kolu spoke, Fahzie wished Kolu would spend time with Maa Gaamai. Just then, Fahzie's prayer was answered for Kolu said excitedly, "I especially love to spend time with Maa Gaamai. That old mom is incredibly brilliant. When she talks, one can tell she is not only experienced but has a kind and loving heart. I definitely will spend time with her."

"Thank you God," Fahzie whispered. "Cupid please go to work. Please, please get busy."

"Well Sis Fahzie, I will hang up my things and be on my way," Kolu said standing up. "Oh, I forgot to mention that when I told Mom and Dad that I would like to spend weekends here, they have decided to renovate your place. Quite frankly, that bothered me somewhat."

"What? Renovating my place bothered you? Why?"

"Not exactly," Kolu interjected. "Maybe that came out incorrectly for I did not mean it that way. My point is, they had never offered to renovate your place until I said I would be spending more time here. Doesn't that bother you?"

"I'll accept whatever it takes to renovate my poor home except by criminal means," Fahzie said laughing. "If that's what it takes, that's what it takes."

"I'm glad you see the issue from a positive perspective," Kolu stated earnestly. She revealed that she finally convinced her parents to sign off on the deed to the land on which the house stood. Now, the land, house, and store were solely Fahzie's.

Naturally, Fahzie was glad to hear the news. She admitted however that all along, although the deed had not been transferred to her, their parents had not shown any interest in the property and for that, she was most thankful. With that said, she and Kolu walked outside and Kolu was on her way back home to be there in time for dinner. She prayed her parents had not invited Zawu to dinner again.

∞ ∞ ∞

During her visitation tour, Kolu always stopped last at Maa Gaamai's house and this day was no exception. The old lady had just gone inside after warming herself nicely under an afternoon sun when Kolu arrived. "Maa Gaamai, Ya na?" As usual, the old lady was very happy to hear Kolu's voice.

"Kolu, Ay Va?" the old Ma replied. Continuing the greeting exchange, she added, "Oh my dear Kolu; welcome. Is your body well?" Kolu answered affirmatively and said she had brought food items and a little gift for the old mom. She gave her three blocks of a nice smelling bathing soap.

"I do not believe this. How did you know I needed soap? I used my last bathing soap this morning and do not know when my grandson will bring me supplies. I do not remember when last he brought me anything. In fact, I do not remember when last he visited me." Kolu thanked God for bringing the right thing in time.

The old lady and Kolu conversed a while before Maa Gaamai asked, "My dear Kolu, you know I love you very much and truly appreciate your visits and kindness toward me. However, as beautiful as you are, I have never heard you talk about a boyfriend. Why is that?" the old lady laughed lightly.

Kolu was taken aback. This was the last thing she expected from Maa Gaamai but knowing this lady had a heart of gold, she did not mind the question. "Well Maa, I am not sure the man I am dating can be called my boyfriend."

"Why not?" the old mom inquired.

Kolu hesitated as to how much to tell the old mom. Was it possible that whatever she told Maa Gaamai would soon spread all over town? She did not think so but, at the same time, she did not want to take any chances. She had to speak guardedly and warn Maa Gaamai that whatever she said was to be kept to herself.

"Well Maa," Kolu began. "I do not know how much to tell you but whatever I say must stay with you alone because I love and trust you dearly."

"Kpoo, my little one," the old lady started, "I talk with very few people and besides, I am not one who runs her mouth. Therefore, I assure you that whatever you say stays in this house. My aim is not to dig behind you[10] and tell everyone about it. Quite the contrary, I am interested in your wellbeing for you are a sweet and caring person."

Kolu believed the old lady. She truthfully disclosed that she had been dating a young man from Gizisu. However, she was losing, no, more correctly, she had lost interest in him because he drank too much. Worse, she was sure the young man used drugs too. She stopped and thought a minute before completing her brief narrative. "I got turned off about him when, on several occasions, he became violent when I did not give him to his sexual advances. I could not do that out of respect for myself. Besides, I really had not known him to be convinced he deserved my body."

The old lady laughed although she now appeared to have only a faint memory of sexual encounters. She nonetheless registered some degree of recollection and accordingly, offered a word of advice. "When it comes to sex my dear, men are worse than hawks but if he is being violent, you definitely do not need him."

Kolu was grateful for the old ma's understanding. In a soft voice, almost as if she did not want to talk, she said she now had to find a new boyfriend. She revealed that she was almost eighteen and at the end of the following school year, she would be a high school graduate and pushing nineteen.

Maa Gaamai sighed. She thought for a couple of minutes while Kolu watched curiously. She wondered what was going through the old lady's mind. "Come here my little one," Maa Gaamai ordered. She averred that, as much as Kolu had been nice to her, she owed her no less than the purest of her blessings. "I have nothing to give you but my blessings

---

[10] To dig behind someone is to search everywhere for one's secrets with the aim of spreading such secrets as broadly as possible.

from the ancestors and ultimately, from God," the old lady pronounced in very sincere terms.

Kolu went to the old lady. "Here I am Maa. What do you want me to do?"

"Kneel down my granddaughter." Kolu did as she was told. The old lady laid her hands on Kolu's head. "Oh the God of the ancestors, the God of the highest Heavens. I present my granddaughter here to you. I pray she meets and marries a young man who truly loves her; a man with a clean, kind, and caring heart; a man she will be proud to be her children's father! May she focus on a man who loves her, not necessarily whom she loves for such persons often break hearts; God, may no man ever break her heart! May she have long life, peace, happiness, and prosperity! May you, Oh God do these and more in the life of this dear one and may all be so! Amen!"

When commanded, Kolu stood up feeling new and refreshed although she did not understand why. She was just grateful to Maa Gaamai for such a wonderful blessing. She gave a few coins to the old Ma as a token of her appreciation before heading home. Inexplicably, when she reached home, she was very happy, even exuberant. When asked why such an unusual mood, she simply replied, "It has been a great day; a great day indeed."

∞ ∞ ∞

Akoei and Zawu were headed to their usual spot but without Kolu. When they were seated, they ordered food and drinks. "We cannot afford to drink much tonight," Akoei admonished.

"Oh no," Zawu agreed. "I want to be a part of the drama. No one can convince me that this (using the B word) is not responsible for Kolu's bizarre behavior." He regretted that Kolu would not go with him to their usual spot nor would she go anywhere else with him. For a while now, when he had dinner with the Fahpeh family, she excused herself early, returned to her room and locked herself in. "It's all weird Akoei," he pounded the table. "I love Kolu and will not lose her for anything or anyone, certainly not for that idiotic peasant." He claimed that, because of his love for Kolu, he had done everything right to ensure he did not lose her. He therefore would not allow anyone to snap her away from him, no, not if he could help it in any way.

"I just do not understand it," Akoei averred. My parents feel the same way. We have no choice but take good care of this fool."

Zawu said that was why he was not drinking more than two shots. "I need just enough to get me going. As athletic as he is, I am sure he works out regularly; so we must be prepared."

"Fear not Brother," Akoei assured. The old man has paid little money to two robust dirt-poor peasant guys to join our football team. In fact, they will play most of the game." Both laughed and headed for the door.

It was a cool and quiet evening. Sayzay and his father were conversing calmly around the fireplace when a little boy knocked on their door. "Sayzay Kargbo," the boy called, your friend Golo asked me to come call you. He says he is facing a serious problem and will appreciate you going to his place immediately."

Sayzay jumped to his feet. "Thank you little boy. I will go right away to see what Golo wants. I pray he is alright."

"He really needs you," the boy emphasized once more.

"I heard you. I'm on my way." Sayzay threw on a shirt, put on sneakers, and dashed toward Golo's house. When he was just a few yards from his destination, a gang attacked him. The first person struck him with a stick. He dropped. Incredibly, he stood back on his feet to face his attackers. He fought back fiercely, hitting one attacker after another but he was struck once more. He fell over bleeding in the mouth and nose. As if that was not enough, one attacker said, "Get this Dummy; never go around Kolu again." Nonetheless, he continued fighting back fiercely but, unable to say anything, he took blows and kicks from several attackers even when he lay helplessly on the ground.

Eventually, his attackers left him half dead. In fact, they thought he was dead; otherwise, they definitely would not have left.

Sayzay was lucky in that a man with a flashlight who had just left his girlfriend's place at night spotted him on the ground. Alarmed by The body of a young man on the ground seemingly dead, and a pool of blood in the area, the man raised an alarm. People easily identified Sayzay. Fortunately, he was not dead but seriously wounded. He was rushed immediately to the regional hospital in Biahlaw.

Sayzay was unconscious for several days. His father, Tayzu as well as his buddies Golo and Gayduobah stood by his side in tears. A team of doctors said he was likely to survive but could not predict his condition thereafter, at least not yet. They said that although the young man suffered multiple fractures, he did not lose a lot of blood externally; rather, his internal bleeding was their greatest concern.

News of Sayzay's merciless flogging made national headlines. The regional and national police were put on the case. They promised a swift and thorough investigation. "The cowardly criminals who committed this barbaric act against a nationally renowned athlete will be brought to justice and punished appropriately for their heinous act," a police spokesman promised.

After intensive treatment, Sayzay gained consciousness to the delight of his father and closest friends. When he was able to talk, the police asked him several questions. Slowly and sluggishly, he narrated the story as best as he remembered. He mentioned one of the last things he heard: "Get this Dummy; never go around Kolu again."

"Did you recognize the voice that uttered those words?" a police sergeant asked. Sayzay said he did not but he said he recognized the second voice. "What did that voice say?" the sergeant pressed on.

"This dog must not live through this to come near her," Sayzay said in a trembling voice.

"You said you recognized that voice?" the sergeant asked again. Sayzay nodded in agreement. "Who was the speaker?"

Sayzay did not hesitate. "Without doubt, it was Akoei. I know him well."

The room went quiet when Akoei's name was called. Mr. Kargbo had teary eyes. For sure, it did not take a security genius to know the source of the attack.

"Most likely, the first voice was Zawu's, the man who has been dating Kolu," Sayzay surmised and the police took notes carefully.

Sayzay's revelation made his father furious; it was difficult for him to control himself. Without just dwelling on anger, Mr. Kargbo went to the Fahpeh residence to demand justice—compensation for pain and suffering as well as payment of Sayzay's hospital fees which were expected to be huge given the fact that he had to undergo several surgeries. "I do not know law but as some good people have already advised me, this grievous bodily harm and attempted murder will not pass with impunity," Mr. Kargbo growled as he approached the Fahpeh residence.

Upon hearing that Mr. Kargbo was at his gate, Mr. Fahpeh did not bother to come out to meet his childhood buddy. Instead, he turned to a bodyguard and said, "Go tell that dirty idiot to get away from my gate. If he does not get away, and I mean soon, he will be worrying about two hospital bills for a peasant's life is not worthier than a pig's. Worse, the life of a peasant who is a real dog is not worth anything; tell him I said so." After that direct order, he lay back in a nice recliner and ordered a drink. His workers complied immediately and he joyously drank to his heart's content.

CHAPTER SIXTEEN

Sayzay's recovery was slow and long. Various people from Fasawoba visited him while others volunteered to help his mother in his stead. Kolu and Fahzie wept over the matter. Fahzie words stuck with Kolu: "Even though you had no hand in the matter and therefore it was not your fault, the truth still is, that young man almost got killed on account of you."

Kolu therefore made up her mind to visit Sayzay and make whatever little contribution she could.

Kolu had wit about her not to ask her parents' permission directly to visit Sayzay. This was because when, at dinner, she showed her parents a newspaper article of the governor's visit to Sayzay's hospital room, her father was furious. "That governor is an absolute idiot! Why would he spend taxpayers' money to visit an idiot who only got what he deserved? In fact, he deserved more but I guess it takes one idiot to visit another."

"So no one from Fasawoba ought to visit him?" Kolu asked in a scary voice.

"Well, there are many idiots from that dirty town. I therefore will not be surprised if some visit him." He said if given a million dollars, he would not foot at that hospital and he dared any member of his family to step there. As if this was not enough, he predicted with certainty that the worst was still to come for a peasant dog who dared defy him. With unmistakable certitude, he vowed that, no matter what was said or done, the dog's days were numbered.

Everyone was sure Mr. Fahpeh was not likely to fail; failure was not in his repertoire. This was why no member of the family doubted him in such situations. When he vowed revenge, he got revenge. When he threatened to teach someone a hard lesson, he made good on his threat. So, accomplishing his goal of "permanently silencing the dog" was now only a matter of time.

Despite her father's tough stance, Kolu was not deterred. She bribed Jimmy, her loyal driver to take her without telling her family. Jimmy was more than glad to oblige for he got a good tip, the kind he, even in his dreams, would never get from Mr. Fahpeh.

Jimmy's willingness to oblige was not a surprise because he loved to work for Kolu; she treated him well. Besides, everyone knew that, despite his vast wealth, Mr. Fahpeh paid his workers peanuts and even that was not on time. It was not unusual for his workers not to be paid for two or three months and they dared not complain or stay away. None dared participate in, let alone organize a strike action. Such would rain doom not only on the person but on his or her entire family as well. There were many previous examples of such counter actions by Mr. Fahpeh so no one needed a reminder.

As quickly as he could, Jimmy got Kolu to the hospital. Sayzay was shocked to see her. "Thanks for coming," he said in a groggy voice, obviously in pain. He apologized for not being able to sit up as he had tubes stuck in him in all places. She said she understood.

"Are you Kolu?" asked an older man in Sayzay's room. When Kolu answered affirmatively, he said, "I am Sayzay's father; I am pleased to meet you." Kolu responded politely.

The room was quiet for a while when a young lady spoke. "I am glad to meet you too Kolu; my name is Tayzu." Kolu's eyes lit up. Fahzie had mentioned the name Tayzu and given her background as Sayzay told her.

"I am pleased to meet you too." Kolu tried not to be caught staring but she looked at Tayzu repeatedly. My goodness; she is very beautiful, Kolu thought.

"It is really nice of you to come Kolu but tell me honestly, does your father know you are here?"

The question took Kolu by surprise but she was glad Mr. Siefa Kargbo asked. "No, he does not," Kolu answer. "I would not want him to know either that I came here."

"I perfectly understand," Mr. Kargbo said. "We have appreciated all the friends who have come to see Sayzay including this young lady (referring to Tayzu) who has gone all out to help. However, I just want you to know again that I truly appreciate your visit. Your father and I grew up together so I know him well. I therefore know it took a lot of guts on your part to come." Kolu nodded but did not know what to make of Mr. Kargbo's reference to her father.

After visiting for a couple of hours or so with very little exchange between Kolu and Sayzay, Kolu expressed desire to return to Fasawoba. Sayzay thanked her again but before she left, she asked to speak with Mr. Kargbo privately.

Kolu and Mr. Kargbo stopped in the hallway away from Sayzay's room. Almost in tears, Kolu said, "Sir, I am truly sorry for Sayzay's injuries especially when they were on account of me. I wish I could heal him instantly but I can't. So, here is little money to help with his hospital bills. If I can find another time to sneak away, I will come back." Then she broke down and cried bitterly. Mr. Kargbo put his hands around her.

"You are a very honorable young lady and I cannot tell you how much I appreciate this. Indeed, this is a lot of money although we expect my boy's hospital bill to be huge." Mr. Kargbo confidently stated that they were not worried about Sayzay's hospital bills; God would provide as He always did for His children. He said their major prayer centered on Sayzay regaining full health. Kolu tearfully reechoed the prayer while Mr. Kargbo too was in tears. Kolu gave him a big hug before she walked down the hallway and out into the parking lot where her driver was waiting.

When Kolu returned home, she told Fahzie about her visit but especially about Tayzu. "Sis Fahzie, she is extremely pretty. I do not understand why Sayzay would not kill to get such an angel."

"I do not understand either," Fahzie said. However, it seemed she was trying to say something but choked on her words. After what seemed like a second try and a change of thought, she said, "I am sure Fasawoba High School will miss him this year." Kolu nodded.

When school reopened in Fasawoba and around the nation, Sayzay still was in the hospital. His buddies Golo and Gayduobah were offered several athletic scholarships but opted to play together; they therefore went to the same university on athletic scholarships. Kolu was back in school as a senior.

Sayzay's recovery was slow but he had been moved from the intensive care unit, ICU, to a regular ward. However, he would need long-term physical therapy before returning to Fasawoba. It was therefore a surprise one day when he received an unexpected visitor, Dr. Koboiku, the chief surgeon and Medical Director of the hospital.

"How are you doing Son," Dr. Koboiku asked. Without waiting for Sayzay's response, he added, "My goodness; God is with you. You came through wonderfully but, as the nurses have told you, you will need long term physical therapy."

"Thank you Doctor," Sayzay said in a groggy voice. "I appreciate all you and the entire hospital staff have done for me but how long will my therapy be?"

"That's why I'm here," Dr. Koboiku said. He disclosed that Sayzay would need physical therapy for two to three months and staying in the hospital during that period would increase the already very high hospital bill. "The hospital's business manager is concerned about this especially since we do not know how your huge bill will be paid." He emphasized that because of the incredibly tight budget of the hospital, the business office was strict in collecting bills. "If your bills are not paid in one way or another, I doubt if they will let you out of here. As such, the more we can minimize that bill, the better." The doctor further explained that in some places, a rehabilitation facility was either adjacent or attached to the hospital. "Unfortunately, we do not have such facilities here. Therefore, we must find alternatives."

Tears streamed down Sayzay's face. "But as you say, I need the therapy badly. Oh God help me; I did not deserve this!"

"I know Sayzay and that's why we would like to help," Dr. Koboiku declared. He informed Sayzay that he and his family were willing to take Sayzay into their home for the two or three-month period at absolutely no charge and with no strings attached. "That's the least we can do," the doctor concluded.

More tears ran down Sayzay's face. He lay quiet for a while before saying, "Thanks Doctor but please give me chance to discuss this with my father."

"That's fine Son but remember, we just want to help for one thing because we have always admired your athleticism and for another thing, we have a child your age; if she's ever in a similar or same predicament, God forbid, we hope someone who is able will offer similar assistance."

When the doctor left, Sayzay turned to the wall and sobbed unceasingly. He knew for sure Tayzu had engineered the whole thing; now, he was caught between a rock and hard place. On one hand, he needed the therapy but could not afford it, especially so while living in the hospital. On the other hand, knowing he loved Kolu and Kolu only, he could not stomach the thought of living in Tayzu's house. What was he to do? "Oh God," he cried. "Why didn't they kill me once and for all?"

When he arrived for another visit, Mr. Kargbo was shocked to see a horrible melancholy look on his son's face. "What's the matter Sayzay? Did the doctor give you a terrible news?"

Sayzay shook his head in disagreement. Instead of first asking about his mother, grandmother, and uncle, he plunged into the matter, explaining what he termed a horrible dilemma.

Mr. Kargbo listened intently to his son's explanation. However, Sayzay did not mention the true reason for a dilemma. "So, what's really preventing you from accepting this generous offer especially when we have no idea how we will pay the huge hospital bill?" Mr. Kargbo questioned. The bill was already huge; to get even bigger was unimaginable. Sayzay's tears rolled again. "I do not understand why you are in tears. Dr. Koboiku and his family are simply trying to help us," Mr. Kargbo registered his frustration and lack of understanding. Sayzay managed to pull himself up a little so he could lean backward on the hospital bed. He earnestly disclosed his reason for not wanting to go to the Koboikus'. "Their daughter, Tayzu, says she is in love with me. As you know, I love Kolu, and Kolu alone." He said he was sure Tayzu proposed the arrangement. He therefore felt uncomfortable going to the home. "I know we do not have money Papa but I do not want to be forced into accepting a relationship I do not want."

Mr. Kargbo thought for a while. "I still do not understand my little one. You say you are in love with Kolu but she is not in love with you. Don't you think God is opening up a way for you?" Mr. Kargbo informed his son that God would not come down on earth from His Heavenly throne to give instructions, directions, answers, etc. Rather, He works His miracles from Heaven.

"I thought you were going to say something like that," Sayzay bemoaned. I will swallow the bitter pill and go but I assure you Papa, I will not be a happy camper."

"Just go. Our aim is to get you fully recovered. Somehow, I am sure God will make a way for us to pay the hospital bill in full."

When Dr. Koboiku came around to do his round, he asked Sayzay what he thought of the offer. "My father and I have agreed that I come. We thank you and your family for such a generous offer; frankly, we cannot thank you enough."

"Well, that's the least we can do for a young man like you. I will tell my wife and daughter. I am sure they will be pleased to have you stay at our house for a little while. Believe me, you will be a welcome member of the family, and when your father comes to visit, he will be more than welcome to spend a night or two." The doctor then disclosed that Sayzay was not the first nor would he be the last to receive such an offer from the Koboiku family. "Oh no," he said. "Several people have stayed at our house from time to time. Some come back and thank us while we never see others after they leave; but that's the name of the game." He said he had no regrets because they did not provide such services to gain anything but this was their way of thanking God for bringing them thus far; their way of giving back to society; their way of serving others.

When Sayzay arrived at the Koboikus', the family had a brief meeting with him to make him feel as welcome as possible and to acquaint him of everything in the home. They introduced to him the home's two workers, a male and female. The family informed Sayzay that they arranged for one of them to drive Sayzay to therapy once or twice a day. "That's one thing you do not have to worry about," assured Dr. Mazu Koboiku. "Everyone in this house can drive and that includes our two wonderful workers who are considered vital members of the family."

The Koboikus and their two workers could not be more hospitable. As promised, one of them drove Sayzay to therapy and when Mr. Kargbo came to visit, he was allowed to stay a night or two. Mr. Kargbo said he had never seen such a luxurious home. He jokingly encouraged Sayzay to stay a little longer so he (Mr. Kargbo) could enjoy tasting the fruits of true opulence.

While at the Koboikus, Sayzay read a lot to minimize boredom. He also watched television but did not care for what he called "stupid and boring shows". On the other hand, not surprisingly, he enjoyed football games and other sporting events on TV.

Sayzay was afraid Tayzu was going to flirt with him daily. He dreaded that because he did not want to offend her but, at the same time, he could not tolerate her flirting because he loved Kolu and Kolu alone. On her part, Tayzu accommodated the family guest well. She never flirted with him but on all, or almost all occasions, remained official, even distant. This was particularly true when her parents or the two workers were around. When they weren't she occasionally give Sayzay looks that made him freeze. Yet, she never asked for a hug, and certainly not for a kiss. One day, however, while driving Sayzay to therapy, she said rather unexpectedly, "Sayzay, please never forget the fact that I love you dearly and will marry you someday; I know that for sure. You're the only man I have ever loved; I doubt if I will love another."

Sayzay's demeanor changed noticeably. "This was what I was afraid of."

"You need not fear anything," Tayzu assured him. She said while living in their home, he was a guest and had to be treated as such. Besides, he needed therapy and she did not want to scare him away or do anything to detract from his treatment. "But as soon as this treatment is completed, I will be in your arms again as my true love and future husband."

Sayzay remained speechless as Tayzu drove. When they reached the hospital, he managed to get out with a walker and make his way slowly toward the therapy room. "I'll be back to pick you up in two hours," Tayzu shouted as Sayzay opened the door of the hospital. He simply nodded to accept the offer but wished someone else was picking him up.

In a little less than two hours, Tayzu was at the door where she dropped Sayzay off. When Sayzay opened the door of the hospital and spotted Tayzu, the looks on his face said everything. He nonetheless walked slowly to the car and got in. "How was therapy?" Tayzu asked, not looking at her rider.

"It was alright; seems to be getting better and better. Soon, I hope, I will not only be walking on my own but actually running; I can't wait. However, I must say earnestly that I'm very grateful to you and your parents for such a generous offer."

Tayzu laughed. "I'm thankful to God you accepted the offer. It means I get to see you every day." She also swore she had nothing to do with her parents' offer for Sayzay to stay at their home. "Believe me, it was a total shock to me, a pleasant news nonetheless. Of course, I welcomed it jubilantly."

Sayzay nodded doubtfully as Tayzu drove off. Without noting his demeanor, she returned to her original topic. "Look Darling," she said and that was the first time she referred to him as Darling since he entered their home. "I have no doubt that this makes you feel uncomfortable. While that hurts, I'm willing to live with it because I know there's a bright light at the end of the tunnel." She promised not to bring up the topic until he left their home. Meanwhile, she informed him that, for the first time, she told her parents that she was in love with him. "But I also promised them that I would treat you as a guest, not my love, until you complete your treatment."

"You say 'for the first time'. So they did not know when we came to your house after the championship game?"

"No," Tayzu said. "They may have suspected something but I did not tell them anything about you and me." She said if the governor suspected something, it would not be a surprise for her parents to do the same. Again, she stated earnestly and emphatically, "Honestly, I did not tell them anything about you and me."

The words, 'you and me' kept ringing in Sayzay's ears; he wished he had heard different words. He remained silent for a while. He kept wondering. "Are you alright?" Tayzu asked and Sayzay answered affirmatively. "Would you like to stop somewhere for lunch? I will pay and it will be a pleasure to have lunch with you alone and away from our home." Sayzay remained quiet, not knowing what to do. Certainly, if he had his will, he would rather go home. "Oh come on," Tayzu nudged. "Just one; that will not kill you. If that vicious attack did not kill you, my dear, certainly having lunch with me will not; by God's grace, you are with us for a long time."

"I think that will be alright," Sayzay gave in begrudgingly.

Tayzu left the steering wheel and clapped jubilantly. "Lunch with you at last. I prayed for that for months. One step at a time."

The two settled in a posh restaurant for what Tayzu considered a romantic lunch. "What would you like to eat my dear?" Tayzu asked. Sayzay said he did not know. Tayzu looked over the menu. "The last time I came here with Mom and Dad, I had salmon with steamed vegetables and a small side dish of salad; it was good. Mom and Dad had salmon too but theirs came with rice which they said was very delicious." She cited other dishes she had at the restaurant at different times but probably did not realize she was only confusing Sayzay the more.

"I think I want something with rice," Sayzay murmured. "What would you like with the rice?"

"Soup or grains with meat," Sayzay stated softly, looking over the menu.

"Oh look at this," Tayzu pointed out excitedly. "Potato greens with beef served on brown rice; that sounds delicious. If you want, you can have two or three pieces of boiled chicken with that. The chicken is boiled in garlic and olive oil; again, that sounds good. Of course, you may have a small, medium, or large salad as well. However, you must leave room for dessert; this place has some of the best desserts in town."

Sayzay's mouth began to water although the choices offered him made him increasingly confused. Eventually, he settled for the rice dish and accepted two pieces of chicken to go along. Choices of drinks brought another confusion and so did the choices for dessert. However, since both did not drink anything alcoholic, they quickly decided on drinks. For dessert, Tayzu talked him into having pecan pie, her favorite and he did not mind that choice at all. Yet, he accepted a small piece of banana bread as well.

By the time Tayzu and Sayzay left the restaurant, they were both full. Back in the car, the conversation was a little livelier and that's precisely what Tayzu wanted. As such, instead of driving directly home, she went around the city for a while, pointing out places to Sayzay. She drove to the university and from a distance, showed Sayzay different buildings—one in which she took most of her classes, and another in which her mother worked.

Back home, Tayzu kept her words. She never once mentioned her love for Sayzay and this made the young man's stay comfortable in the Koboiku home. One day, however, Dr. Folomo Koboiku was home from the hospital. He offered to drive Sayzay to lunch instead of eating at home. Sayzay gladly consented.

Seated in the same restaurant where Sayzay and Tayzu had lunch, the doctor said, "I think I know you would like something with rice; so do I." The doctor pointed out different rice dishes. Eventually, they both settled for the same thing, rice and cassava leaf with fresh meat and chicken. For drinks, in addition to the water glass, which a waitress filled for each of them, Sayzay had a glass of juice. The doctor had a glass of wine.

As Sayzay and Dr. Koboiku ate, the doctor went from one conversation topic to another—how he admired Sayzay's athleticism, how he wished many young people roaming the streets and doing drugs and alcohol could go to school and become useful men and women, etc.. Eventually, the conversation centered on his daughter. Without saying Tayzu had told him anything, he said the young lady was their only daughter but everyone knew that. He went further by stating that anyone who married her would have half of their wealth and the other half upon their death. "I will not say exactly the kind of wealth we have but we are very grateful to God that, although both of us come from very humble beginnings, I mean we grew up dirt poor; yet, God has blessed us enormously; praise be to Him."

Sayzay remained quiet for this conversation was ruining his delicious lunch. Whether the doctor noticed the young man's change of demeanor was not clear for he went on and on about his daughter and possible future spouse. Sayzay only managed to say, "I think that's wonderful. I'm sure she will get a great husband."

"I hope so," said Dr. Koboiku. "Everyone needs a nice family and a decent home; we cannot wish anything less for our daughter."

The two enjoyed their dinner and soon, they were back in the car headed home. Amazingly, precisely as Tayzu did, the doctor drove Sayzay around town showing him places.

After a little more than three months of treatment--six weeks in the hospital and two months of physical therapy--Sayzay was allowed to return home. Miraculously, his medical bills were covered. It seemed people in the governor's office and from the hospital's director's office had pulled various strings to cover the bills much to the delight and appreciation of Mr. Kargbo and Sayzay himself. As such, when he returned home, Sayzay wrote long letters of thanks and appreciation to the governor, to the Chief Medical Officer of the hospital, and to the Koboiku family for their hospitality.

After returning home, Sayzay had to continue treatment and therapy until fully recovered. Knowing that, and as Tayzu drove her own car, she visited Fasawoba regularly taking supplies and pharmaceuticals to

Sayzay. Sayzay was somewhat uncomfortable with this continued generosity as he insisted that his only love was Kolu. "I know," said Tayzu. "She is your love and you are mine. You are taking a risk on her and I am taking one on you. Moreover, I am confident that it's only a matter of time when you will be in my arms forever as my lifetime partner, friend, and lover. I do not have the faintest doubt."

Sayzay was once more uncomfortable with the interaction and Tayzu's kind gestures. He wondered again, what this meant. This was the second time Tayzu had said such a thing. What in the world did she mean? As before, he could not find an answer.

Sayzay's recovery was going well. He visited the hospital regularly and soon, he was able to perform minor tasks on his father's farm. Before one knew it, he was fully recovered. He practiced football with the high school boys regularly. Occasionally, football clubs known as citizen teams' recruited him to play for them. As always, he performed superbly between the poles.

Kolu also continued her visitations with elderly ladies. Maa Gaamai always talked about the realities of life. Once in a while, she briefly talked about Sayzay and his family but when she did, she would quickly move on to another subject as if it were an unimportant topic in passing. One day when Maa Gaamai mentioned Sayzay again, Kolu asked, "Does he know I visit you Maa Gaamai?"

The old lady was not expecting this question but was glad it was asked. "Yes," she said with excitement in her voice. "He even left some kind of paper here just in case you might be willing to look at it."

"Oh Maa; why didn't you mention that before?"

"As I say, I was not sure if you might be willing to see it," the old Maa repeated. She did not say whether the note had been there for weeks, perhaps months. Kolu asked for the note.

The old lady kept the note securely in a basket underneath a roll of cotton. She handed it to Kolu whose anxiety could be cut with a knife. It read: "Dear Kolu, I cannot thank you enough for visiting me when I was in the hospital. Honestly, it meant a lot to me. My father also told me of the huge financial contribution you made. Words are inadequate to thank you for such generosity. I hope, however, you will give me a few minutes to talk with you in person. If this is fine with you, I will meet you at Maa Gaamai's at any time you please. Thanks Kolu and God bless you richly. Sayzay.

"What did he say," Maa Gaamai inquired. "You book people are amazing. I do not know how you understand those small small things on the paper. When I had a better eyesight, I remember seeing them like little ants with different shapes." The old Maa laughed and repeated her question. "What did he say?"

"He wants to meet me at your house Maa. Do you agree?"

"Of course my darling. If you are willing to talk with him here, I will have no problem with that." Maa Gaamai then went on and on talking about Sayzay's wonderful family. "I do not know if you are aware," she said, "but Sayzay's grandmother helped raise your mother Kebbeh."

"Really Maa? Mom has never said anything like that. In fact, she and Dad seldom talk about their upbringing in Fasawoba. No, they avoid the topic like a plague. So, although we live here, my brother and I know nothing about what is definitely our home town and certainly nothing about our culture." She said if she learned anything about the culture, she learned it from the old ma and her sister Fahzie.

"Be sure to ask your mother about Maa Luopu when you go home," Maa Gaamai encouraged. "But what do you say to Sayzay's request? Are you willing to talk with him even once?"

"Tell him I will talk with him here at about noon next Saturday." Kolu could not believe those words crossed her lips but she would make no attempts to take them back. Before the meeting, she would talk with Fahzie and get some sound advice as always.

Back home, Kolu asked her mother if she knew an old lady named Luopu Taapulu.

Mrs. Fahpeh hesitated. "From where did you get that name?"

"Someone mentioned it to me in town and thought you might know her."

Mrs. Fahpeh seemed reluctant to talk about Maa Luopu. When her daughter pressed on, she said, "I have heard of that lady but really do not know her much."

"Well, what have you heard about her?"

Mrs. Fahpeh seemed annoyed but did not want to show it. Clearly, she did not want to talk about this lady. "I heard she was a mean old lady. Some even think she is a witch. I will not advise you to go around her nor do I ever want to hear her name again."

Kolu's mother's words amazed her immensely. If indeed Ma Luopu raised her mother, what did the old mom do so much to her mother to be hated with a passion? Was this mere ingratitude on the part of her mother or was her mother simply going along with her husband to detest the town and all its people? What could it be? As Kolu did not have any answers, she said nothing about the matter. Instead, she visited Fahzie to discuss her upcoming meeting with Sayzay.

CHAPTER SEVENTEEN

There was no doubt that both Sayzay and Kolu anxiously, even nervously, anticipated their first meeting. Sayzay fasted, prayed and prayed about it, hoping God would make this meeting the break-through point regarding his relationship with Kolu. "My goodness," he whispered, "After twists and turns, trials and tribulations, she has finally consented to meet with me. I cannot thank God enough for this golden opportunity. It is the meeting of my life." He therefore visited Ma Gaamai three times to seek her blessings regarding the upcoming meeting of this life. He fasted and prayed about it, faithfully putting his trust in God.

Kolu too was in deep thought about the meeting. Did she really want to see him let alone date him? Was she making a mistake perhaps trying to make up for the disappointment regarding Zawu? Fortunately, she had an older sister who not only gave sound advice but prayed fervently about the matter. "Go with an open mind, a listening ear, watchful eyes, and above all, a strong faith," Fahzie advised. "If it is God's will, He will direct you. You know what the Good Book says; 'Lean not upon your own understanding. In all thy ways, acknowledge Him and he will direct your path'[11]"Kolu agreed and prayed about the meeting.

On Saturday, Sayzay arrived at Maa Gaamai's an hour in advance. The old Maa told him to wait inside while she warmed herself outside. As he waited, the minutes seemed like years. At the same time, a million thinks ran through his mind. On one hand, he was in total disbelief that he would be talking with Kolu on this day while on the other, he had known that this day would come.

---

[11] Prov. 3:5-6

As Sayzay thought hard, Kolu arrived. Maa Gaamai signaled her to go inside. Sayzay was all smiles when Kolu walked in. He wished he could hold her in his arms and kiss her repeatedly but he did not want to scare her away and ruin his first chance of talking with her. Instead, he stood in respect.

"Hello Sayzay," she greeted. She did not stretch her hand for a handshake. He too refrained from doing so as he did not want to do anything that would upset the moment. However, handshake or not, no one could describe his joy for hearing her voice; it was melodious music to his ears. He never gave up hope of hearing that angelic voice addressing him directly in close proximity.

"Hello Kolu. How are you?" Kolu answered politely.

Kolu looked incredibly beautiful with her tailored made outfit--a designer blue blouse and a form fitted black skirt--with matching gold clutch and shoes. Her huge gold chain was dazzling calmly between her breasts. She smiled broadly and took a seat one chair over from Sayzay's. With cherry lips and gorgeous eyes, she faced him directly still smiling. "We are here. What did you want to talk about?"

Sayzay was speechless; in fact, he almost passed out as he focused on her. "Gorgeous! Heavenly!" he whispered very softly. He managed to take a deep breath but no doubt, he was shaking up but he fought hard to hide that evidence of fright and/or uneasiness. The fragrance of her sweet cologne only made matters worse.

As Sayzay struggled to appear cool, calm, and composed, he wondered whether he was dreaming or truly awake. Convinced he was awake, he knew this was a once-in-a-lifetime opportunity; this was a make or break occasion. He knew he had to pour out his heart with sincerity and conviction. He therefore presented his case as a good lawyer in a closing argument intended to convince and persuade a jury. To that end, he presented his case strongly and fluently as if he rehearsed it for days. Maybe he did. His shaky expressions were recaptured and reworded for clarity and emphasis as follows. "Kolu, thank you for agreeing to talk with me for a few minutes. I'm aware of the pressure you are under. I am stressed too but my pains and aches are insignificant compared to yours. Even if they were ten times, indeed a hundred times more, they would be worth bearing for your sake.

Kolu, I loved you from the day I first laid eyes on you. That day, something within me aroused my feelings and they have never been and will never be dampened. True, we have differences but also many similarities and the similarities of our God-given human characteristics are what count, not differences."

"Similarities like what?" Kolu interrupted.

Well, we are from the same ethnic group and from Fasawoba. Of our genders, as our names indicate, we are first borns; I mean, I am the first-born boy of my mother and you are the first-born girl of yours. Above all, we are both humans regardless of our ethnicity, social status, and the fact that we come from the same town. In other words, I am not in love because of some intellectual or logical analysis or similarities or worse, dissimilarities between us; that's intellectual love, which can, and often falters, and therefore has no basis in true love. I'm not in love because of your family's financial holding from which I wish to benefit; that's dependent love. By any measurement, you are an extremely beautiful young lady, a fitting queen for any king or kingdom, but, although appreciated highly, your looks are not the basis of my love; that's sensual love which can fade when looks do. I love you because of something deep within me, something within my heart and my soul; that's intuitive love which is manifested on first sight and that's precisely how I fell in love with you. If you are looking for someone rich, vastly educated, mesmerizingly handsome, or for other reasons, I am not the man. However, that man will never give you what I will—true love not only with all my heart, but with every breath in me as the lady of my dream, my waking hours, and my entire life. I do not have material things to give you but true love and happiness. I do not woo you because no other girls want me; I do not want them but you. I am aware of the opposition of your parents and family but have said repeatedly that anything as precious as you is worth fighting for, even dying for. This is why I endured heavy beating and severe injuries inflicted by your brother, your suitor, and their cruel accomplices but bore no malice. I love you Kolu and no one else. Without a doubt, you are my Zeemai. However, I care for your happiness so much so that if you will find happiness in loving someone else, do so but rest assured that if I do not marry you; I will marry no one else until I die. God bless you my love in your decision. Remember, life is not full of beds of roses; some of the best things in life come through difficult means. Remember also that if God directs you, as I'm sure He has directed me, no family opposition can prevent our lifetime togetherness. With that said Zeemai, may I at least shake your heavenly hands and then wash not my hands for a week, indeed a month?

Kolu feebly stressed her hand. Sayzay took it, felt up it, and down with both hands before she pulled it away. "I will think about your words Sayzay, I promise," Kolu said. To say this was music to Sayzay's ears would be a gross understatement. They both left Ma Gaamai's house shortly thereafter.

Kolu explained everything to Fahzie who gave words of encouragement. This made Kolu to accept meeting Sayzay at Maa Gaamai's occasionally. Soon, occasionally became a regular occurrence although they were careful not to make any erotic moves. This was particularly true of Sayzay who did not want to ruin an excellent opportunity. Also occasionally, Kolu's mother accompanied her on the visitations but whenever no bodyguards accompanied her, she would slip away for an extended period and without explanation.

As Kolu met Sayzay regularly, she did not know her father had one of his junior bodyguards checking on her. The bodyguard told Mr. Fahpeh when and where Kolu met Sayzay. "I will kill that dog," Mr. Fahpeh said and he meant it. He grabbed his pistol and headed for town.

No doubt, Mr. Fahpeh saw himself as a mini god who could do anything in Fasawoba and get away with it. He had proven so by getting away with many criminal acts. There seemed to be no match for him in town or in the region. More than that, his exaggerated ego made him think he had no match in the nation and throughout the world. Given that, he was sure the time was ripe to eliminate the young man he called a dog and so would not miss this chance. Nothing and no one would stop him.

Kolu and Sayzay had not yet kissed but for the first time, they sat close to one another and held hands. A thousand thoughts ran through Sayzay's mind. He was glad to put his trust fervently in God for little by little, God was answering his prayers. Whatever pains he had endured for Kolu was worth it. On her part, Kolu had minimal experience with men. Her only comparison was between Zawu and Sayzay but Sayzay was light years positively different from Zawu.

As Kolu and Sayzay sat close in Maa Gaamai's house both thinking about different things, Mr. Fahpeh showed up. He directed the driver to stop the car a little way off and he walked to the house. When Maa Gaamai greeted him, he did not say a word; rather, he went into the house. Seeing his daughter and Sayzay sitting together boiled his blood like fire. He quickly reached for his gun, took an aim at Sayzay, and pulled the trigger.

Zawu and his driver showed up early at Akoei's house in anticipation of their long trip. Since they decided to take one car, Zawu's driver transferred things from their car into Akoei's while Zawu helped Akoei pack. They were both looking forward to having a good time for at least a month. Accordingly, their luggage included bottles of expensive liquor and more.

The two youngsters planned to stop in several cities before ending up in Coastal City. In the capital, although Zawu assured Akoei's parents they would stop with his parents, they planned to rent a motel room because Zawu later told Akoei his parents were in Gizisu. Even if they were in town, the young people wanted as much independence as possible. After all, thanks to Mr. Fahpeh's largesse and Akoei's skillful thievery, they had enough money for the trip and intended to 'live it up'.

For two weeks, Zawu and Akoei had wonderful times in various cities. They had their lion share of wine, women, song, food, and illicit drugs. They usually went to bed late and slept most of the day. Thank god they had a patient and experienced driver. The driver enjoyed the trip too because when the young men were drunk and/or drugged, they gave him money he had never dreamt of and, of course, that was fine with him.

By the third week of their journey, Akoei and his buddy reached Coastal City, the capital. They rented a motel room and set out to have fun, real fun. On the first night, Akoei became interested in a young lady whom he met at the small bar in the motel. However, a young man who seemed to be the girl's boyfriend impeded his advances. Zawu and Akoei bought drinks for the young man until he was drunk. Although they themselves were already significantly charged but not drunk for it took lots of booze to reach that level, they took him behind the motel and beat him mercilessly. A motel guard heard the young man's cry and went to his rescue. He saw the two young men delivering blows to the man's head. Not surprisingly, the man was wounded terribly by the time the guard finally arrived on the scene. They rushed him to the hospital but he died the next day. Akoei and his buddy were arrested and charged with premeditated murder. As it turned out, not only the motel guard witnessed the brutal flogging of the deceased victim; several other individuals partly or totally did. Several of them, unwilling to intervene given the extent to which the victim was wounded, took pictures on their cell phones while others called the police. These eyewitnesses were likely to ensure the conviction of the two assailants and if found guilty, the least they could expect would be many years imprisonment, if not a life sentence. The maximum penalty was execution. They were thrown in jail while authorities made efforts to contact their parents although both were above eighteen and past the age of mincrity.

On numerous occasions, Mrs. Fahpeh had heard her husband swear he would kill Sayzay if Sayzay made any advances toward his daughter. She casually mentioned this to the chief bodyguard who made no comments. Rather, as he seemed to know Sayzay, he removed bullets out of Mr. Fahpeh's three guns and hid all ammunitions. Thanks to this move, when Mr. Fahpeh pulled the trigger on Sayzay, the gun did not go off. He considered attacking Sayzay physically but thought twice when he remembered Sayzay was not only younger but, as an athlete, was in a far better physical shape than he was. Abandoning that option, he used profane language at Maa Gaamai who was sitting outside. He angrily kicked the old lady's chair throwing her to the ground. "You stupid old lady," he insulted. "You are the idiot providing a meeting place for that dog and my daughter. You will die soon as poor as your mother bore you." Shaking with fury, Mr. Fahpeh headed toward his car, got in, and took off.

Kolu and Sayzay had tears in their eyes as they helped the old lady up. Maa Gaamai was crying bitterly. She was injured. Kolu ran to the store and bought bandages and medicine to help the old lady. After feeding and treating her, Kolu and Sayzay got someone to spend the night with the old lady. Before leaving, they laid her in bed and promised to come back the next day. They also planned to find a nurse and permanent helper for the oldma.

Seeing her father almost killed Sayzay and that he injured an innocent old lady, Kolu could not be angrier with her dad. When she reached home that evening, she spoke with no one nor did she eat. Rather, she took a shower in her private bathroom and went to bed.

Mr. Fahpeh did not care Kolu did not eat with them. Instead, he called for a huge quantity of liquor. When served, he expressed fury for the fact that anyone dared take the bullets out of his guns. Of course, no one admitted. "I should have killed that dog," he blotted. "What? A peasant dog flirting with my daughter? He should be dead and gone. It's not late. I will get that dog and nothing, I mean nothing, will come out of it." He once more swore that the days of the peasant kid he called a dog were numbered. His wife not only nodded in agreement but encouraged him to ensure he made good on his threat.

As Mr. Fahpeh fumed and drank, his phone rang. He signaled a worker to answer. "It's a man named Mr. Subah," the worker informed.

"I am sure that's the father of my future son-in-law, Zawu. I will definitely talk with him. I hope he has something positive to say about my business proposal." He smiled broadly and whispered, "It's about time I got another sucker."

Mr. Fahpeh grabbed the phone from the worker. "Hello," he greeted and it seemed the person at the other end returned the greeting and plunged into the reason for the call. As he listened, his breathing increased. "I'm very sorry to hear that. We will be there tomorrow."

"What is it Darling?" Mrs. Fahpeh asked.

Mr. Fahpeh was undoubtedly shaken up. He had to sit down before speaking. The only thing that flooded his thought was his business and the likelihood of losing money because of what he called "a silly stuff."

"What is it Darling? Please tell me."

"Oh Darling, I just hope I do not lose much money again. Such a silly thing should have occurred at another time." He bowed his head and sucked his teeth before gulping his drink. His wife was still staring at him and pleading for explanation.

"It's your son Darling."

"What's about him?" Mrs. Fahpeh stood up. "What Dear? Please tell me. Is he alright?" Knowing what her son was capable of doing and had actually done in the past, a million things went through Mrs. Fahpeh's mind. Was this related to girls? Was Akoei busted again for drugs? Did he harm someone or was he in a car accident? What could it be? Mrs. Fahpeh's fears increased astronomically.

"He is alright but in jail."

"For what?" Mrs. Fahpeh was now shaking violently. What had her son done to land him in jail again? What would the lawyer say again after warning them on numerous occasions about their son? Whatever he did, and she could care less, how would it affect their business? "Oh Lord save us," she cried. "Darling please tell   me.

What is he busted for again?"

"For murder," Mr. Fahpeh uttered the dreaded words.

"Oh no!" Mrs. Fahpeh fell over weeping bitterly. They woke Kolu up and told her the horrible news. She too started crying bitterly.

"We will go to Coastal City tomorrow," Mr. Fahpeh announced. "We have to find the best lawyer for him and Zawu. I will call Gawvehgo, one of my business partners to start looking for a good lawyer. I will pay any money to keep my son out of jail. Regardless of who he killed, and frankly, I do not care, I have no doubt he will be out by tomorrow. When money talks, people walk, and when people suck, money works." He pushed a button and out ran a lady. Before he ordered more drinks, he gave her a backhand slap for allegedly wasting time.

CHAPTER EIGHTEEN

After a long ride, the Fahpehs pulled up in front of the Subah residence in Coastal City. It was a nice house but did not look like the mansion Zawu described.

Mr. and Mrs. Subah, wearing casual clothes, ran out to meet the Fahpehs. "Welcome," Mr. Kokulo Subah said. "I'm sorry we had to meet under these regrettable circumstances."

The Fahpeh went in. again, it was a very nice house with modest-looking furniture. Certainly, it was kept very clean.

When the visitors were seated, Mrs. Subah offered drinks. She served whatever they preferred. The Fahpehs were somewhat hesitant. What? No servants? They only had to wait a few minutes to find out.

"This is our modest home," Mr. Subah said. "We have lived here since we got married some twenty-five years ago. We thank God for these years but again, I am truly sorry for the problem we have at hand."

Mr. Fahpeh shifted his attention from the problem at hand to knowing a little more about the Subahs. "So where do you work?"

"I am the manager for a large grocery store in town. I do not make much money but I thank God for a job. It has paid the bills and sustained us over the years."

"And your wife?"

"Well she is a lecturer at a community college. She loves working with young people partly because of Zawu, our only child."

"Your only child?" Mr. Fahpeh repeated as if he did not hear correctly.

"Our only child," Mr. Subah also repeated himself contrary to what Zawu had said to the Fahpehs.

"Where does Zawu go to college?" Mrs. Fahpeh asked.

"He does not," Mr. Subah said sadly. He relayed that Zawu was an extremely brilliant student. He topped his classes from first through tenth grades. However, at age sixteen, he started drinking heavily and dropped out of school. Mr. Subah emphasized that this was baffling for him and his wife for neither of them drank. "Anyway," he went on, "our son has never gone back regardless of our repeated enticements. This is why I rather give him my car and driver. I know if allowed to drive, he will kill himself and maybe someone else."

Mr. Fahpeh followed up. "Did he and our son come to you when they came to Coastal City? He said they would."

Mr. Subah said he did not know the two young men were in town until the police called him. If he had known, he would have set some guidelines. Most likely, he thought that was why the young men did not go to his house when they arrived in Coastal City.

Although Kolu and her parents could not believe their ears, they took everything in strives. Naturally, their concern centered mainly on Akoei. "Well, we have made arrangements to stay at a hotel," Mr. Fahpeh informed the Subahs.

"But you are welcome to stay here; we have rooms to accommodate you. If nothing else, we hope you will have dinner with us," Mrs. Yama Subah offered. Before the Fahpehs said anything, she disclosed honestly that her husband was a far better cook than she was. She therefore had no problem allowing him to do the cooking. "Quite frankly," she continued what seemed a family affair, "I enjoy it.

The Fahpehs accepted the invitation and had a wonderful dinner, which included whatever drinks they wanted. Although the Fahpehs did not mention the driver, the Subahs were concerned about him; they fed him too but, on Mr. Fahpeh's insistence, in another room.

After dinner and some visitation, and that included repeated drinks by the Fahpehs, the Fahpehs' driver drove them to a hotel and returned to the Subahs for the night. Before going to bed, the driver thanked the

Subahs for their hospitality. "I tell you in confidence," the driver began, "since I started working for the Fahpehs some twelve years ago, this is the first time I have been treated like a human being. My boss and his wife never think I exist when we go places." He said he was often forced to sleep in the car or stay in sleazy motels at the risk of his life. "The only thing they care about is their car. To them, the car is far more important than my life." The Subahs listened without comment.

The next day, Mr. Gawvehgo joined the Fahpehs for breakfast at their hotel. "From here," Mr. Gawvehgo said, "we will reach the lawyer's office. He is one of the best criminal lawyers in town or the country."

Following breakfast, Mr. Gawvehgo led the Fahpehs to the lawyer's office where the Subahs were already waiting. An extremely attractive young lady who worked in the front office greeted them warmly. She identified herself as Boryea and offered soft drinks, water, tea, or coffee. They declined the offer stating that they just had breakfast. The young lady, probably a law school student or aspirant, tempted them further with freshly made doughnuts and variety of breads. They further resisted the temptation. However, they were extremely impressed with the lawyer's front office, not only because of Boryea's superb service and professional appearance, but also with its sophisticated computers and elegant furnishing. Mr. Fahpeh whispered to his wife, expressing his delight for being in such an office. Yes, this was their type of environment. They were therefore grateful Gawvehgo found this lawyer.

Boryea casually conversed with the visitors until the lawyer called them into his office. Like the front office, it was elegant. Not surprising, there were tons of law books on the shelves.

The middle-age lawyer warmly shook hands with the visitors. "My name is Musa Blamo and, after you sign some retention agreements, I will be representing your boys. It's a very serious charge but we'll do our best."

"Mr. Fahpeh's facial features changed noticeably. Did you say your name was Musa?" He asked before everyone took a seat.

Ignoring Mr. Fahpeh's strange looks, the lawyer answered directly. "Yes, I am Musa. My father is Kru and my mother is Fula, two very different ethnic groups. Don't ask me how this combination came about; all I know is that they are my parents, and they are wonderful parents. I could not ask for a better combination of parents." Without waiting for another question presumably about his religion, the Lawyer added, "Since I was raised by my mother, I am Muslim." He also did not mention the fact that the community in which he grew included various mixed-race children--children from Japanese, Chinese, Indian, Middle-Eastern, and other Asian as well as European, North and South American backgrounds. Likewise, there were children of various inter-ethnic relationships. Amazingly, they were doing well in school and society. No one, or almost no one noticed differences among them and many really appreciated that unconditional and universal acceptance.

"May I talk with you a moment?" Mr. Fahpeh asked Mr. Gawvehgo. "Sure," Mr. Gawvehgo answered. "But I do not think Mr. Blamo expects you to pay anything more than a retention fee."

When they stepped out of the room, Fahpeh, intolerable of external differences, voiced his resentment. "This is not about payment. If we get the right lawyer, I will pay whatever he charges. I called you out here because I will not have that man represent my son."

"Why not?" Gawvehgo was taken aback but perhaps not surprised, knowing Fahpeh.

"He's not from our ethnic group and I do not care for that religious stuff, be it Muslim or Christian. At the very least, I will accept someone who is Christian but definitely none of that Muslim stuff." Gawvehgo spoke plainly. "Fahpeh, when will you break out of this senseless prison of narrow-mindedness? When will you break away from the shackles of tribalism and bigotry? When will you free yourself from the egocentric delusion that you know everything and no one else knows anything although you yourself know you did not graduate from high school? When will you free yourself from the disease of discrimination and ethnocentrism? Will you ever understand the oneness of humanity and especially the people of this nation as one big family? Do you understand, let alone appreciate the purpose, power, and positivity of diversity? I don't believe you; I really don't. I probably should not be but I'm shocked to know you do not understand, let alone appreciate the inter-connectedness of our people. Oh, the Heavens save us. This man is one of the best lawyers in the entire country. Are you looking for a good lawyer or ethnicity and all that other nonsense? When was the last time you went to church to talk about religion? Of all people, you Fahpeh talk of religion when you constantly say you do not believe there is a God? Thank God you do not represent our ethnic group of liberal and level-headed people."

Gawvehgo caught his generalization and admitted that his ethnic group had its share of conservatives. On his part, Mr. Fahpeh stood speechlessly, apparently not knowing what to say. Without waiting for Fahpeh to respond, Mr. Gawvehgo said if Mr. Fahpeh did not accept Mr. Blamo, he (Gawvehgo) was leaving and no doubt, Mr.

Fahpeh's son would be headed toward the firing squad. "For that, my dear, not-so-learned, egocentric, self-centered, ivory tower but ignorant friend, you have only yourself to blame."

"O.K., if you say so, I guess I will go along."

"You have to; you have no choice. Look Fahpeh, this is not Fasawoba where you are judge, jury, and executioner. Here in Coastal City, we insist on the rule of law; therefore, your pocketbook, supposed influence, lies, or baseless threats are totally immaterial here. Unlike other places, no one in his or her right mind even dreams of, let alone attempts bribing judges, lawyers and jurors. I'm not saying it does not happen here but when found out, such will be met with a full force of the law. So, Fahpeh, for once, you must play the game fairly and squarely."

It was clear Gawvehgo did not know Fahpeh well because Fahpeh was not full of empty threats; he often, if not always, carried out his threats. Yet, Gawvehgo deserved commendation for very seldom, if ever, did anyone talk to Fahpeh as he did. Clearly, he was a man of self-confidence and most likely, a man of very good financial standing.

Back in the room, the lawyer explained their chances. "No matter what we do, these boys will serve time." Of course, he made it clear, his first attempt was to ensure the boys did not but he also knew that the evidence against his clients was overwhelming. He said his next effort would be reducing the charge and thereby reducing the length of service. The lawyer said he was sure however, he would prevent the youngsters from going to the firing squad.

In court, as Counselor Blamo expected, the prosecutor presented overwhelming evidence, including eyewitness accounts and pictures showing the two men brutally beating their victim. On the strength of his evidence, he insisted on the charge of premeditated murder and therefore prayed the court for the execution of the two young men.

Mr. Musa Blamo posed a fierce defense. He argued that, as the two young men were drunk, as evidenced by the police report, they could not have possibly formed a specific intent to commit premeditated murder. He therefore threw out that charge.

Like a good lawyer, Mr. Blamo withheld fire to be ignited at the appropriate time. For instance, he anticipated the prosecutor insisting on the boys going to the firing squad because they kidnapped and later murdered their victim. "Therefore, Your Honor," Mr. Blamo could hear the prosecutor, "this is not just murder but kidnapping and murder which, by law, carries a death sentence. The state therefore prays the court to that effect."

Mr. Blamo had an appropriate rebuttal but much to his pleasant surprise, the prosecutor did not go there. Mr. Blamo therefore took the prosecutor to another test. He argued for voluntary manslaughter but the prosecutor would have none of it as, according to the prosecutor, there was no evidence of provocation or heat of passion. Mr. Blamo bit his lips, a very good show. Of course, he expected that rebuttal for almost any first year law student would have argued the same; yet, he took a chance.

The trial continued with both lawyers displaying their lawyering skills although clearly, Mr. Blamo had the upper hand as he was far more experienced than the prosecutor was. In the end, the two young men were spared from both the firing squad and life imprisonment. However, inasmuch as he tried, Counselor Blamo could not prevent the young men from serving considerable number of years.

After the trial and sentencing, the Fahpehs and Subahs met with Mr. Blamo. They thanked him sincerely for his zealous defense. He said he deemed it a duty to keep such young people from the firing squad but lectured both parents about raising children properly. He said he was a father of two but would never allow his children to do what the convicted young men did. The Fahpehs and Subahs nodded in agreement, although for them, it was already late, too late.

After Mr. Fahpeh paid Mr. Blamo and before the Fahpehs left for Fasawoba, Mr. Blamo said he had one more thing to talk about. One could cut the curiosity in the room with a knife. What was on the lawyer's mind? To whom was it directed? It was anyone's guess.

People in the room did not have to wait long. "I noticed," Mr. Blamo began, looking directly at Mr. Fahpeh, "you did not want me to represent your son probably because of my ethnic background and religion. Isn't that the truth?" the lawyer asked as if cross- examining a witness.

"How did you reach such a conclusion?" Mr. Fahpeh fired back. "Are you a mind reader?"

Mr. Blamo laughed while Mr. Gawvehgo and the others remained serious. "It's not a matter of reading minds. Just answer me directly," the lawyer insisted. "You did not want me to represent your son, and that's the truth; isn't it? Please answer me!"

"To be honest, no, I did not," Mr. Fahpeh answered earnestly. "I did not know you and so had some doubts but my friend here, Mr. Gawvehgo, convinced me otherwise. I went along out of respect for him; he and I go back a long way."

"Come on," the lawyer mocked. He admonished Mr. Fahpeh not to kid himself. "It had nothing to do with knowing or not knowing me; rather, it was all about my ethnicity and religion and you know it! Be a man, and be honest with yourself and   tell the truth."

Mr. Fahpeh was beginning to be irritated. "Well, what if I did not want you to represent my son because of your ethnicity or religion? It was my money and I had a right to choose who to hire to represent my son. After all, you are not the only lawyer in town; no, there are many others and you know it too."

"Mr. Fahpeh, please do not dodge the point. Sure, there are many lawyers in town, and very good ones too but that's not the point. The point here is that you resented my representation because of my ethnicity and religion and you are admitting that; right Mr. Fahpeh?"

"It was my right to choose who I wanted to spend my money on and I did just that; you just happened to be the lucky one who got my money and should be glad you did."

"This discussion is going nowhere," Mr. Gawvehgo jumped in. He said he advised Fahpeh to recruit Mr. Blamo because he knew the latter's record of accomplishment, sensitivity to others, and overall affable character. He therefore encouraged Fahpeh to come clean. "You know you did not want Mr. Blamo to represent you because of his ethnicity and religion. I had to knock some sense into you to accept his representation." Mr. Gawvehgo then apologized to Mr. Blamo but also thanked him for standing by his principles and fiercely representing the two young men.

Once more," Mr. Fahpeh attempted to repeat himself. "I do not know how many times I need to tell you but it was my money and I had a right to know on whom I spent it. Yes, I had some doubts; I mean serious concerns about this man's weird ethnic background and religion. Frankly, I cannot stand both; so there you are. You heard it from the horse's mouth, no beating around the bush. I am a man and will always be."

Mr. Blamo was once more direct. "I hear you loudly and clearly Mr. Fahpeh and honestly, I believe you. It's nice of you to come through with the truth for I knew it all along."

"Now that you know the truth, are you going to eat me up? In other words, what in the world can you do to me Mr. Lawyer Man?"

Mr. Blamo made it clear that it was not a matter of eating anyone up. Once more looking directly at Mr. Fahpeh, he said, "Mr. Fahpeh, my dear compatriot, you must think again. First, you ought to know that this is a nation of laws and regulations; no one is above the law. Secondly, in this nation, we teach unity as opposed to sectionalism, tribalism, racism, classism, and the like." He regretted that Fahpeh and his kind still wallowed in a world of bigotry, tribalism, sectionalism, and elitism. "In spite of your demonstrated nauseating air of superiority, I did not turn down this representation because in reality, you are not my client. Sure, you were expected to pay but I represented two young men who had made serious mistakes and whose lives were in jeopardy. As I have said, this was partly due to horrible parenting but I won't dwell on that point."

"Look Mr. Lawyer, I do not need a lecture from you about parenting," Mr. Fahpeh growled. "I hired you to perform a duty, you did, and I paid you. What's more?"

Mr. Blamo said he was not in law simply to make money. "Of course, I need money not only to survive but more importantly, to take care of my family adequately and contribute to society as much as I can. Stated differently, Mr. Fahpeh, making money is not my only aim. If it were, I would not have taken on your case as there are big corporations seeking my service and with whom I could make much more money." He said he took on the case partly because of his respect for Mr. Gawvehgo and partly because of his desire to assist young people like Akoei and Zawu, hoping they would learn from their mistakes and become useful men and women in society. "I also took an oath to represent any clients as zealously as I can and so, while I lamented the loss of someone's life, I represented these young people in that spirit, your horrible attitude notwithstanding."

"Again, Mr. Blamo," Fahpeh jumped in, "you did a job for pay and were paid. If you do not want to represent us next time, that will be your choice. I must be going because I do not deserve this nonsense of yours."

"Mine may be nonsense now but legal representation in general may not be so in the future. As such, before you go, please allow me to give you a word of advice as a friend and a brother."

"First, you are not a friend and definitely not my brother. In actuality, you were my employee for a specific duty for which you were paid. Therefore, I do not need your advice," Mr. Fahpeh snapped. "Keep that for your next client whom you will charge another huge fee. I can afford it but feel sorry for the poor people whose last pennies you take without shame."

"This man just saved our sons and you are alleging that he charged huge fees, and that he has no shame? Shame for what? Is there anything worthier than the lives of our boys?" Mr. Subah questioned. He appealed to Mr. Fahpeh to listen to Mr. Blamo. Further, he expressed gratitude for the fact that Fahpeh paid for both boys but he and Fahpeh owed Mr. Blamo a lot. "If nothing else," Mr. Subah stressed, "we owe him gratitude and thanks."

"You be quiet," Mr. Fahpeh shouted. He said Mr. Subah's wayward son got his son Akoei in trouble, thanks to Subah's lousy parenting ability. More than that, he said Mr. Subah was so broke that he did not have a penny to bail his son out. "Shame on you," Fahpeh scolded. "You walk around here like some big shot when your pocket is not only empty, but it's torn to pieces. I need not associate with a lowly one like you. Otherwise, some of the idiocy and lack of dignity that go with lowliness may rob off on me and I certainly would not want that."

"A 'lowly one'? Are you talking about the lowly one with whom you were dying to do business but who rejected you because of your lies, shady deeds, and trickeries?" Mr. Subah berated. "Look Fahpeh, I do not deserve and therefore will not take insults from you; you can rest assured that any more insults from you will be met with greater force. In addition, understand that I can pay back anything you spent on behalf of my son, and my money is earnestly earned. Moreover, you and I need to listen to Mr. Blamo's advice regarding parenting; frankly, we have done lousy jobs so do not shift blames. Shame on you too! In addition, from what I know, you better beware because, with all your pomposity, trickeries, and drunkenness, you are sitting on a time bomb."

Mr. Gawvehgo added his voice. "This is not necessary. Fahpeh, you really need to get off your high horse and listen to people sometimes. I have advised you over and over to be law abiding, listen to others, respect others, be humble, and treat others right; you find all of these and more impossible; you must not continue life like that regardless of how much money you have." He paused shortly before adding softly, "You know Fahpeh, as I have told you often that money is not everything. Please remember that."

"You are dead wrong, Gawvehgo and you know it. It is pure nonsense to say money is not everything; of course, it is. This is why I am fortunate, unlike you, to have money to back me up; therefore, no one, I mean no one can do me a thing in this country, and that includes you Mr. Blamo, and I care not whether you are the world's best lawyer or not. I have enough money to pay lawyers who know ten times than you do. If I want to hire ten such lawyers, I can; so there!"

Mr. Blamo smiled. He advised Fahpeh not to continue with this air of pomposity and arrogance, and not to perpetuate his sickening sense of superiority. Likewise, it did not help when Fahpeh carried on as he pleased, paying attention to no one, respecting none, and unmindful of laws and regulations. "Mr. Fahpeh," Mr. Blamo continued, "I agree with Mr. Gawvehgo. Believe it or not, money is not everything; money cannot do everything. Besides, as a mere mortal, you have no idea what lies in the future. You have no idea who's watching you. In my practice and in the beauty of literature, I have seen or read about many who were up there, virtually untouchable but came down like a falling tree. Therefore, my dear brother and compatriot, please be careful. Life has its twists and turns."

"I must be leaving," Mr. Fahpeh once more snapped. "I do not need your stupid lectures. Good day to you and once more, don't you ever call me a brother. You are not my brother and never will be."

"Before you leave," said Mr. Subah, "I would like to know my share of the legal fee." Mr. Blamo turned to his computer, hit a few keys and announced the exact amount. Mr. Subah handed a check for it to Mr. Fahpeh who accepted it with a broad smile. He said he was sure that after the check cleared, Mr. Subah and his family would not eat for days. Mr. Subah refused to comment.

"Also before you leave, let me just say next time you need a lawyer or any other support, please do not call on me; I have much better use of my time and a reputation to protect," Mr. Gawvehgo said angrily. "You are your own god and therefore you know your present and future; good luck to you."

"Big deal Gawvehgo," Mr. Fahpeh laughed. "If, after a long and fruitful friendship, you want to dish everything because of some crooked Muslim lawyer, that's fine. Do not call on me for anything either. With friends like you, who needs an enemy?"

Mr. Gawvehgo shook his head in disbelief. Mr. Fahpeh dashed for the door followed by his wife and daughter. Before they left town, they stopped to see Akoei at the prison but did not say a word to Zawu.

CHAPTER NINETEEN

The ride back to Fasawoba was unusually long. Occasionally, Kolu and her mom sobbed quietly for Akoei while Mr. Fahpeh drank his liquor from a bottle with a straw. No one wanted to stop for a bite. Back in Fasawoba, Mr. Fahpeh was in a horrible mood for days. The workers felt the brunt of his lousy mood but Kolu and her mother were not spared either. Kolu minimally endured the venom of this lousy mood as she spent considerable time at Fahzie's store. Regularly, she visited her elderly friends but particularly Maa Gaamai. She and Sayzay felt horrible that the old mom endured injury on their account. They therefore did all they could to take care of her. For instance, Kolu paid someone to cook and provide other regular services for the old mom. On the other hand, the old mom's situation provided an opportunity for Sayzay to meet Kolu regularly, an opportunity he welcomed dearly.

No matter how long Kolu tried to stay away from home, she could not stay away forever. One day, her father had an emotional outburst. "Kolu," he barked, "come here!" Kolu had never heard her father call her in that manner. Mrs. Fahpeh was equally concerned when she heard the call.

"Yes Dad," Kolu complied immediately.

"From today, I no longer want to see you visit those dirty and dirt poor children and stupid old people. I am not responsible for their idiocy nor did I condemn them to perpetual poverty. Besides, you have gone against everything I taught you. Understand?"

"Yes Dad," Kolu said sobbing. "But Dad, what have I done to indicate that I have gone against everything you taught me?

"Shut up! Never talk back to me; that's your clear example." Kolu and her mother were stunned. "Another is the fact that you keep talking with that dog Sayzay. I regret for not blowing his brains out but it's not late. What I said I meant and will be sure to silence that dog."

"Thank god you did not kill him for you would have been in jail with your son," Kolu said boldly.

"So are you glad he is alive?"

"I am glad for anyone who is alive because, as John Donne says, every man's death diminishes me. Unfortunately, Dad, you killed another person although you will never be charged for it. The injuries you inflicted on Maa Gaamai will kill that old lady, a death she does not deserve."

"You are mad," Mr. Fahpeh shouted. "Even if that stupid old lady dies, it will be a well-deserved death. She provided a place for you to see that dog."

"I'm sorry Dad; I do not mean to annoy you in any way but please do not call another human being a dog. He is created like you and me in God's image."

"I told you to shut up! Never tell me about your God; there is no God but your idiotic and illogical imagination."

Kolu bowed her head and sobbed violently. In the midst of copious tears, she said a prayer for her father. Domestic workers hid away while Mrs. Fahpeh wept bitterly.

"One more thing," Mr. Fahpeh shouted. "My demand still stands. I do not ever want to see you with that dog. He is nowhere near our social class and will never be."

"Evidently we have not learned our lesson about social class and I will not say, 'I told you so'," Kolu once more stated with audacity. "I just wish we could also understand what the Bard once wrote: 'All that glitters is not gold'."[12]

"What did you say?" her father demanded.

"Kill me if you will but I meant that," Kolu was not giving up. It seemed she had been pushed beyond her saturation gap and no longer cared what her father did or said. People often are pushed to their saturation

---

[12] This is from Shakespeare, The Merchant of Venice, Act II Scene VII.

gaps and, beyond such gaps, like a balloon, they will explode. This was why Kolu no longer cared. Her father could cancel her nursing school prospects, close her account, or do whatever he pleased. None of those things mattered to her any more.

Mr. Fahpeh did not say another word; he grabbed a bottle and dashed for his room. Kolu also headed for the door. "Where are you going?" Mrs. Fahpeh asked tearfully.

"To Sis Fahzie. Am I allowed to do that or is she off limits too?" Mrs. Fahpeh did not answer.

Fahzie was playing with her two boys when Kolu arrived at the store. Sumo and Sopo ran and hugged their aunt who, in traditional terms, was considered their mother.[13]"How are you today?" Fahzie asked. "You look very different. This must be serious."

Fahzie took her sister by the hand and led her to the back room of the store. Kolu narrated her encounter with her father. "So, I am not to visit my dear dear friends but sis Fahzie, I will never stop visiting Maa Gaamai. Because of me, Sayzay was almost killed in cold blood and that nice old lady got hurt and may never recover from her injuries. I will never forsake her, even if it leads to my death."

Fahzie had never heard her little sister speak with such strong emotion. She knew Kolu meant every word. "Did he say you are not allowed to visit me too?"

"Not yet but if you will excuse me Sis Fahzie, I am off to see Maa Gaamai."

Strangely, Maa Gaamai was not sitting outside when Kolu arrived. Kolu became terribly concerned. She rushed in the house. Maa Gaamai was lying on her bed looking very sick. "I am not well, Oh dear Kolu." The old lady said her sores hurt and her entire body was aching.

---

[13] In this tradition, a child's mother's sister is considered mother in the same way a child's father's brother is considered fa ther. Thus, one's only aunt is his/her father's sister and one's only uncle is his/her mother's brother. That's why, in this work, Kolu and Fahzie are not cousins but sisters. The word "cousin" does not exist in this culture.

"I understand Maa. I brought you some food and medicine." The old ma ate and felt much better. Kolu cleaned her sores and bandaged them. She also gave her a new supply of pain tablets.

"My grandson has not been here for weeks, perhaps months; I have lost track. I do not know what the deal with him is and quite frankly, I no longer care."

"Kpor Kpor!" someone knocked at the door. Neither Kolu nor the old lady answered but the person went in anyway. "Maa Ya na?" said the visitor.

"My goodness Kolu; I do not believe in coincidence but this is my long lost grandson. Kollie, this is my granddaughter Kolu who has cared for me more than I can explain. Where have you been and what did you bring for me?"

"Things have been rough Grandma; I did not bring anything but this young lady is very beautiful. Are you married Kolu? Actually, I care not if you are married; I want you, not your husband if one exists. Again, are you married pretty one?"

"No and I am not looking. If I were looking, I'd not be looking at you."

"But I am looking at you. Who would not admire an angel like you? Please tell me, when can we get together? Gee, you are gorgeous. I cannot wait for the first kiss and then Mmmmmm! I mean, it will be great to touch those hips and believe me, I'm extremely experienced. Yes, Baby, I've got the magic touch and the move with the groove. So When? You name the time and place and I will be there before the wind arrives. Once there, Cupid will take over and off we go into the magic world beyond imagination. Trust me, I will take you into another world; just give me a chance. You dig?"

Kolu was furious. "Do I look like a wandering girl to be picked up by any oddly-dressed vagabond? Don't bring your nonsense to me," she snapped.

"Look Kollie," the old ma said angrily. "That's the only thing you know, look for women and have fun. I want you to know that if anything happens to me, this house belongs to this young lady." Kolu was shocked. This was the last thing she expected from Maa Gaamai. "Really Maa?" she asked breathlessly. "Why would you do that for me?"

"You have been everything to me and that's the least I can do, especially after I have left this world to join the ancestors and there, enjoy my rest in peace."

"That's alright Grandma," Kollie said. He informed his grandma that he was not willing or able to take care of the old house anyway. Besides, he wanted his grandma to know he was moving away from the area and would not be back for a long time. He said he might never come back to Fasawoba or the entire region again.

The old lady's tears fell. She recalled how she raised Kollie's mother who, unfortunately, predeceased her. She then raised Kollie but he did very little or nothing for her. Instead, while growing up, he often got into trouble and the old mom had to bail him out or beg on his behalf; this was a constant occurrence. Now, he was leaving and might never be back, not even to bury his grandmother, let alone talk about who would look after her while he was gone. Evidently, he cared less about a grandmother's precious blessings. "That's alright Kollie; the good God gives and the good God takes. He has given me this wonderful granddaughter and for that, I am most thankful," Grandma said tearfully. Kollie, not the least perturbed, nodded and walked away. It would not be a surprise if a fashion police arrested him that is if such an agent existed.

Mr. Fahpeh's inability to get rid of Sayzay was to him a failure, defeat and humiliation, none of which was fathomable. He therefore renewed his determination to get rid of 'the dog'. To that end, he bought a small but extremely powerful pistol unknown to his wife and bodyguards. He hid the gun from everyone and kept it loaded at all times. Whenever he ventured out of the house, he took it along under his coat. He also devised plans as to how he would come face- to-face with Sayzay.

After all, it did not take much to know Sayzay's schedule. For instance, he knew for sure Sayzay still met Kolu at Maa Gaamai's house. He was therefore sure that the next time he confronted Sayzay, the young man would be a dead duck. After all, if nothing else, he knew

Sayzay's house. He vowed that if he ever visited that house to carry out his threat, Sayzay's father would not survive either for their two lives were not worth the price of peanuts.

It was difficult to doubt Fahpeh because he seldom failed, if at all, in his machinations. In this case, he flared up not only because of Sayzay's interest in his daughter but also because he could not stomach the thought of someone he called "a peasant dog" defying him and getting away with it. He therefore resolved that this anathema would not pass with impunity. Accordingly, he controlled his anger and planned carefully to ensure success. Definitely, he would not fail.

After perfecting his plans, Mr. Fahpeh sat in his favorite chair and ordered drinks. He had taken his first, second, third or fourth shot but who was counting? Suddenly, Kolu walked in. She greeted her parents and headed for her room. "Where are you coming from?" her father snarled.

"From Sis Fahzie's store," she told a half-truth. "Is that off limits too?"

"Come here Darling," Kolu's father change of tune was intriguing. "Sit down," he demanded. He apologized for the harsh words but insisted that Kolu's visitations were called off.

"Very well Dad but I have one request." When asked to elaborate, Kolu asked if she could visit Maa Gaamai alone. "Dad, when you knocked that old lady down, she was injured. At her age, and without proper medical treatment, she is not likely to recover from those wounds. The least I can do for her therefore is to take care of her until she dies. May I please be allowed to do that?"

"That sounds like a reasonable request Darling," Mrs. Fahpeh said. "I beg on my knees for and with my daughter."

Mr. Fahpeh hesitated. "Well, I guess you may do so." He considered telling her not to meet Sayzay at the old lady's house but he did not because, as he planned it, that was exactly what he wanted. Also, perhaps out of guilt, if he had any, he considered offering money for the care of the old lady but again, he refrained from doing so.

"I also understand my sister Fahzie's place is not off limit; right? Remember, you and Mom already gave your permission for me to spend time with her even after I come home from nursing school."

"I remember that," Mr. Fahpeh recalled. "That has not changed."

"Forgive me Dad but one more question. I am grateful you paid my entire nursing school tuition, covered books and fees, and deposited money in the school's account for me but are you still depositing money in my private account in Coastal City?"

"Of course Darling. Why would I stop that? I want to make sure you have enough funds throughout your nursing school. As a result, for your information, during the last few months, I doubled the amount I promised to deposit in your account monthly. In fact, I will triple it; and don't worry, you are the only signatory on the account. In addition, I have given a huge sum of cash to your mother to give you before you leave for nursing school. If you use that money wisely, it will last you a few months while your account accumulates interest. Coastal City is expensive and I do not want you to be stranded for anything while you are there."

"Thanks again Dad. I promise to do my best."

Fahzie was full of smiles when Kolu said she could not stay as she was headed to Maa Gaamai's house. She had met Sayzay there many times but this was a special appointment. "Poor Maa Gaamai," Fahzie chuckled. "It seems her name is used to camouflage another name."

"No camouflage necessary Sis; I will see both of them." Indeed, Maa Gaamai's home had become a regular meeting place for Kolu and Sayzay. Both of them were looking forward to this important planned meeting.

Maa Gaamai was sitting out front when Kolu arrived. She greeted the old lady warmly. "He's inside waiting for you," Maa Gaamai pointed toward the door as if Kolu needed directions into the house. Kolu hurriedly went in. She was wearing a gorgeous dress and her uncovered hair was brayed elegantly.

"Hello Zeemai," Sayzay said, smiling broadly and stricken by awe and disbelief. "It's wonderful seeing you. You always look incredibly beautiful." In addition to a nice haircut, he was wearing a white short sleeve shirt, which perfectly matched his gray pants and black shoes. He looked very handsome.

"Thanks," Kolu blushed. No doubt, she was very pleased to see Sayzay. He moved slowly toward her and, for the first time, held her in his arms. He hugged her with all his heart and love. As Kolu hugged back with all her heart, she could feel tears running down his cheeks.

"I love you Kolu, I always have. I could not wait for this day and hour although, no matter the hazards and setbacks, I knew they would come. God never fails." His tears of joy flowed like a river.

"I know; I know Sayzay. Believe me I do but I love you too. It took a while but thank God I now know the truth. Yes, I have seen the light. Oh yes, while there's still room for improvement, thank Heaven I have matured substantially." Both of them cried as they hugged. Sayzay pulled out a handkerchief and wiped Kolu's tears. Then he took her in his arms and kissed like there was no tomorrow.

They kissed, kissed, and cried again. It seemed they could not get enough of each other.

"When and where did you learn to osculate?" Kolu asked smiling. "What does that big word mean?" Sayzay inquired, feeling somewhat embarrassed he did not know.

"It means to kiss," Kolu laughed teasingly. "You kiss sweetly and romantically; so answer my question please," Kolu was still laughing lightly. Sayzay swore truthfully that Kolu was the first lady he ever kissed. He explained that he had heard Golo and Gayduobah talk endlessly about hugging and kissing. They meticulously described the process to him on numerous occasions and those were his lessons. On the other hand, it did not cross his mind to ask Kolu where she learned to kiss. In fact, that was not important; hugging and kissing his true love was Heaven on earth.

The two took breaks from their romantic interactions to talk seriously. After meeting at Maa Gaamai's many times, they were now sure where they were headed with their relationship, come what may and they definitively decided to that effect. Returning to their romantic encounter, they kissed and kissed with a passion that could burn a kingdom.

The new lovebirds stopped kissing when they heard a car pull up and stop suddenly in front of Maa Gaamai's house. They pulled apart when they heard the car door open and slammed quickly followed by someone jogging lightly toward the house. Kolu was sure it was her father. She knew her father's recent change of mood was smartly calculated; she therefore feared something like this all along. She could not understand what made her father vindictive and oblivious to statutory and customary laws as well as intolerant of all cultural guidelines. Everything had to go his way or no other way; even if it meant committing a heinous crime like murder. And what for? Because he did not like Sayzay?

To say Kolu was furious would be a gross understatement. She was determined to prevent the murder of the man with whom she finally and deeply fell in love, even if that caused her own life. In her mind, the relationship she just established with Sayzay was worth dying for because all of a sudden, she understood what it meant to be in love deeply and sincerely.

In the midst of her fury, Kolu advised Sayzay to hide under Maa Gaamai's bed or head for the attic. "No time for argument Darling, go!" she insisted.

Up to this point, with the help of friends and relatives, Sayzay had taken extraordinary precaution to save his life but now, it was clear he was in eminent danger; this was possibly the end of his young life. Yet, hearing Kolu call him, "Darling" for the first time made him forget the danger totally and smile broadly. Finally, she had come around; she was now definitely his. No matter how long that would be, it was worth the moment of a lifetime. However, he quickly recovered himself. When he thought of all he had endured for Kolu, he was not moved. He refused to run or hide. He said if Mr. Fahpeh killed him because of Kolu, it would be a worthwhile death. He therefore stood still staring directly at the door knowing any time, Mr. Fahpeh would dash in. He knew that the likelihood of being lucky twice was very slim and yet, he did not move.

Kolu could not believe her sweetheart. "Well then Darling," she said breathlessly, I will go out there. He will kill me before he reaches you." She said her love for Sayzay was only a minute long but that minute was longer than a millennium. Her newborn love was higher than Everest, stronger than The Rock of Gibraltar, and deeper than a well in the Sahara. It therefore was a love worth dying for. With that said, she once more hugged and kissed her love. "If this is the last kiss of my lifetime," she said, "it will be worth my life. I love you Sayzay and that love is worth dying for you." With that said, and swearing to attack her father if necessary, she dashed for the door.

Next to Maa Gaamai was a man bending over the old lady. Kolu was sure her father intended to get rid of the old lady before entering the house to carry out his dirty deed. She was determined not to allow either murder. She therefore dashed toward her father hoping to reach him before he pulled out his gun. Behold, it was a middle age man delivering goodies a charitable organization had sent to Maa Gaamai. Kolu stopped cold in her tracks.

"Are you her granddaughter?" the deliveryman asked in amazement after seeing Kolu's elegant clothes and huge gold chain. Aware that Maa Gaamai was not looking at her, Kolu quickly concealed her angry face and shook her head in disagreement not wanting to give the stranger a false impression. She thanked the deliveryman and took the boxes into the house.

When Kolu returned to her love, it took a while for them to calm down. Then, they both burst out in an interminable laughter. "Still alive!" Sayzay shouted. God is good! We are alive! We are together!" he rejoiced. He took his love into his arms once more and kissed passionately. They pulled apart when they heard Maa Gaamai coming in.

"Are you finished talking?" Maa asked.

"Not yet Maa but you may come in," Kolu answered. It took a few minutes for the old Maa to reach Kolu and Sayzay. When she finally did, she sat near the young people and offered words of wisdom.

The young people thanked Maa Gaamai with deepest sincerity. They had news that would gladden her heart. They informed her that they had agreed to get married someday and when they did, they would renovate her house as their first home. This is where they first met in the truest sense of meeting, and this was where they first kissed. "So, no matter who or what we become, this will be our first home," Kolu said in tears.

Fighting back tears, Sayzay agreed. "We cannot find a better way to honor you Maa Gaamai; this is the least we can do."

It was the old ma's turn to weep. Tears of joy flowed down her cheeks. She asked the young couple to kneel for her blessings. She blessed them with a fervent prayer.

When Sayzay returned home, he told his parents who wept for joy. "I thank god to have lived to hear this news," his mother said. She asked Sayzay to come home with Kolu at least once so she could see her and give her blessings to both of them. To say Sayzay was overwhelmingly jubilant would be a gross understatement.

"That young lady is very special. I thank god too for this news," Sayzay's dad said.

Fahzie too cried a river of tears when she heard the news. She advised Kolu to handle their father's opposition smartly. "I pray that eventually, he too will come on board. Meanwhile, I would like to see the two of you here for some advice, if that's alright with you." Kolu gladly consented.

On another occasion, Sayzay and Kolu agreed to meet at Sayzay's house at a specific time. When they did, Mrs. Yasa Sianeh Kargbo was very happy to meet Kolu and her husband was no less so. Both of them briefly relayed stories as to how they grew up with Kolu's parents. Kolu was shocked to know people in the town intimately knew her parents.

After the brief history lecture, Mrs. Kargbo blessed Kolu in a special way as tears streamed from Sayzay's face. Mr. Kargbo and Kolu did not have dry faces either.

CHAPTER TWENTY

For fear that, he might make a fool of himself, as he would be noticed easily during the day, to visit Fahzie's shop; Sayzay did not wear his disguise. As a result, he entered through the backdoor. "Where is the old man today?" Fahzie asked laughing.

"The papay"[14] is taking a rest," Sayzay replied, also laughing. Fahzie led him to the living room where he sat comfortably in a corner.

"So, God has come through for you; I am very happy for you," Fahzie declared.

"Frankly, 'happy' is not the word; I'm overwhelmed," Sayzay asserted. "Right now, I'm taking everything in strive. Sometimes, I think I'm dreaming But I thank God. I had never doubted Him."

"No doubt, I admire your tenacity and strong faith; both of those are weapons of success," Fahzie praised.

Sayzay said he would always give the praise and thanks to God. "Kolu was, is, and will always be my only love. The thought that she has agreed to marry me comes with indescribable joy, and once more, I am very thankful to God."

As Fahzie and Sayzay conversed, Kolu's driver pulled up in front of the store. Kolu wondered what was going on. Fahzie was neither in front of the store nor behind the counter. Was she home at all? Where in the world could she have gone when Kolu made it clear she and Sayzay would be at the store this afternoon?

Dressed in an elegant skirt and blouse, Kolu ceased speculating and ran to the back of the store. "There you are!" she shouted when she saw Fahzie. "I was wondering where you went. You know my

---

[14] Respectfully used with reference to an older man.

sweetheart will be here soon." Just then, she spotted Sayzay in the corner of the living room. She dashed toward him. He stood up to receive the love of his life. She landed in his arms and both kissed as if their lives depended on it. "Mmmm!" Kolu murmured. "I love you Sayzay; I really do."

"I love you more than words can say Kolu and God knows it."

That is very sweet to see," Fahzie declared with tears of joy running down her cheeks. "God be praised and may He bless your union richly! After your smooching, we really need to talk."

Initially, the lovebirds did not pay much attention to Fahzie as they continued kissing heavily. Eventually, they sat down to talk with Fahzie. "Before we begin talking, does anyone want something to eat or drink?" Fahzie asked. The two said they would accept a soft drink or juice but did not want to eat anything big. "Very well," said Fahzie as she rose up to get the drinks. Kolu offered to help but Fahzie had everything under control.

As Kolu and Sayzay waited for their drinks, Sumo, Fahzie's older son ran into the living room. He jumped into Kolu's lap; Kolu was sitting next to Sayzay holding hands. "Auntie Kolu, is this your boyfriend? Oh Auntie Kolu got a boyfriend!"

"Yes Darling, this is my fiancé, your future uncle but in our culture, he will be your father."

"Father?" the boy asked.

"Yes, father," Kolu repeated. "You may not understand it now but I will explain when you get a little older."

Sumo was not interested in understanding family relations. Rather, he curiously asked, "What's a fianson?"

Sayzay and Kolu laughed just as Fahzie reentered the room with drinks and munchies on a tray. "That means someday I will marry him."

"Oh Auntie Kolu got a boyfriend! Mom, Auntie Kolu got a boyfriend," sumo carried on and on.

"Yes Sweetie, Mommy knows. Now go to your room and play with your brother." Sumo ran off. "Oh children," Fahzie chuckled, "never underestimate them. It seems nothing passes by them. Believe me, they are capable of grasping and discerning far more than we realize. Bless his heart for his auntie, or more correctly, his mother."

Fahzie took a seat across the room from the two lovebirds. Again choking on her words, she expressed thanks to God that Kolu and Sayzay decided to get married someday. "From the time I met Sayzay," she stated with a very serious face, "I never doubted his deep and sincere love for you, my little sister. I therefore prayed that, with such deep love, Cupid would wave her magic wand to bring you together regardless of oppositions and obstacles."

"Thanks a million Fahzie," Sayzay said also almost in tears. "My first and greatest gratitude goes to God but frankly, I owe you a lot as well. You were always there with a listening ear, a shoulder to hold me if I were falling, and best of all, with nothing but sincere advice. You took risks to allow me in your home although I had to come in disguise. You are a wonderful and honorable person and I too pray God's blessings on you."

Kolu was shocked to hear about Sayzay's disguised appearances. "Did you really come to my sister in disguise?"

Sayzay answered in the affirmative and Fahzie confirmed. "I did not want your sister to get in trouble with your parents on my account so I disguised myself each time I visited her even though I always came late at night."

"Sis Fahzie, you never told me of those visits," Kolu stated in continuing amazement.

"No, I did not," Fahzie admitted. "You had many things to think about so I did not want to confuse you further."

"You are a true angel Sis Fahzie," Kolu praise. She started sobbing softly. Sayzay pulled her into his arms and wiped her face gently. When she pulled her face from Sayzay's chest, she looked directly at Fahzie. "Sis Fahzie, I mean it; you are a true angel. I do not have adequate words to thank you for your love, support, and above all, logical and sincere advice. You have been a wonderful older sister and only God can repay you for the manner and extent to which you have been there for me, and for what you have done for me."

Fahzie thanked the couple for their words of gratitude but reminded them that there still were forces against them and their relationship. "Therefore," she emphasized, "the work has just begun." She said she knew her parents, especially her headstrong dad. "Because of his wealth and social status, he feels no obligation to anyone, not even to God. He does whatever he wants. When he sets his mind on anything, it must be done and done his way, nothing else."

Kolu nodded in agreement. "This means Darling we must do all we can to convince him to allow us to be married. If all fails, we must be prepared to forget his humongous wealth and fend on our own. I'm prepared for that because as long as I have you in my arms, nothing else matters. I can sleep on the floor in your father's house and will be just fine as long as you are with me."

Sayzay's tears of joy flowed like a river. Wearing a beautiful gray and white dress with matching shoes, Fahzie stood to address the pair as if she could be heard better standing up. "As I have said, our parents will oppose this relationship strongly but as I'm sure God has blessed it, it will flourish. I therefore advise you to put your trust in Him for with Him, there is no failure, no disappointment, and no loss." She advised Kolu never to disrespect or disobey their parents. "Give them no reason to stiffen their opposition."

While Fahzie was speaking, a car pulled up in front of her store. She looked out the window and there was her father coming toward the store. "It's Dad!" she exclaimed. "Sayzay, please, please, run out the backdoor; this man is vicious."

"I will not. If he will kill me, so be it."

Kolu stood up to join Fahzie while Fahzie continued pleading. "Please Sayzay, this might cost you your life. Moreover, this is not just for you; it's about my children and me. Please Sayzay, go. Remember, I took a risk to allow you to come here during the day. Now, my worst fears have been realized. Please, please save my children and me while you save yourself at the same time. Please Sayzay go!"

"If you truly love me Darling, you will go and avoid a disaster, an unnecessary disaster that will feed my father's ego and bring him satisfaction. Please Darling, go."

Kolu did not end her sentence when Sayzay dashed for the backdoor. He was out in a twinkling of an eye. Just then, Mr. Fahpeh entered the living room. "I saw a man leave as I came in. Who was that?" he questioned sternly. Kolu and Fahzie remained quiet for a while and Mr. Fahpeh repeated his question. "Who was that?"

"Dad, that was Seywala," Fahzie lied to cover up.

"But I know Seywala; why did he flee when he saw me coming?"

"Dad, he was afraid you might harm him out of anger. He left me with two children and therefore the burden shifted to you. Although as a dad you provided for your grandchildren and me, he still was afraid that the way he treated me angered you and therefore you would seek some kind of a revenge."

"Call the young man back. I will not harm him but just knock some sense into his head. Now, if he repeats that stupid thing, that will be a totally different story; no doubt, he will get the wrong side of Kolubah Fahpeh, and no one in his right mind should ever wish to see that."

Fahzie took a few feet toward the backdoor, looked out, and shouted, "Dad, he's gone! I doubt if he will ever come back here."

Mr. Fahpeh asked Fahzie if she was aware of the renovation plan for her house. Fahzie answered in the positive and expressed her thanks and gratitude. "Well, I just came to look around to make sure the various areas needing renovation are properly identified. He showed her the list. "Is there anything more you want us to do?"

"No Dad, this is more than enough. Again, I am truly grateful to you and Mom for doing this."

"Well, we are glad you will allow your little sister to spend time here. This is the least we can do. Materials and workmanship for these jobs have been paid. In addition, we have ordered some merchandise for your store; you do not have to pay back a penny. You have demonstrated fiscal maturity and a keen sense of business like your dad and we appreciate that." He disclosed that the merchandise ordered cost several thousand dollars.

Fahzie's jaws dropped. "Thanks a lot Dad; I really appreciate that," she said in a shaky voice. She offered her dad something to drink but clarified quickly that she only had soft drinks and juice.

"I do not drink that dirty sugar water. Don't you have something with a little bit of spirit?"

"No Dad," Fahzie laughed. "No ghosts are allowed in this place." She continued laughing for she knew exactly what her father meant. "O.k.. Then, I must be going. I must go to a place where ghosts are allowed for they are great company for me." He majestically walked out of the store and in a minute, his driver took off.

Kolu and Fahzie looked at one another in disbelief. "Can you imagine how this day would have ended if Dad met Sayzay here?" Fahzie asked.

"I cannot imagine; no Sis Fahzie, I cannot imagine. I just thank God my sweetheart listened to me and left." She said she did not have a definitive proof but something told her that her dad moved around with a hidden weapon. He was determined to get rid of Sayzay and knowing him, he would not rest until he accomplished his aim. "Oh good God, do not let him; please don't let him touch my sweetheart." Fahzie shifted her thoughts from a headstrong father to the new lovebirds. "Kolu my dear sister; that young man truly loves you. Again, I will pray hard for a bright future for the two of you. You can rest assured that what God approves no human being can disapprove. Therefore keep praying to Him with unbending faith; He never fails."

"I know; I know Sis Fahzie and I pray the same too." With that, she too left the store to return home. As Jimmy, Kolu's driver, sped down the highway toward home, she once more did not say a word until she reached home. She barely ate anything during dinner. Afterwards, she took a quick shower and went to bed.

In a few weeks, Kolu graduated from high school as valedictorian of her class. On her advice, Sayzay attended the graduation ceremony but at a very low profile, almost at an unrecognizable level. This was difficult to do as Sayzay was popular in the school and in Fasawoba but he accepted Kolu's advice as it made sense to him. She wanted him to avoid Mr. Fahpeh at all cost. Therefore, when the program ended, he quickly and unceremoniously slipped away.

Following the graduation ceremonies and for the rest of the long summer vacation, Kolu and Sayzay met regularly. Occasionally, thanks to Mrs. Fahpeh who complied with her daughter's unexplained and uncharacteristic requests for considerable sums of money, they took out of town trips. They did so by leaving Fasawoba separately and meeting in another place, usually in Gizisu, which was only five miles away, and Sayzay did not mind getting there even if he had to walk the distance. In fact, this was within his jogging distance. On several occasions, Jimmy and Kolu picked him up while walking or jogging to Gizisu. On his part, Jimmy, Kolu's driver looked forward to these trips as he got great tips not only to drive but also to keep his mouth shut.

Kolu knew without a doubt that her father was checking heavily on her. He was determined to get rid of Sayzay and nothing would stop that. To prevent any disaster, Kolu bribed the bodyguards and they promised to cooperate as much as possible. Yet, when she and Sayzay got away, they had to be smart and creative to avoid Mr. Fahpeh catching up with them. Knowing that at different and odd times, he went to various parts of the Northern Region and beyond, Jimmy often drove them to Biahlaw, the regional capital. They would then book Jimmy in a motel, give him money for food, and then rent a car. Initially, Kolu, whom Jimmy had taught how to drive, drove and that disguised them further; Mr. Fahpeh had no idea that his daughter could drive. He therefore would have never imagined his daughter driving around the region. Eventually, Kolu began teaching Sayzay how to drive; in no time, both were excellent drivers.

On a number of occasions, Kolu and Sayzay disguised themselves as Caucasian tourists wandering about. As long as they were in the car, they only needed to cover their faces and wear wigs to match their white faces.

When Kolu and Sayzay returned to Biahlaw, Jimmy usually took the steering wheel as they headed home. Once, after another rendezvous, the three were comfortably seated in the car. Kolu and Sayzay were in the back seat with arms around one another. Suddenly, Jimmy spotted Mr. Fahpeh and his driver on his tail. "Kolu, your father is chasing us," Jimmy announced.

"Take off Jimmy; be sure to lose him," Kolu demanded.

"I have it under control," Jimmy assured confidently. With that, he took off and so did the other driver. Of course, both drivers knew each other well but Jimmy seemed to be more experienced and he showed it.

When Jimmy left Mr. Fahpeh and his driver in the dust, he made it to Gizisu where Sayzay ran out of the car to save his life. Fortunately, he knew people in town so he hid quickly.

Shortly after Sayzay left the car, Mr. Fahpeh and his driver pulled up on top speed. The driver stopped with a squeaking noise. Mr. Fahpeh jumped out with his gun drawn. "Where is that dog so I may blow up his dirty brain?" he asked in an angry voice. Indeed, his whole body was shaking with anger and his eyes were red as fire. "Do you mean you still associate with that dog against my advice? How dare you? There's only one way to put an end to this; I will definitely silence that dog and anyone who dares to inquire about his welcome exit from this world. I will do so now, even in public; I do not care!"

Kolu too jumped out of the car with her hands in the air. "You want to kill someone? Shoot me. Shoot me Dad and be satisfied at last."

Mr. Fahpeh froze in his tracks. He put his pistol back in his jacket pocket. "Why would I want to shoot you Darling?"

With tears streaming down her face, Kolu informed her father that because of his rigid stance and condemnation of everyone, she could not date whom she wanted. Consequently, even as a high school graduate, she had to leave town to see her new boyfriend. "Dad, when will you think that other people matter as well? When will you stop thinking that your money and social status are the only things that matter? Please Dad, shoot me for I'm sick and tired of this life, and, it was you who made me sick and tired of this life. So shoot me, please shoot me and send me to my eternal rest."

Mr. Fahpeh's face dropped. "I'm sorry Darling. Please call the young man. I will be glad to receive him. I even have money for him." He pulled out a bundle of notes. "Here Darling, give this to him."

"Dad, I do not want your money nor does he. I want to be free, happy, and respected but none of that matters to you especially where others are concerned. Keep your money."

"Then call back the young man Darling. I swear, I will not harm him."

"No I will not. He is not of the social status you expect because to you, everything is money, social status, luxurious goods, expensive drinks, and on and on. Dad, it is difficult to believe as to how you think less of others. You have even forgotten where you grew up, and the people you grew up with. You know the cultural rules and regulations, you know the laws of the land but, because of your wealth, you ignore everyone and everything as if you were a god by yourself. Please, Dad, shoot me. You do not care about my happiness and me but only think of yourself. So please shoot me and send me to my eternal rest." Weeping violently, she raised her hands in the air again.

Mr. Fahpeh had tears in his eyes. "Please Darling, forgive me. Get in the car with us and we'll talk."

"No, I will not," Kolu declared defiantly. "I'm out of your house from today on. Enjoy your luxury and all that comes with it. I need my peace, freedom, and those rare commodities are just as precious in poverty as they are in riches." With that, she jumped in the car and ordered Jimmy to drive to Fahzie's store.

Fahzie, Sumo and Sopo were playing in front of the store when Jimmy pulled up. Kolu jumped out of the car and ran into her sister's arms weeping bitterly. "What happened? What's the problem?" Fahzie's curiosity burned.

As she wept, Kolu could only murmur a few words. "It's Dad; it's your dad."

Fahzie began to shake. She thought something happened to Mr. Fahpeh. "What's about him? Is he all right? Please tell me." She led her little sister into the store and to the back.

Kolu was still sobbing when they took seats in the rear of the store. Fahzie's mind ran to a thousand possibilities, none of which was good. Finally, Kolu explained that she had to get away from town to see Sayzay. Even then, they had to disguise themselves and hide. "Today," she sobbed on, "he spotted us on the highway and chased us. Thank god, Sayzay ran out of the car before he got there. Sis Fahzie," she cried harder, "he came out with his gun drawn. He was shaking with rage and his eyes were as red as fire. I have never seen him with such an angry and wicked look."

"Oh my goodness!" Fahzie screamed. "He actually had a gun?"

"Yep, he did," Kolu answered as her sobbing subsided. She wiped her face over and over but one could feel her anger. "I cannot date whom I want; I cannot go wherever I want; I cannot do anything because of this one man. Believe me Sis; I'm sick and tired of it. I'm not going back to his house. Let him and his wife enjoy their luxury; I need peace, love, health, and happiness in my life. Wealth without those precious commodities is worthless." Fahzie nodded in agreement.

As Kolu and Fahzie talked, they did not hear a car pull up in front of the store. Shortly after, their father walked into the living room at the back of the store. "Good afternoon Fahzie Dear; how are you?"

"Dad!" Fahzie exclaimed. "What happened?" Mr. Fahpeh did not seem to hear a word. He stood still looking directly at Kolu as if he could fish the answer out of her although she refused to look at him. Fahzie repeated herself. "What happened Dad?"

Mr. Fahpeh still did not move his eyes from Kolu but answered, "I don't know Dear; I really don't know." When Fahzie asked if her dad drew a gun on Kolu, he lightly shook his head in disagreement. "You know I love your sister Dear. I will never do anything to hurt her.

Instead, I am willing to pay any amount of money to make her happy."

"Once more Dad, that's your biggest problem; you think you can solve every problem with money. Go home and enjoy your money. I am not coming there; no never!" Kolu shook with anger, still not looking at her dad.

Fahzie walked to her sister and held her by her hands. "Don't say that please Kolu; Dad and Mom need you. You must go home."

"No, I do not have to," Kolu protested. "If you do not want me in your home, I will find someplace else, anywhere but that home, I mean that house for it s only that, a house, not a home."

Mr. Fahpeh appealed to Fahzie to please talk to her sister and encourage her to go home. "You are right Dear; your mom and I need your sister home." After a lengthy discussion, but mainly out of respect for Fahzie, Kolu finally agreed to return home. However, when asked to name the young man who was in the car with her, she refused adamantly. Likewise, when Jimmy was asked if he could identify the young man, he swore he did not know him. In fact, he had never met the man. This lie was sure to earn him a few coins later for he took a heavy risk. He lied even when he knew Mr. Fahpeh could have ordered his flogging, firing, or worse, his elimination.

CHAPTER TWENTY ONE

The head coach and officials of Eleven Brothers United, EBU, an internationally renowned professional football team were seated once more at a planning meeting. "We need a goalkeeper but I have not been able to find one. In three weeks, we have a major game and yet, we do not have a reliable goalkeeper. This really disturbs me," declared the head coach. "We need someone for at least three months while we look around for a permanent goalkeeper."

"I do not know how this sounds," Said one assistant coach, "but I suggest we try Sayzay, the young man who led his team to national championship."

"I thought of him but he is just a high school kid," the head coach countered. The assistant coach rebutted that Sayzay had been out of high school for more than a year and during that time, had played for various teams. He said from what he heard, Sayzay had not lost a single game.

"I really think we give him a chance because this young man is incredible between the poles. We all know that so, to me, it only makes sense to go with him, even though he came out of high school only a year ago. After all," he went on, "we do not have comparable alternatives nor do we have time to do a nationwide search for a goalkeeper." Everyone agreed. Consequently, the assistant coach was dispatched to Fasawoba to recruit Sayzay first for three months and, depending on his performance during that probationary period, on a permanent basis.

Sayzay was talking with his father when someone knocked on his door. He rose to find out who it was. "You must be Sayzay Kargbo," the stranger said. "I can recognize that face anywhere."

"Yes I am," Sayzay agreed, knowing a number of journalists had come to see him. "Who are you?" The assistant coach, wearing a business suit, introduced himself and disclosed the purpose of his official trip. Sayzay was shocked.

"God is good," he praised. "I thank Him for allowing my mother to live long to hear this, even if this will be for only three months." Wearing a t-shirt, short pants and a pair of slippers, he turned to the visitor and asked, "Are you spending the night?" the assistant coach answered affirmatively. "Then, I will seek advice and travel with you tomorrow."

Sayzay discussed the matter with his father. He secretly visited Fahzie to tell her the news. She promised two things. First, she would telephone Kolu to meet him the next day at The Den. This was a reference to the Den of Lions,[15] their code for Maa Gaamai's place. Next, she would find someone to help Maa Gaamai and Sayzay's mom while he was gone.

The next day, Kolu met her love at the Den. She was extremely delighted to hear the news. She kissed her love repeatedly. "I thank God for you, Sayzay." She thought of her father's words that a professional team would never recruit Sayzay. She quickly shifted her mind from her father to Sayzay who was about to embark on a new life. "You will need a lawyer Sayzay; do you know that?"

"That's what the assistant coach said."

"Then I will get Mr. Gawvehgo's number for you. He found a very good lawyer for my brother," being careful not to mention Zawu's name. "Even though he fell out with my father, and that's nothing new, he looked like a nice gentleman who will not turn you or me down because of my father."

"I will appreciate that but the most important thing is you approve. If you did not, I would not touch it with a ten-foot pole."

"Oh don't be silly. Why would I oppose such an excellent opportunity? I just hope you get drafted fully."

"I must confess one thing to you Kolu."

---

[15] This is a reference to Daniel who was thrown into a lions' den found in Daniel 6

Kolu laughed. "About your former girlfriends?"

"No, no, no! I never had any girlfriends.

"Liar, liar pants on fire," Kolu teased. "I knew about Tayzu; I even met her. My goodness, she is beautiful."

Sayzay explained that Tayzu was in love with him while he was in love with Kolu. Further, he said however, the professional team business turned out, he wanted Kolu to know he started playing football because of her. "I heard you liked music and sports so, to impress and attract you, I went into music."

Kolu thought of Zawu's horrible singing performance but said nothing. "Go on," she nudged.

"Well, I was terrible at it so the next thing was sports. I tried football but was horrible at it too."

"You were not!"

"I was," Sayzay reiterated. "I tried playing on the field but just could not make it. One day, when no goalie could be found, the coach took a chance on me."

"And the rest is history," Kolu rejoiced. "It is particularly delightful to know you did it all for me. Just for that, I will say extra prayers for this professional team business."

In Coastal City, Sayzay found Mr. Gawvehgo who in turn, found a smart contracts lawyer. For a small fee, the lawyer negotiated Sayzay's short- term contract.

Sayzay's pay for the three month probation period was far more than most people earned in a year, even in two or three years. He was therefore determined to prove himself as a good goalie and thereby get a long-term contract. Fortunately, during the three-month period, Sayzay did not allow a single goal against Eleven Brothers United, EBU. With him on the team, EBU won major games both within the country and around the region. The football club therefore happily offered him a five-year multi- million-dollar contract. His signing bonus was several million dollars, far more than many upper class people earn in years. After taxes, the money was deposited in an account the lawyer had helped to establish for him. The banker did not only make sure, only

Sayzay knew his account number but warned him to protect same tightly. "Guard it as you do your eyes, indeed, your life for there are lots of identity thefts out there," the kind banker stressed. He also warned against crooked investors, lions in sheep's clothing, and bogus charitable organizations.

Sayzay could not wait to tell Kolu and his parents. Meanwhile, he immediately donated a good sum of money to a genuine charitable organization, which championed the education of poor children, and another organization that focused on children with disabilities. Likewise, with the banker's help, he started investing his money carefully. Later, he got advice from reputable stockbrokers and investment experts.

Back in Fasawoba, Kolu was on cloud ninety-nine when she heard of the five-year contract. "God is good Darling. Before this contract is up, I would have graduated from nursing school to marry the man who loves me with his heart, head, hands, and soul. Who can ask for anything better than that? God be praised; I pray He forgives me for everything I did and said." Sayzay nodded with joy and thanks.

With a long-term contract, Sayzay prepared to move to Coastal City. On his way, and driving his own car, he stopped to see Golo and Gayduobah who were very happy for him. They were even more excited to hear of his firm relationship with Kolu, the only woman he loved. "I can't wait for her to move to Coastal City to start nursing school," he told them. Through Fahzie, he arranged for permanent paid helpers for his mother and Maa Gaamai. Sayzay took another major step. He registered with a university in Coastal City to take courses part-time so that, by the end of his contract, he would be completing his first degree.

∞∞∞

"Go Sayzay go!" was the chorus often heard around the country and the region when Eleven Brothers United took to the field. No kidding, Sayzay was awesome between the poles. The first two years of his professional football life were incredible. He broke and set one record after another. In fact, because of his outstanding performance, his lawyer asked to renegotiate his contract or he would insist on Sayzay being traded. Eleven Brothers United could not afford to lose Sayzay; it seemed no team could. Therefore, the renegotiation proceeded and Sayzay received an incredible raise while the lawyer was paid handsomely. Sayzay never dreamt of such an amount for his entire lifetime.

Kolu too had spent two years in nursing school when she was home for the summer vacation. Determined to get out of her parents' way as much as she could, she spent most of her time at Sis Fahzie's store where she had moved most of her things. One afternoon, however, while resting at home, she was awakened by a loud noise of a police siren. She threw on designer jeans and sneakers and rushed outside. She was shocked. At least ten cars and probably twenty-five cops and bank officials surrounded the entire building. Two persons were talking with her parents at the door.

"Mr. Fahpeh," the first man said, "I am from the bank. We have found out that you defrauded the bank of hundreds of thousands of dollars over the years. In addition, you defrauded many customers who will file joint or separate complaints against you. On our part, we have frozen all your accounts, at home and abroad. We will seize every property you have to use them to repay the bank. We also have seized your shares in department stores, restaurants, and companies. Likewise, we have seized your deeds to all your real estate properties. So, as it is, the only thing you own now are those clothes on your back and even that ownership will not be long as you will soon exchange them for prison clothes. Step out of the house and hand over the keys to the house and all your cars."

"And I am from the National Revenue Agency," said the second man. "We also have liens on your property for failing to pay taxes for years. Our records show that you falsified your tax filings for more than fifteen years. Additionally, charges await you regarding money laundering, forgery, and sale of illicit drugs. You, therefore, are under arrest and will face prosecution. You have a right to remain silent for anything you say will be used against you in court. You also have a right to legal representation. If you cannot afford a lawyer, we will provide you with a public defender." The man pulled out a pair of handcuffs and placed it on Mr. Fahpeh.

Kolu and her parents were in tears and so were the domestic workers. Everyone was ordered out of the house for the doors to be bolted. All the vehicles were seized. In a twinkling of an eye, Mr. Fahpeh had lost everything he owned. Mrs. Fahpeh and Kolu had to go to Fahzie's house.

Before the doors were bolted, Kolu wiped her tears and stepped forward. "Excuse me Sirs," she called the two gentlemen. She said she was a first generation college student; she had just completed her second year in nursing school. She asked if she could retrieve her notes and books from the house. "Please, please," she pleaded. "I need those books and notes as well as a few possessions to continue my schooling."

"Nursing student?" the man from the revenue agency asked. "I am impressed. My wife is a director of nursing in Coastal City and I know how much nurses mean to this country and to the world."

"I say 'Amen' to that," said the man from the bank. "I have a daughter about your age and wish she took her school work seriously. I am proud of you."

The two men allowed Kolu back into the house not only to retrieve her books and notes but permitted her to take three suitcases full of her possessions. They offered to drive her to wherever she wanted to go.

Kolu got the three big suitcases and packed her things as well as some of her mother's. They had so many things that she could not pack them all but she gathered as much jewelry, precious pictures, and other valuables as she could. She covered them with clothes and books.

When she and her mother were dropped off at Fahzie's, Kolu called Sayzay on her mobile phone. In tears, she explained what happened to her father. "I'm truly sorry to hear that Zeemai. I will send a car to pick you up. Does your mother need a car too? I will be glad to provide her with one. Is there anything else I can do to help?"

"A car for Mom?" Kolu asked. When Sayzay repeated his offer, at least for the moment, Kolu could only say, "No Baby but I will get back with you."

"Who was that?" Mrs. Fahpeh asked.

"Sayzay Kargbo, the goalie and my fiancé," Kolu said.

Mrs. Fahpeh sat quietly. She could not accept the car because she could not drive and could not afford to pay a driver. "Sayzay?" she asked as if she had not heard Kolu. When Kolu confirmed, Mrs. Fahpeh seemed bemused. "How can Sayzay afford a car? I'm not even sure if he has ridden in one."

"Mom, he has just signed a multi-million dollar contract as a soccer star. He can afford a hundred cars if he wishes. I will not marry him on that account but on account of my deep and sincere love for him, a love I had denied on account of the sickening disease of social status." She explained further that Sayzay loved her with all his heart and was willing to die on her behalf. "With such love, Mom, I am very blessed. I only ask God to forgive me for all the insults I heaped on that great and wonderful man, a man who nearly lost his life on my account and yet, did not give up his suit."

With tears running down her cheeks, Mrs. Fahpeh asked, "Do you think he can help with your father's legal defense? We do not have money anymore." She broke down and wept bitterly.

"To show you the kind of man this great man is, I am sure if I ask him he will help," Kolu stated with certainty. "Mom, he does not keep grudges. However, based on what the two men told Dad, I doubt if any lawyer can save him; but, we will try." Kolu was sure she could not defend her father's deeds but, regardless of what her father said and did, and despite all people said about him, he provided for his family generously. Therefore, the least she could do was to do all she could to save him.

For sure, when Kolu asked if Sayzay could help with her father's legal defense, he obliged. However, when Mr. Fahpeh's case came to trial, Kolu and her mother were shocked to see Mr. Musa Blamo as the chief prosecutor. He had been promoted to the position of Attorney General of the nation. He smiled lightly at Kolu and her mother before taking his seat.

When Mr. Fahpeh, the defendant, realized that Mr. Blamo was the chief prosecutor, he was almost in tears. He whispered something to his court assigned defense counsel. Based on that, before the trial got on the way, the defense counsel moved for a change of venue on ground that he did not think his client would get a fair trial in Coastal City. Furthermore, he moved for a replacement of the chief prosecutor on ground that the Attorney General bore a personal grudge against his client.

"Your Honor," Mr. Blamo began, "there is absolutely no basis for moving the trial. Defense Counsel has not provided any evidence that the defendant will not get a fair trial in Coastal City." He argued further that he bore no grudge against Mr. Fahpeh. "Your Honor, in my private practice, I represented the defendant's son; I was not in opposition and I was paid in full. Why then would I bear a grudge against him?" The defense counsel's motions were overruled and the trial got on the way.

Mr. Fahpeh's trial was swift but fair. He was shocked to see former business partners, bankers, oversea traders, and former employees, including bodyguards, testify against him. In the end, he was found guilty on all counts so there was no possibility he would get any of his property or money back. Worse still, he was not only handed a huge fine but had to serve a long term. In prison, he attempted suicide unsuccessfully.

Kolu visited her father and brother regularly and did all she could to comfort them. At the same time, she continued nursing school while Sayzay played with Eleven Brothers United. Eventually, she graduated with honors. Because of her superb performance on her first job, a year after Kolu graduated from nursing school, she was appointed supervisor of nursing in one of the major hospitals in Coastal City.

Shortly after Kolu's appointment, she and Sayzay were married in a simple ceremony attended by their families and best friends. While Kolu's father could not attend because he was incarcerated, her mother attended and Fahzie was her maid of honor. On the other hand, Sayzay was thrilled Golo and Gayduobah stood with him. In addition, he was most delighted that, despite an unusually protracted long illness, his mother lived to witness this ceremony although her health was going downhill. His father could not be more excited either.

A few weeks after his wedding, two important things happened. Sayzay completed his first degree. Secondly, he signed another five-year contract with Eleven Brothers United with an increase in pay that almost doubled his already huge multi-million dollar annual salary. Yet, he refused to hire a driver; he drove himself at all times unless under special circumstances.

In addition to his huge official salary, Sayzay renegotiated old endorsement deals and signed new ones; these deals amounted to ten times his official salary. By this time, they had a nice home in Coastal City but more importantly, their dream home in Fasawoba was totally completed and fully furnished. Of course, Maa Gaamai's house was their first home, which they renovated. Unfortunately, two years prior to the wedding, Maa Gaamai passed away and was buried honorably. Six months after the wedding, Sayzay's Mom also passed away and was buried with honors. On the other hand, there was joy and thanksgiving when Kolu and Sayzay had their first son. They named him Gazubalay.

Sayzay and Kolu also relocated and expanded Fahzie little store into a huge one. The new FBC, Fahzie's Business Center, had restaurants, barber shops, women's and men's stores, and more. Fahzie could not be happier.

Because of Sayzay's intervention, Mr. Fahpeh was released from prison. He returned to Fasawoba. Given the huge sums he was expected to pay to the bank and government, even after both entities sold every property he owned and confiscated every penny he had, he would have served another fifteen or twenty years. This term would have been increased by another ten years or a little longer because of charges brought by investors, creditors, employees, and other individuals. However, on Kolu's passionate appeal, Sayzay hired another dynamic counselor whose firm fought vigorously for Mr. Fahpeh. The firm succeeded in reducing, albeit only slightly, the amount Fahpeh owed the bank and revenue agency. Sayzay paid the huge remainder. In addition, the counselor filed a joinder motion to conjoin parties and claims against Mr. Fahpeh before seeking a settlement with the parties. Again, Sayzay paid everything including lawyer's fees. Altogether, he paid a little more than two million dollars. Yet, when Mr. Fahpeh returned to Fasawoba, and despite the fact that Sayzay and Kolu not only lived in a huge and luxurious house but had three adorable children— two boys and a girl—he preferred to live with Fahzie.

Mr. Fahpeh was sure his time with Fahzie would be temporary. As an astute executive, he was bound to bounce back even if he did not return to his pre-imprisonment status. This possibility, however, was impeded by two factors. As an ex-con, his former creditors and business partners, most of whom he defrauded, avoided him like the plague. In light of that, and owing to the fact that he had no seed money, it was virtually impossible for him to start any business. His second choice was to find a job. Again, as a convicted felon, it would be very difficult for him to gain employment anywhere. To make matters worse, he had very limited formal education to enable him gain a decent employment. For the first time, he wished he had at least graduated from high school. Without a high school diploma, he had no choice but depend on Fahzie.

No doubt, Fahzie was generous to take in people she called Mom and Dad, people who educated her and set her up with a store. However, she was now married to a very nice man, and thanks to God, she now had four children. She and her husband had a boy and a girl. Yet, given the expansion of her store, although taxes had to be paid and workers remunerated, and in light of her parents' situation, she said it was a privilege and an honor to take care of them. "No matter what," she said, we will manage whatever resource god has provided generously through Mom and Dad, and through Kolu and Sayzay."

Sayzay was impressed by Fahzie's generosity. However, he knew the complications she was facing. Therefore, in the presence of Kolu, Fahzie, Mr. and Mrs. Fahpeh, he offered to take care of his in-laws until they died. Already, he had not only visited Akoei several times in prison but, in response to Akoei's complaints about horrible prison food, and given the busy schedules of Mr. and Mrs. Subah, he paid someone to cook one decent meal a day for Akoei and Zawu. He was Akoei's only hope of an early release. He also offered Akoei and Zawu a place to stay upon their release. Furthermore, he offered to continue paying for their drug and alcohol rehabilitation programs, which they began in prison.

Sayzay's father went farther. He appealed to Mr. Fahpeh and his wife to move in with them since he, Sayzay, and Kolu lived in a bigger and better house. "After my wife passed away," he said, "I was glad to move in with my son and daughter-in-law. Kolubah, despite everything else, we are, and have always been, one family and I think it will be better for you and the Mrs., to move in with us. The children's house is incredibly huge and luxurious; believe me, there's room for you too. Likewise, as before, there are servants to wait on you."

In appealing to Mr. Fahpeh, Mr. Kargbo did not state that Kolu and her husband treated their workers with utmost respect and paid them regularly, often offering them bonuses and sending their children to school. In fact, retirement benefits were established for each worker. Furthermore, Kolu, Sayzay, and their children did their share of domestic work. In addition, Sayzay retained and expanded his father's farm and never stopped farming. The children not only learned the language, culture and history of the land but they too learned to farm.

Mr. Kargbo also did not mention the persuasions and attitudes Kolu and Sayzay adopted. To cite a few, they taught their children to respect everyone and appreciate the oneness of humanity irrespective of any 'external differences'. They told their children no one was better than they were. Likewise, they were not better than anyone was; therefore, they were to fear God, appreciate who they were and what they had. Likewise, they were to respect everyone but fear none. On his part, Sayzay was determined that, while he would continue to fear God, love and respect everyone, he resolved not to do two things; not to offend anyone knowingly and not to try pleasing everyone but live with as clear a conscience as he could.

Mr. Fahpeh, who had lost weight considerably and looked much older than Mr. Kargbo, listened intently. In response to Mr. Kargbo's invitation, he shook his head in disagreement. Conversely, Fahzie graciously accepted Sayzay's offer and encouraged him to do all he could to release Akoei. At the same time, she was very worried about her father. She knew, and Mr. Fahpeh himself was aware that, without bodyguards and given his deeds in the community and region, there was no doubt that the ghost of revenge would haunt him and his son. This was particularly likely since he had no friends, not even among people otherwise considered relatives. Therefore, in private, he could not stomach the tormenting reality that his days were numbered. Consequently, He largely kept to himself but in that seclusion, as evidenced by medical tests Sayzay and Kolu covered, his blood pressure skyrocketed, his advanced liver Sclerosis ate his liver away, while a horrible ulcer fermented, and doctors said there was little they could do. Worse still, he was sitting on a time bomb in that he had no idea when the ghost of revenge would land at his door; all he knew was that there was no doubt about such a visitation. Knowing this, Sayzay and Kolu placed him under a suicide watch.

Epilogue

Undoubtedly, it had been a long road to marriage. Sometimes Sayzay loved talking about the process but other times, he rather forgot it all and enjoyed the moment. For instance, it was difficult to forget Tayzu. This was because prior to his wedding, Tayzu sent him a note that read:

Dear Sayzay, I am writing to congratulate you for your marriage to Kolu, the love of your life. Sayzay that is what every sane human being needs— to marry one he/she loves. So, although I dearly wish I were marrying you, I am sincerely happy for you and wish you all the best. But Sayzay, I want you to know you are the only man I have ever loved. I do not think I will ever love anyone like you. In fact, I may never fall in love again but, because of my sincere love for you, I hold no malice or grudges toward you. Besides, you do not deserve any. Love is a beautiful thing. It should take its course naturally. I asked God to settle this and in His infinite wisdom, He has done so; I therefore will not question Him. Rather, I accept His divine judgment and wish you and Kolu well. Thank you again for making me taste the sweetness of love. God bless you and Kolu richly. Sincerely,

Tayzu.

This letter touched Sayzay enormously. He could not get it out of his mind. He could empathize as he thought of how he dearly loved Kolu and wanted to marry her.

On another afternoon when Sayzay was home for a break from the games, Uncle Gayvlor also brought out the past. "You know Nephew Sayzay, I admire you for the way you fought for Kolu."

"Thank you Uncle but she was the only woman I loved and I truly believed she would be my wife, no matter what. Sometimes people thought I was crazy and other times they thought I was just outright stupid."

Sayzay's uncle revealed that Sayzay did not know a few things. At Sayzay's nudging, Uncle Gayvlor explained that Kolu's Mom had an old boyfriend in town with whom she met at Uncle Gayvlor's house despite her high social status. "That's because, my dear nephew, when a man satisfies a woman, nothing and no one can keep her away from him. I guess the same is true of a man whom a woman satisfies."

Sayzay was shocked. "Uncle, knowing Mr. Fahpeh's character, you were taking a huge risk."

"I told you; Fahpeh knows me in other capacities. He could not do me a thing. Instead, by isolating and insulting us, he hurt himself in the end." When asked to explain, Uncle Gayvlor said he and a few people knew that Fahpeh's chief bodyguard was a planted agent. "I know the young man well. In fact, he is closely related to us but I could not tell Fahpeh because of his arrogance, conceitedness, and exclusivity. My dear nephew, remember this, no human being is a god; there is only one God. He jokes not when He says, 'Be still and know that I am God'. In addition, as we mere mortals strive for maturity, 'No one is an island' regardless of power, position, or possession."

ABOUT THE AUTHOR

Originally from Liberia, West Africa, Sakui W. G. Malakpa is a career educator. From his teenage years, he wrote short stories in English and Loma, his language- something he still does.

He graduated from Florida State University cum laude. He then earned a masters degree from FSU with a 4.0 GPA. After which he matriculated to Harvard University from where he earned a second masters degree and a doctorate. After a while, Dr. Malakpa returned to school and earned a law degree. He then moved to the University of Toledo as a professor where he is now a full professor with tenure.

Dr. Malakpa is a public speaker who has presented academic papers throughout the United States, Africa, and Europe. He also frequently speaks to civic and political organizations. He served as visiting professor to the University of Zululand in South Africa and Cuttington University in Liberia.

His publications include a novel and one academic work. He recently published the biography of H.E. Joseph N. Boakai, Vice President of the Republic of Liberia.

Other Titles By the Author

The Village Boy

From Foya to the Capitol: His Excellency Joseph Nyuma Boakai Sr., Vice President of the Republic of Liberia

Empathetic Planning Implementation: Inclusion, Retention and Success of Under-represented Groups